EX LIBRIS

SELMA SILVERMAN

# The Wedding Guest

# The Wedding Guest

## DAVID WILTSE

DELACORTE PRESS/NEW YORK

Published by
Delacorte Press
1 Dag Hammarskjold Plaza
New York, N.Y. 10017

Manufactured in the United States of America

Third Printing—1982 _

Designed by Judith Neuman

Library of Congress Cataloging in Publication Data

Wiltse, David.
  The wedding guest.
  I. Title.
PS3573.I478W4      813'.54      81-12447
ISBN 0-440-09443-7              AACR2

*To Nancy*
*with love and gratitude*

# Shah Leaves Iran for Indefinite Stay: Crowds Exult, Many Expect Long Exile
## Fighting Continues in Tehran

# Prologue

There wasn't enough shooting for it to be a war.

Someone was firing in the streets below, unloosing random, desultory shots, one at a time. There would be a shot, a pause of a minute, sometimes several minutes, then another shot. There never seemed to be a response. If this was a battle, it was a very one-sided one. Sobhani had always thought of a war as something lethally intense, a rain of gunfire that would be impossible to walk through. He could not only walk through the lazy firing on the streets below, he could dance, stopping to tie his shoes. There seemed as little chance of getting hit as there was of being struck by a thunderbolt.

This was supposed to be a revolution, though, not a war. Perhaps that made the difference. Perhaps in a revolution you only killed occasionally, and spent the rest of your time making speeches. There had certainly been enough of those. Denunciations of the Shah had been heard on every street corner for weeks. If a tenth of what they said about him was true, he was a monster incarnate. If half of it was true, he was too evil to have lived. If it was all true—how had Persia survived?

Mohi Lane Sobhani was not inclined to believe any part of

3

the vilification of the Emperor, for if it was true, then he had been working for the government of the Evil One for three years. He was only a dispatch clerk, he had never met the Shah, but those who traffic with the Devil, however distantly, will be singed by his fire. Sobhani did not feel singed. Sending and receiving messages in the communications room had not left him burned and blistered. At twenty-three he felt untainted by the sins of his elders and superiors.

Another shot rang out in the street three stories below. This one sounded as if it came from in front of the building. That would be the troops, defending the ministry, although what exactly they were defending it from, Sobhani could not say. He saw no one on the streets, no sign of life at all save for the occasional shot. There were those who were taking it all very seriously, however. The deputy minister of finance himself had come in not ten minutes ago to inform Sobhani that the building was being held by the troops only until the employees inside could evacuate. The deputy minister had seemed very frightened as he told Sobhani, but he was making an effort to keep his panic from his subordinate.

The deputy minister had given Sobhani a message to send via satellite to the United States. He was to wait for confirmation, then leave the building by the back exit and make his way home as best he could on his own.

"And tomorrow, sir?" Sobhani had asked, wondering if he should come to work.

"Tomorrow?" the deputy minister asked in amazement. "Let us pray there is a tomorrow."

Sobhani sent the message. It was unusual, because it was sent in the clear; the deputy minister had said there was no time for code. If that was the case, Sobhani wondered why he had to wait for confirmation. Sobhani read the message carefully before sending it out. It was brief: "Commence

David Wiltse

Operation Sanctuary. Merchandise installed." A series of numbers followed; 1, 2, 3, 4. It would all mean something more to
the person receiving the message, of course, but Sobhani had
some idea what it was about. He had been involved in Operation Sanctuary before, sending transfer orders to Switzerland,
then Tunis, then the Bahamas, and only yesterday to Mexico,
then back to Switzerland again. Sobhani vaguely realized that
information of this sort would be very valuable to someone,
and he made a mental note to remember it.

He heard the metallic chatter behind him and realized the
message had gone through. He took the handwritten note the
deputy minister had given him, glanced at it once more, then
shredded it. He turned off the equipment, looked around the
communications room again, then turned off the lights. It was
hard for him to believe it was the last service he would render
the Shah. He had no way of knowing it was the last service
he would render anyone.

Mohi Lane Sobhani had been given his middle name by a
sycophantic father who wished to flatter a particularly powerful CIA agent. In those days, the mid-1950s, CIA agents had
been welcome everywhere in Iran. They had been the power
behind the throne and often in front of it as well. In the past
few weeks the CIA had been conspicuous by its absence. Any
Americans left in Tehran kept a very low profile, and Sobhani
no longer went out of his way to boast of his middle name.

Sobhani took the rear exit and emerged from the ministry
onto Rajai Street. The street seemed empty, but he could see
someone sitting in a doorway half a block away. As he walked
toward the man in the doorway Sobhani realized it was a
beggar, his hands held limply in his lap, his head downcast,
one of his legs twisted into a bizarre, crippled attitude. Sobhani
was surprised to see a beggar this close to the ministry. The
Shah had long since banished them from the government

5

buildings—they offended the foreigners who dealt with the government, especially the Americans. It must be a very hard life for a beggar in America, Sobhani reflected. A very fastidious people, the Americans.

As he drew abreast of the beggar, Sobhani stopped. For a moment he feared he could not breathe, his heart seemed to have stopped beating in his chest. The beggar was the deputy minister. There was a bullet hole in the middle of his forehead, and another on the very crown of his head where someone had apparently shot him after he slumped to the ground.

Sobhani stifled an impulse to scream. There was no one on the street. He began to run. When he turned the corner, there were several men pressed back into doorways, pointing rifles at something in a building behind Sobhani. For a second the presence of rifles made him think they were the troops, and that he was safe. But then he realized they were not in uniform. He stopped running, and one of the revolutionary guards came toward him. The guard pointed his rifle toward Sobhani, and Sobhani instinctively lifted his hands.

"Papers," the man demanded.

"I have done nothing," Sobhani started, but the man jabbed him in the solar plexus with the barrel of the gun. As Sobhani gasped for breath, the man seized his papers.

"You work for the government," the man accused.

"I am just a clerk," Sobhani gasped. "It's just a job." The man seemed to consider, but then a shot was fired in the distance. The man struck Sobhani savagely in the throat with the rifle butt. Sobhani fell, clutching his throat. He could see a mullah hurrying toward him, his long robe sweeping the street. A man of God would help him, Sobhani thought. Whatever madness this was, the mullah would protect him.

The man with the rifle showed Sobhani's papers to the

mullah. The priest glanced at them, then glared down at the fallen clerk, his eyes ablaze with rage. He began to denounce Sobhani, calling him a cancer, a devil.

Sobhani raised a hand, pleading. "I have done nothing," he tried to say. His throat was crushed; nothing came out but a gargled moan.

The mullah ranted on, his fury rising with every word.

"I can help you," Sobhani tried to say. "I know about Operation Sanctuary, I sent the message! It must be important information, I'll tell it to you." Blood filled his throat and no intelligible sound came out.

Sobhani bent his head down, trying to choke out the blood. His eyes fixed on the sandaled foot of the mullah. He reached out to touch the foot. A gout of blood came out of his mouth, spattering off the pavement into his face and onto the priest's toes. "Sanctuary," he said, the words clear at last. They were his last words. The man with the rifle shot him in the head, then pushed his body into the doorway, out of the way. He did not die instantly. Sobhani lingered for nearly an hour. No one knew he was still alive, of course. Had they known, they would have shot him again. The revolution was humane.

# Shah Reported Planning to Move But Is Advised Not to Visit U.S.

# 1

The bright red Camaro turned off Route 18, moving left across the oncoming traffic. Tom Nardo stepped on the accelerator, praying that for once the automatic shift would work smoothly enough so he didn't have to sit there like a suicide for that precious extra second, with the traffic bearing down on him. And as usual the car let him down, not badly enough to kill him but late enough to scare another six months or so off his life. The gears finally engaged, and the Camaro lurched off the highway onto the side road, leaving the angry drivers and blaring horns behind. Another few moments of terror and humiliation that money could avoid, Nardo reflected. If this piece of junk were a real sports car instead of a ludicrously weak imitation, a "sporty" model, he could do his therapeutic sweating in the sauna, and not on the highway.

After fifteen minutes of winding side roads Nardo pulled the Camaro to the gates of the estate. He pressed the button on the intercom and identified himself to the disapproving metallic voice of Martha Sawyer.

"The Man is expecting me, Martha," he said wearily.

"I'll check my book," came the answer. Nardo drummed his fingers impatiently on the steering wheel, but tried to keep his face composed for the benefit of the closed-circuit television camera mounted on the brick gatepost. *The old bitch knows I have an appointment,* he thought bitterly. *She's known it every week for five years. I work for the Man, for Christ's sake! But she'd never admit that she knew I was coming. That would indicate I was someone worth remembering, that would show too much respect.*

"Yes, I see it," came the voice. "Drive through, Mr. Nardo." At least she called him mister. She didn't mean it, he suspected, but the formalities helped nonetheless.

As he drove toward the main house he reflected again that the former President could have installed him here, in the mansion or even one of the outbuildings. Lord knows there was enough room, the place had been built, at taxpayers' expense, to entertain foreign dignitaries and their retinues. That would have shown that the Man held his services in some regard. And it would have saved him some rent, not to mention driving back and forth on the highways in that insulting piece of tin.

Tony's panel truck was in front of the house when Nardo pulled up. *I'll bet Tony doesn't have to wait at the gate for la Sawyer to look him up,* Nardo thought. *He comes only every two weeks, but the fat wop waltzes right in.* Nardo braked too hard. The Camaro dieseled after he turned off the switch, the engine continuing to run for almost three seconds before it died.

Tony Curtini dragged his electronic equipment into the far corner of the Man's study. He slowly moved the probelike antenna across the wall, adjusting his earphones, fiddling with the read-out dials. He looked a bit like a man sweeping for

12

land mines, a job he had in fact held during a brief stint in the Army.

"What are you getting, Tony?" asked the former President of the United States. He stood by his desk, leaning on it with one hand, watching Tony intently. He was excited. The regular biweekly electronic sweeps constituted one of the few exciting events in his days now, and it had always thrilled him to do battle with his enemies, on any level.

"What are you finding?" he asked again.

Tony ignored him, concentrating on his equipment. He stopped, the probe hovering above the electrical outlet set into the polished oak baseboard. Tony bent with some difficulty because of his huge paunch, and unscrewed the plate on the outlet.

"You got one!" said the former President.

Tony gently, gingerly put a finger into the hole that housed the outlet. He reached his finger up, inside the wall. The Man moved hurriedly around the desk, trying to see past Tony's bulk.

"Nope," Tony grunted, pulling his hand away and replacing the plate. "But it's close. They must be using the electrical wiring of the house for an antenna."

"The bastards," said the former President.

Tony picked up his probe again. Checking his readings every foot, he followed the baseboard to the Man's desk. The readings on the dial jumped dramatically at the electric typewriter. Tony picked up the machine and turned it over as the short little man moved anxiously around behind.

"In my typewriter?"

Tony was unscrewing the bottom plate of the typewriter as Nardo walked in. "Look here, Tom!" said the former chief executive, oddly pleased. "The cocksuckers are bugging me again!"

"Jesus, sir," said Nardo, trying hard to muster the appropriate sense of shock. He felt these regular sweeps were just pandering to the Man's paranoia. He had to feel they were still out to get him, it was a measure of his importance. *Who the hell wants to know what an ex-president is up to so long after he's been booted out of office?* Nardo thought. He was certain that Tony was producing the bugs himself to justify his job.

Tony pulled the tiny microphone transmitter, small as a shirt button, out of the typewriter. The Man grabbed it. "Look at that!" he said gleefully. "Those cocksuckers!"

*He loves the cocksuckers,* Nardo thought. *He loves the game.* "That's terrible, sir," he said.

"Terrible? It's fucking awful."

"Yes, sir," said Nardo.

"Will they ever leave me alone?" the Man asked, balling his fist dramatically.

*You hope not, you stupid bastard,* thought Nardo. How had he spent so many years working for such a jerk?

"Ah . . . Tom, . . . I believe you know Tony Curtini, don't you?" said the Man in the curiously formal manner that alternated with his more natural mood of obscenity and vituperation.

"Yes, sir. How are you, Tony?"

Tony managed a nod in Nardo's direction and began to pack up his gear. *Know him? I've been dealing with the obese dago for thirteen years, I see him here every two weeks doing this little charade.* As he had done more than once in the last few months, Nardo worried if the Man was slipping. Was he getting infirm? God, if the old man died, where did that leave Nardo? Without a job, that's where. *Hell, I'll be his chief mourner,* he thought, *and I can't stand the man.*

Tony left, his huge bulk barely clearing the doorway. Tony

had been with the administration in some low-level capacity or another throughout its duration and through the scandal that the ex-President referred to, in his inimitable fashion, as "the shitstorm" or, sometimes, just "the shit." As with everyone else, Tony had gone before the congressional committee, had testified, had had his fat face broadcast to a nation of bloodthirsty viewers, but somehow had come out of it all unscathed. Nardo had never understood how all those people throwing shit had missed such a big target. For some reason the Man trusted Tony. Nardo wouldn't trust him any farther than he could throw him, which was no distance at all.

"Well, Tom," said the Man, virtually rubbing his hands with pleasure, "we caught them at it again. Do you know I sent this typewriter out just last week to be repaired? That's when they must have done it." He held up the transmitter at eye level, then dropped it to the floor and crushed it under his heel. "What makes them think I'm stupid?"

*It's a matter of public record*, Nardo thought. He said, "Sir, I can't begin to understand these people."

Once outside the estate Tony drove for one block and pulled into a closed and shuttered gas station. He drove his panel truck past the dismantled pumps, past the old Buick sitting up on cement blocks, the tires gone, and around to the back of the building.

Tony knocked once on the back door, paused, knocked twice, paused, then knocked three times. *Some code*, he thought contemptuously. *Got to be able to count all the way to three to do it.* Tony had no respect whatever for federal agents—he'd spent most of his professional career outwitting them—but when one opened the door, Tony smiled.

Agent Stone stepped aside so Tony could squeeze past, and even then his great stomach brushed against him. Stone felt faintly repulsed as he followed Tony into the room. The entire equipment bay of the garage had been converted into a listening station homed in on the Man's estate. Quigley, Stone's partner, sat with one earphone on, one off, the headset on his bald scalp. He was listening perfunctorily to Nardo obsequiously pandering to the Man's ego as the giant Uher tape machine turned and dutifully recorded every word.

"So, Tony, how'd it go?" Stone asked.

"I put a new bug in the electrical outlet in the baseboard in his study. . . ."

"Yeah, I'm picking that up now," said Quigley.

"Clear as a bell, right?" Tony asked. "It uses the electrical wiring as an antenna. . . ."

"Yeah, what else?" Stone asked impatiently. He was anxious to get Tony out of there. Being in a room, even one as large as the equipment bay, with someone as fat as Tony made him feel claustrophobic.

"I was getting to it. I took the phony piece out of the type-writer. I checked the plants in the living room and on the two outside phone lines. He didn't see them, so I didn't see any point in changing them."

Stone said, "Couldn't you just once tell him there's nothing planted? It makes us look like such assholes if you're supposedly always finding our work."

Tony shrugged. *You are assholes,* he thought. He smiled, lifting his massive shoulders. "He's paying me. I want to keep him happy."

"We're paying you too. Keep us happy."

Tony said, "Ah, hey, have some respect. The guy's a former President of the United States."

When Tony left, Quigley shifted the earphones to his other ear, then shoveled some more potato chips into his mouth. Stone was concerned about Quigley's nonstop consumption of junk food. For some reason it didn't seem to affect his weight,

16

but Stone feared it would all catch up to him, he would balloon grotesquely overnight, and Stone would be stuck with a partner as fat as Tony Curtini.

Quigley said, "This guy Nardo says 'sir' more often than anybody outside of boot camp. What a groveling mutt."

"You ought to hear what he says about you."

"I mean, he doesn't ever come up for air. He sticks his nose in the Man's backside as soon as he walks in the room and keeps it there. . . . Christ, listen to this!"

Stone hurried across the room and picked up the other headset. It took him a moment to gather the sense of the conversation, then he looked up at Quigley, mouth agape.

"Is he saying what I think?" Stone said.

Quigley nodded slowly. The two agents listened, spellbound, until Nardo left. Stone finally removed the headset, rubbing his ear as if trying to remove the effect of what he had heard. Both agents moved slowly, stunned, still trying to take it in.

"There's no end to that guy," said Stone with awe. "There's just no end."

"We've got to report this right away," said Quigley.

Stone thought for a moment. "I'd better take it straight to the Head of Station. There's no time to play around with this." Both men knew that whoever got credit for this discovery was in for a commendation at the very least.

"Why don't I take it in," Quigley said. "I was the one who heard it."

"Someone's got to stay here."

"You stay here," Quigley said. "I'll get Anderson to relieve you."

"Who's senior here?" Stone demanded.

"Balls to that!"

"Who's senior?"

"Three lousy months!" roared Quigley.

17

Stone shrugged with the confidence of a man who knows
he's going to win. "The important thing is to get the word to
the Head of Station right away." Stone was already halfway
out the door. "I'll be sure to mention your part in this."

"You bastard!" Quigley said, but Stone was gone.

Nardo's hand was shaking as he put the key in the Camaro's
ignition. This was it, at long last, the opportunity for the
killing! He snorted at the irony. He'd been with the old
bastard since the first campaign, through the glorious, golden
years of the administration when people knew Nardo's name
and were forced at least to put on a show of respect. And
then through the scandal, the shitstorm that entertained the
nation and seemed to make everyone connected with it rich,
no matter which side of the fence they were on—except Nardo.
When everyone else was making hay with insider's deals or
bribes or the dozen other ways to make a profit while serving
the government, no one approached Nardo with a proposi-
tion of any kind. And later, when it was all over, the un-
kindest cut of all. He was scrutinized briefly by the inquisitors,
then rejected as not worth their effort, labeled as a harmless
toady in among the sharks and barracudas. This final lack of
respect had left him tagged forever as a hopeless incompetent,
good for little else than bootlicking.

It was only because of his reputation that he had remained
with the Man. Oh, he could get some kind of job, sales rep
or PR man for some conservative manufacturer who still
thought the Man had been railroaded. But that was where
he had started, and since then he had supped at the table
with kings and princes, or at least *from* the table of kings and
princes, and he was not about to take scraps in the kitchen
again. He had moved with power once, and he preferred to

stick close to the remnants of power rather than resume his anonymity in the wider world.

And now it looked as if the Man had a lot more power left—and only faithful Tom Nardo to rely on. Thank God for the Man's endless spite.

"I don't want the money for myself, you understand, Tom," the Man had said, switching to his sanctimonious role. "Wealth has never meant much to me."

*Then why had they caught you with your hand in the till,* Nardo thought. *You've been after money like a hog for mud ever since you got elected. But your sources are drying up, aren't they? Your pension wouldn't even cover the overhead here, and how many times can you write your memoirs?*

"Yes, sir, I know that," said Nardo aloud.

"It's for my daughter," said the Man.

"Your daughter, sir?"

"Yes."

"You have two daughters, sir."

"That's right," said the Man. "It's for my daughters—and so those other bastards don't get it."

The only bastard who was going to get it was Nardo, if he had anything to do with it. All he had to do was find someone to kill a man.

## 2

The crocodile was fifty feet from shore, floating, only the tip of the snout and the gimlet eyes showing above the surface of the murky water. If the croc was aware of the log drifting slowly toward it from the rear, it made no sign.

The log was a dugout canoe, chiseled painstakingly with hand adze and mallet from an ebony tree. Peter lay flat on the rough and splintered bottom, his chin and cheek pressed against the side as he tried to maneuver the periscope. It was an awkward device that Peter had fashioned himself from the cardboard tubes of toilet paper rolls, and shards of mirror. It wasn't fancy, but it worked, allowing him to stay completely out of sight as he drifted toward the quarry. Peter hated taking the crocs in the water. The ones basking ashore were easy, one shot from the hypodermic gun from a safe distance, and the croc was theirs for the taking. Occasionally one of the reptiles would slither, startled, into the water, but the tranquilizer would take effect before it got more than a few feet. The men would have to wade out to the croc, never a happy prospect in this lake, to be sure, but still much preferable to what he was doing now.

21

Peter reached out with his free hand and touched the long wooden shaft that held the hypodermic lashed to the end. It was crude and risky and offered little reassurance. A hand-held spear didn't have the force to penetrate the bony plates on the dorsal side of the crocodile, so the animal had to be turned and the relatively softer underbelly presented to the needle. Turning crocodiles over, fifty feet from shore, while trying to stay upright in a dugout canoe—a procedure the crocodiles invariably disapproved of—was not Peter's idea of fun. But it was for science. Peter could hear Dr. Arnoff's high-pitched little giggle as he said it. Arnoff justified all manner of unpleasant work by invoking science with a self-mocking giggle.

Peter glanced again in the homemade periscope. They were within a few yards of the crocodile. The beast's raised bulbous eye blinked, staring at the log. The nictitating membrane, the croc's third eyelid that allowed it to see safely underwater, slid horizontally across the eye. The croc was prepared to dive.

Peter touched the toe that was inches from his nose. "Tim" Tsimbabwa looked back at Peter from his position in the front of the canoe. The two men made eye contact. Tsimbabwa gripped the pole in his hand tightly, raising the wire loop on the end a few inches from the bottom, ready. Peter nodded and the two men struck with practiced speed.

Tim came to his knees and in the same motion looped the wire noose over the crocodile's snout. The croc reacted immediately by diving. The huge tail lashed the water and hit the side of the canoe. Peter was nearly knocked overboard by the blow, but he hung on to the gunwale with his left hand, raising the hypo spear high with his right hand, ready for the thrust. As the beast's snout plunged underwater, Tim jerked up and sideways, twisting the pole. The torque worked two ways. The croc was turned onto its side in the water, neck pulled toward the surface—but as its superior strength took hold the pole was wrenched from Tim's hands and the native was slammed against the side of the canoe, his waist hitting the gunwale, splinters ripping his bare skin.

Peter had less than a quarter of a second to jab the needle into the underbelly before the croc righted itself and plunged deeper underwater. He could feel the impact of the pole against the croc's hide, the lesser tremor of the spring-loaded hypo going off, shooting its dose of fast-acting tranquilizer into the animal's stomach muscles. Peter released the spear at contact, knowing from painful experience that as the croc heaved itself back onto its belly the wrenching leverage on the spear shaft could be enough to dislocate his shoulder.

The spear crashed against the boat, shattering the shaft. At the same moment Tim recoiled too rapidly, fleeing the lashing tail. The canoe tipped, pushed even higher by the swell created by the angry, thrashing animal. Tim fell over first, a cry stifled at once as his head went underwater. Peter scrabbled desperately at the smooth edge of the canoe, trying for a handhold in the unyielding ebony. He hit the water, butt first, legs tucked in instinctively. The capsizing edge of the canoe hit him on the knees, jerking him forward, and his head slammed against the rounded bottom of the boat.

The boat saved his eye. The crocodile's tail slashed the wooden hull as the animal swirled to attack. As the tail flicked angrily away the knobby carapace ripped through Peter's skin, cutting a jagged strip from the hairline at his right temple to the edge of his eyebrow. His eye was spared by the shielding curve of the hull.

At the thrashing in the water a cloud of thousands of waterfowl took to the air with alarm, squawking and cawing their mutual distress. From the shore a dozen basking reptiles slithered quickly into the water, sensing prey in trouble. Others already in the water turned and moved toward the canoe.

Peter clung to the canoe, stunned, trying to clear his head. The first thing he saw clearly was Tim's face as his mouth flew open in shock. The crocodile rammed the native in the side. It was intended to be an eviscerating bite, but the wire noose held the animal's jaws shut. Bewildered and furious, the croc swiveled its snout from side to side with the same savage motion that could tear the leg off a water buffalo. With each sawing of the head, Tim was being pummeled by the horny hide. Peter was amazed that Tim had not yet had time to register fear. He seemed more annoyed than anything else as the croc tore at him with its claws and bore him under the water.

Peter dove, not knowing what he intended to do but realizing he must do it very fast. The water of Lake Kivu was as dark and murky as old coffee, and Peter could see only inches in front of him. He knew where Tim had gone under, and he swam down at an angle to intercept. Peter could see nothing, feel nothing with his probing hands. The lake was at least fifty feet deep here. Something sharp struck him in the back. He pivoted, expecting to feel jaws closing on him, but instead his flailing hand hit the broken shaft of the noose pole. The croc was on the other end, somewhere out of sight but no more than a few feet away in the murk, and his gyrations were sending the pole through the water like a whipsaw.

Peter grabbed the pole with both hands and kicked for the surface, hoping to pull the beast off Tim and give him a chance to get to the surface.

The wire tautened and jerked at the pole as the slack ran out. Peter kicked and kicked again, clutching the pole. He could see the light at the surface, just inches above his head.

His lungs were bursting and he wanted to cry out with the frustration. He either had to let go of the pole and get air, or drown with Tim; there was no way he could pull the croc up if it wanted to go down.

Peter was about to release the pole when he felt the tension go slack in his hands. One more kick and he reached the surface. As he gasped, filling his lungs, something very rough hit his feet, then slithered up along his side, scraping. A form darker than the water rose slowly, then bobbed on the surface. The crocodile was afloat, groggy and stunned by the anesthetic that had been sped through its system by its thrashing— but not yet completely unconscious. One gray-green eye regarded Peter with extraordinary indifference as Peter instinctively kicked away.

Tim's head broke surface next to Peter. He gasped, then began to yell and flail at the water. Like most natives, he could not swim. Peter grabbed him by the hair and dragged them both to the canoe.

When they reached shore, the croc was completely unconscious. The men dragged it ashore and realized for the first time that they had tangled with a giant.

"Have you ever seen one that long, Tim?"

"He tried to eat me, you see that?" Tim laughed incredulously at the nerve of the beast.

They heaved the crocodile onto its back. Tim kicked it contemptuously, but with care, on its belly.

"Heathen fool!"

Arnoff trotted over from the Land-Rover where he had watched the entire episode in safety. He stopped and looked at the giant croc with awe. "Oh, sterling," he said.

"Sterling!" Peter roared. "He nearly killed us both!" Peter wondered for the hundredth time why he liked the man.

Arnoff smiled. "I had you covered."

Tim kicked the croc's belly again. "The heathen fool tried to eat me."

"Not many are called on to die for science," Arnoff said, and giggled. "Particularly among the Rwundi."

Arnoff unpacked a sheet of black plastic and a stomach pump with a long rubber tube. When he looked up, Tim was urinating on the croc.

Arnoff waited with the tube in hand. "Whenever you're finished."

Peter walked heavily to the Land-Rover and took out the field first-aid kit. He examined his cut in the mirror. It was a nasty laceration, not deep but wide, the kind to leave a scar. It might help, he mused. He had never been vain about his appearance, in fact had never fully appreciated how he was perceived by others. As a young man he had been blandly handsome, no more remarkable than any number of other young men with regular features and pleasant smiles. The years had taken their toll, however, although in Peter's case they gave more than they took away. Lines had been gouged out of his face by too much wind and too much sun in too many hot, out-of-the-way places, and by exposure to too many risks that had nothing to do with the weather. His brown eyes, once large and innocent, had acquired a squint, as of someone looking constantly askance at the world. The laugh lines around his mouth had spread outward to form twin ravines running from his cheeks to his chin. A policeman's club had broken his nose in Djakarta, leaving a small lump covered with a tiny patch of translucent skin. And now there would be a scar like a miniature herringbone running from his eye into the dark brown hair by his ear. Despite the changes it still looked like the same old familiar face to Peter; but to the world it presented a visage of hard-won character.

Arnoff squatted beside the crocodile, working the rubber tube down its throat while Tim placed a block of ebony between the croc's jaws. If the croc had the gag reflex, as they usually did, his jaws would snap shut like a guillotine without the ebony block.

Arnoff maneuvered the tube into the esophagus. The croc jerked so strongly its whole body moved. The huge jaws clamped into the block of wood, less than an inch above Arnoff's elbow. The scientist gasped involuntarily, pulling back. He looked up at the sound of Tim's laughter.

"What's so funny?" he demanded.

"For science," Tim said, his teeth flashing.

Arnoff scowled, checking to make sure the wood was securely between the jaws before sticking his arm into the croc's mouth again. Occasionally the crocs bit the wood so hard during the gag reflex that they left teeth behind.

Peter rejoined the others as Arnoff maneuvered the tube even deeper, into the stomach where the digestive acids were so strong that the tube itself would be dissolved if it remained more than a few minutes. The pump went into action, and the first charge of stomach contents spilled onto the black plastic.

"Jesus God!" said Arnoff, as he did every time, reeling backward from black mess. The croc retched again, the second load hitting the first with a splash. Drops of the black bile splashed on Arnoff's boots.

"That is so disgusting!" he cried, wiping off his boot with a tuft of sawgrass.

Tim and Peter stood well clear as the pump finished its job. They watched Arnoff with amusement as the scientist went through his ritual of repugnance. The men had a clear-cut division of responsibility. Very early in their work Tim and Peter had refused to deal with the stomach pumping or the sifting out of the stomach contents, leaving Arnoff to deal with it all himself, muttering angrily the whole time. They would accept the hazard, but not the mess. Peter knew that Arnoff exaggerated his revulsion, making himself look more uncomfortable than he really was in order to make Peter's job seem more palatable. Neither man was fooling the other, but Peter enjoyed Arnoff's show because he knew there was more than a little truth to it.

The scientist had managed to wangle four grants for his study of the crocodiles of Lake Kivu, one from the U.S. government, two from private foundations, and one, miraculously, from the hideously impoverished government of their host country, Rwanda.

Arnoff was theoretically studying the incredibly sturdy digestive system of the crocodile, its imperturbable disease resistance—thus far they had yet to find one that appeared sick of anything—and the beast's role in vermin control; but whether or not the study was of any real scientific importance, whether or not it would aid the crocodile, or the Rwandans, or anyone else, was of no real concern to Arnoff. His one real interest was in amassing enough data to fill the treatise that would justify his grants and qualify him for new ones. Peter knew it, and Arnoff knew he knew it, which accounted for the deprecating giggle. For more gullible ears Arnoff would claim the sacrosanct goal of science with deadpan sincerity.

Arnoff removed the tube and began to sift through the contents of the croc's stomach, using a stick to poke the distinguishable bones into a pile that he would go through later. He spoke his preliminary findings into a tape recorder.

"Arnold 371," said Arnoff. He referred to all the crocodiles as Arnolds, as in Arnold the Alligator.

"One turtle shell, two miscellaneous stones, hides of two

baby crocodiles—the cannibalistic bastard. What a way to make a living."

Peter fastened a tag to the animal's tail, listing the color code for date and place of capture. Later surveys would help them map the migration range and patterns of the entire Lake Kivu population. Tim measured the beast from tail to snout. Sixteen feet, a mammoth.

Arnoff stepped away from the pile of bones and gulped untainted air. "We got a call on the radio in the Rover while you were laboring for science with this bugger." He waved his stick at the croc. "It was from your brother Thomas. He's getting married. He wants you to come home for the wedding. The call came direct, it wasn't transferred through Karallalla. That means he was transmitting via satellite. What kind of pull does he have to be able to do that?"

Peter let the question hang. "You're sure he said Thomas?"

"What's so strange? You do have a brother, don't you?"

Peter nodded. "I have a brother. You spoke to Thomas, he was calling personally?"

"Yes."

Peter studied the bony plates on the croc's tail.

"You don't seem overjoyed," said Arnoff.

Peter smiled, a small, strange twisting of the lips, devoid of humor. "I'm a little surprised. I haven't heard from anyone in my family in five years."

Arnoff chatted on, happy to avoid returning to the gore on the plastic sheet. "Here you are, running around Africa, doing dogsbody jobs, blacksheeping it, thinking of yourself as abused and unappreciated by hearth and home, nursing some cankerous dark secret of rejection." His voice rose dramatically as he worked his way into it. Arnoff was capable of moments of bizarre eloquence. Peter assumed they were in reaction to the dusty prose he was forced to write for his scientific papers. "When suddenly there is a joyous moment in the closed circle, time for a ritual act of unity. The ties that bind are tugged, five years' slack is pulled taut, and off you go, returned to the bosom of your family. . . . You are going, aren't you?"

Peter roused himself from his revery. "Oh, yes, I'm going."

"I suggest you bathe first. Anoint yourself with oils."

"Oh, I'll prepare myself," Peter said flatly. What he did not say was that his brother Thomas had been dead for five years.

They sat by the campfire as the African sun refused to go down. The horizon here was so wide, so distant, so vast and unobstructed on the endless plain, that sunsets seemed to last forever and the twilight at least half again as long. Arnoff sat in the folding director's chair that Peter thought made him look like something from a bad movie version of Hemingway.

Peter cleaned the disassembled hypodermic rifle as he squatted next to Tim. It had taken him several weeks to stretch his thigh muscles enough so the traditional native posture was comfortable. He knew it made him look rather affected to Western eyes, but to Peter, Africa, for the moment at least, was Rome, and he was adjusting his stance accordingly. It was a policy that had moved him through the world with a chameleon's ease.

Tim had gone to the nearest village and brought back a gasoline tin filled with palm wine. He passed the calabash to Peter, who dipped the empty gourd into the tin and drank. The wine was coarse and bitter, with the faint perfume of gasoline, and it made the throat raw before numbing it, as if it were laced with ground glass. Peter had witnessed the local wine being made, and knew that was a possibility too. He passed the calabash back to Tim.

Arnoff leaned back in his canvas chair and puffed contentedly on a pipe of hashish.

Peter continued to work on the rifle, meticulously cleaning the housing assembly.

"You love that gun, don't you?" Arnoff said. "Just look at the way you handle it."

"I respect it," Peter said sharply.

"Touchy subject?"

"I've known people who love weapons. I'm not one of them. Weapons are for killing."

Arnoff puffed again. "I'd call that a defensive weapon."

Peter finished the housing assembly and snapped it into place. "The crocs wouldn't. The only defensive weapon I know is a good pair of running shoes."

"Ah, philosophy," Arnoff said. "It pains me to think I'll have to replace you with a sincere college student."

Arnoff grew serious. "I'll miss you, Peter. I don't know what your story is and you obviously don't want me to know, but I hope you get over whatever ails you. I hope you land on your feet."

Peter said, "I'll get by."

"Oh, indeed," said Arnoff. "I suspect you'll always get by. You're a survivor if I ever saw one, but I wish you something a little better."

"Like what?"

"A job where you wear a shirt," Arnoff said.

Peter laughed, then all three men fell silent as if by agreement. The sun had finally died, and the African night came on as if a switch had been thrown. The stars seemed only feet away and so profuse that in spots the sky seemed solid light. The beauty and serenity of it never failed to impress. The men sat, content with their own thoughts, until the howls of the night animals began, breaking the spell.

Arnoff stood and stretched. "Tim and I have a small going-away gift for you. Nothing very grand, mind you, but the best we could do with such short notice." Arnoff tried to stifle a smile, unsuccessfully. "It's in your tent."

Peter pumped up a hurricane lantern and lighted it with a brand from the fire. He lowered the glass chimney over the hissing flame and started toward his tent. Arnoff and Tim watched him, grinning like conspiratorial schoolboys. When Peter looked back at them, they tried to appear sober and detached, but their pride in their gift was obvious.

Peter turned back the tent flap and stepped inside. The first thing he noticed was the sheen of her skin; then he took in all of her as she rose to her feet and stood silently, regarding him. She was one of the most beautiful women he had ever seen, he thought. She was naked from the waist up, and he guessed that she must be very young by the erectness of her full breasts. Rwundi women mature relatively late because of their poor diet, and their breasts sag early without support. He placed her at fifteen, sixteen, but she carried herself with a dignity far beyond her years. A maiden princess, he thought, regal from the perfect shape of her close-cropped head to the tubular perfection of her limbs. She held herself perfectly still, only the slight tremor of her stomach muscles as she breathed revealing anything of the tension she felt.

Peter approached her, putting the lamp on the folding table. He put out a hand, touched a finger to her shoulder. The skin shivered involuntarily with excitement under his touch, but still her face showed no emotion as she watched him as if from a great height, from a throne. The sheen of her skin was grease, tallow he assumed. She had been prepared ritually as a virgin bride.

Her eyes shifted and she noticed the wound by his eye for

the first time. She lifted her hand and held it just above the wound, not touching.

"You will look like one of us," she said in dialect.

Peter touched the ritual scars that had been worked painstakingly—and painfully—into her cheeks with a needle. He lightly ran his fingers over the raised welts of skin. "Very pretty," he said, smiling. The tribal scarring had been outlawed for thirty years. Whoever had done this to her had been a traditionalist.

She laughed involuntarily, covering her mouth with her hand. "My father says a lion did it," she said. Peter nodded. There were no lions in this part of the country. Then she giggled again, out of control.

No wonder she was so dignified, Peter realized. He sniffed the heavy air of the tent. She's stoned out of her mind. Arnoff has been feeding her his hash.

She was no maiden, either, but that was just as well.

# 3

As Peter approached the checkpoint at the Pan Am terminal in Nairobi, his practiced eye looked for leaks in the security. He immediately saw the three classic ways for getting a weapon past the concealed-arms check. As he passed through the metal detector and his bag was pushed through the X-ray machine, he added another way to his list. The procedure here was very sloppy, any pro would be through it in no time. Peter toyed with the idea of pulling the bored-looking security guard to one side and telling him how to plug the holes in his net. But he dismissed the idea because he knew he would only be making trouble for himself. Security guards don't like being told they're doing things wrong, and the lower their level, the less they like it. He'd be asking for an all-out body search and a lot of questions, at the very least.

Any terrorist who was serious could breach the security anyway, and Peter knew it. The checkpoint was just to discourage the amateurs, the terminal cancer patients who wanted to go out with a splash, the lunatics who thirsted for television time. And the whole rigmarole made the public feel better. The more they were inconvenienced, the better they liked it. Peter reminded himself it simply wasn't any of his business anymore.

After takeoff he settled back in his seat and fell asleep instantly. The native girl had kept him up till very late. As he drifted off he thought he caught a faint whiff of tallow mixed with sweat.

At JFK Airport, Peter rented a car and drove to Connecticut. The day was clear and bright, the midday traffic scanty. In other times, heading for home, it would have been an occasion for speed. Peter would have raced through the flat, open sections of I-95, slowing for the rest stops and service areas where the patrolmen sat with their radar guns humming and their engines turning over. Today, however, he put the rental car in the right lane and let it lead him home at a steady 50 mph, patiently taking the buffeting from the angry diesel truckers who swept by like sudden windstorms. His mind was on home—he was reluctant to get there, reluctant to face his father and feel again the dark wave of enmity and bitterness coming from him. Equally reluctant to feel again the sense of rage and betrayal that rose within himself.

On the outskirts of Greenwich, Peter saw the rolling green lawn, the innocuous-appearing building, the large letters of molded plastic, SSC—Stanhope Security Corporation. There was no way of telling from the highway what went on in the one-story brick structure. There was a time when the SSC building would have been torn down by irate citizens, brick by brick, if they had known what it housed. But that was another decade, another age, Peter reflected. Today they might well laud it again. Fashions in morality changed quickly. When politics did an about-face, national ethics seemed to wheel in tandem.

On impulse Peter pulled off the highway and drove up to

the building. He walked to the front door. A pleasant collegiate type sat behind a low desk in the foyer. Tailoring had changed along with morality, Peter thought. The young man's gun wasn't visible. There was no trace of the pistol in a shoulder harness under his suit coat, no sign of a bulge as he politely rose to meet Peter. Only his ID picture hanging from a pocket marred the expensive tailoring. His name was Richter.

"Yes, sir. May I help you?" the young man said, smiling automatically. From the slight accent Peter guessed he was an Ivy Leaguer. His father still preferred them.

"I just thought I'd like to look around."

The young man continued to smile. "Is there anything specific I might help you with, sir?"

"I used to work here," Peter said. He took one step toward the corridor leading to the right. The young man very smoothly took a step in the same direction, cutting Peter off without giving that appearance.

"Then you probably remember how things work," the young man said. He fingered the button of his jacket, easily, casually, a natural motion, but when his hand came away the jacket was unbuttoned, giving him quick access to the pistol. And still no sign of it.

Peter smiled, taking a step backward, relieving them both. "I remember very well," Peter said.

"May I ask your name, sir?"

"Peter Stanhope."

The young man glanced at the list of authorized personnel on his clipboard. "I don't find your name on the list," he said.

"No. No, it wouldn't be there anymore," Peter said.

The young man remained standing, still smiling, patiently waiting for Peter.

"Is Austin Stanhope in?" Peter asked.

"Mr. Stanhope isn't in today, sir. I believe he's getting married."

"At home?" Peter asked.

"I'm afraid I don't know, Mr. Stanhope."

Peter nodded. "It would be at home."

As Peter walked toward his car he could feel the young man's eyes on his back. Within fifteen minutes he would have traced the car back to the rental agency and have the details of his driver's license. If he was good, within seventeen minutes the family would be alerted that someone calling himself Peter Stanhope might be on his way. But of course they should know it before then, because Peter would be home in ten.

There was a long line of cars parked on the soft, grassy shoulder of the road. Peter pulled his car into the line and walked the two blocks to the front gate. There was no one guarding the gate, but then with close to four hundred guests milling around the grounds of the five-acre estate, a few gate-crashers wouldn't make much difference.

Peter walked straight to the front door, past the pretty girls in their maid-of-honor costumes, past the men in their formal dress. He knew that several of the older people recognized him, but they were either too embarrassed or too uncertain of the lay of the land to say anything. They just watched him pass in surprise.

Inside the house the sitting room had been converted to a warehouse for the wedding gifts. As Peter glanced in, one of the burly off-duty cops sprang to his feet, trying to appear alert enough to justify his pay. Another detective was looking at the bewildering array of silver objects, many of which seemed to have no possible use or function, even decorative.

There would be several more plainclothesmen wandering around outside in their rented tuxedos, mixing among the guests, Peter knew. He nodded to the detectives.

"Everything's in order, sir," said one of them. He didn't recognize Peter, but he knew authority when he saw it. Peter nodded again, with the trace of a smile. Rental tuxedos were not tailored like the suit of the young man at the plant. Peter could detect the telltale bulge on this one's waist.

Peter went straight to his old room. Kneeling in the middle of the floor, his brow touching the carpet, was a man. His lips moved rapidly in silent prayer. He saw Peter from the corner of his eye, but did not appear startled. He rose to a kneeling position, his palms pressed together in supplication, his concentration intent on his prayers.

Peter backed out of the room, but the man held up a hand. While Peter hesitated the man bowed once more, let his hands drop to his thighs, then stood up and faced Peter. He was a short, dark man with wiry hair and a beard that was neatly shaped but seemed to be no more than a week's growth of stubble.

The man inclined his head in a slight bow and smiled easily, as if being interrupted in his prayers were a common experience.

"Thank you," he said.

"Sorry to interrupt you," said Peter.

"Not at all," said the man. "I fear it is I who have interrupted you." He smiled indulgently. "This is your room, I believe." He bowed again and held out his hand. "I am Ghoubadi. Welcome home."

"Have we met?" Peter asked, shaking hands.

"Your brother has told me you were coming." Ghoubadi spoke with the slight accent of an upper-class English school, flattened and nasalized by many years in America. "I hope I did not startle you," he said. He waved a hand vaguely toward the spot where he had been kneeling.

"No," said Peter.

"Devotion is often startling to Westerners," he said.

"I've spent some time in your country," said Peter.

"And my country is?"

Peter paused. The man wanted to play a little one-upmanship. "Persia, I believe." He deliberately used the older name for the country, the name preferred by most natives themselves.

Ghoubadi continued to smile. He nodded again, granting Peter the point.

"We must discuss your impressions of my country sometime," Ghoubadi said. Then, still smiling, he slipped out of the door and was gone.

For a moment Peter wondered if the whole meeting had been carefully staged. It was a big house, after all, and there were many empty rooms where one could go for privacy during prayers. If he knew Peter was coming, why choose his old room unless for a reason? Peter looked at his watch. Nearly one o'clock. The hour for prayer was noon. Ghoubadi must be very devout indeed.

He looked around his old room. The furnishings had been changed, it was used as a guest room now. But in one of the closets Peter found many of his suits, carefully mothballed and hung in plastic bags. How like his father. Not sentimental, but never wasteful either. The rest of his clothes had probably gone to one of the servants, but the really good things, the ones that wouldn't go out of style, had been saved. For him? Or just out of habit? Peter decided it was inborn thrift. His father had not gotten to be rich by discarding valuable possessions . . . except his son.

40

Suddenly the memories that lurked in the room rose up and overwhelmed him. Peter and Thomas had played here, tussling on the beds, hiding in the closet as they waged their warlike games of hide-and-seek. In the middle of the floor they had sat and haggled and joked their way through innumerable card games and board games, passing rainy days. At night they had lain side by side, exchanging dreams, helping each other through youthful fears. When they were young, their father would join them on the floor, wrestling them both, growling like a bear as the boys squealed with delightful terror. And through it all, lacing it together, was Thomas's infectious laugh, making the bad times bearable and the good times better. Peter sighed. How he had loved his brother.

Peter sensed he was in the room before he turned and saw him. His father stood in the door, staring. Peter looked back steadily. For a moment they held each other's gaze, two strong men, bracing. Mr. Stanhope took in the fresh wound on Peter's face, the broken nose, the three-inch scar just under his heart.

"You've aged," Mr. Stanhope said at last.

"You haven't," Peter said. He continued to put on his tuxedo. For a moment he turned his back on his father and saw himself and the older man standing side by side in the mirror. *God, I'm beginning to look just like him,* he thought.

"You've lost weight," his father said.

Peter tugged at the waistline of the trousers. They came away from his body by more than two inches. He was leaner than when he had left home. *And meaner, too,* he thought. *Weight isn't the only thing I've lost since I left home.*

"The young man at the plant seems pretty good," Peter said.

His father nodded. "We're pleased with him." Peter smiled

41

despite himself. "Pleased" was his father's highest accolade. No matter how hard he had tried, no matter how much he had accomplished, he could never drag more than a "pleased" from the older man.

Peter faced his father again as he put the pearl-faced buttons into the shirt. The two men continued to look at each other. The silence threatened to stretch forever.

"You'll want to see your brother," Mr. Stanhope said finally. "He's outside." With that he turned and walked away. Five years of absence, and that was all he could muster.

Peter finished dressing facing the mirror. His face showed nothing, but his hands were shaking. *I haven't seen the man in five years*, he thought, *but after he says three sentences I'm trembling with fury.* The saying didn't have it quite right. You can go home again, whenever you want; you just can't live there.

Sligo hauled himself up into the first fork of the oak tree. He had skinned his shins getting up this far, and he couldn't even see over the damned stone wall yet. He adjusted the barrel of the hunting rifle that was crammed down the back of his pants. *With my luck I'll shoot myself in the ass*, he thought. The climbing was a little easier now that he'd made the first fork, and he quickly lifted himself another six feet.

From this height he could see into the estate, over the eight-foot-high stone wall that ran entirely around the grounds. *Christ, look at all those people!* Who could afford to feed cheese and crackers to that many guests? Sligo rested his back against the trunk, spreading his legs onto adjoining branches. If he got one knee up, he could use that as a brace for the rifle.

He took the scope from his jacket pocket and fitted it onto the barrel of the gun. He slowly swung the rifle over the assembled guests below, peering through the scope, seeking out the private cops he knew would be there. He positioned them quickly. Sligo knew he couldn't be detected unless someone knew where to look. He was two trees deep in the woods that backed the stone wall, and no one would have any idea where to look until after the shot. By the time they got over the panic, Sligo hoped to be out of this tree and on his way to his car.

He shifted his weight too far and nearly fell. *This is a job for a goddamned Boy Scout,* he thought, righting himself. This assignment had sucked from the very beginning. Climbing a tree and shooting from fifty yards with a hunting rifle. What did they think he was, Robin Hood? Sligo specialized in shooting men with his .38 pressed against the bases of their skulls, their hands wired behind their backs. He was an executioner, not a sharpshooter, and he should have told Sam that up front.

But he needed the money, he'd just gotten his son's bill for tuition and a thou would just about cover it. Why his son had to go to a private school when P.S. 37 had been good enough for Sligo, he didn't know. Except he did know. He didn't want his son being ripped off in the school corridors or terrorized by young maniacs with razors and blades. Even Sligo's reputation didn't seem to help there. Those kids were so demented they didn't know enough to be scared. What a world.

He had taken the job, thinking it was pretty good money at the time. But he hadn't realized what a hunting rifle was worth! He'd taken the cheapest he could get, a 30-.06 deer rifle, but the damned scope really cost too. Hell, you could still get a decent handgun for under a bill and an untraceable one for less than two—but of course you couldn't kill a man from fifty yards with a hundgun. Besides, this job was political, if it came through Sam. The politicals had their own methods;

they didn't like it with the personal touch, and they seemed to be in a hurry. His clients usually were.

Austin Stanhope ran up to his brother just outside the vast striped canopy. His face was flushed from excitement. Austin was still in his mid-twenties, Peter realized. He tried to remember when he himself had felt such boyish enthusiasm about anything. Not since Thomas died, at least.

"Peter! Gee, it's good to see you! How are you!"

"Not bad, Austin. Congratulations!"

"Oh, thank you! Come on, you must meet Margo!"

"I'd love to. She's a lucky girl." That much was for public consumption, and it seemed to satisfy the people around them. Austin slipped his arm through Peter's as they walked, a most uncharacteristic gesture, and Peter wasn't sure whether it was to keep Peter from slipping away, or for support.

Austin's voice dropped so only Peter could hear as they walked. "Thanks for coming, man. I know you didn't want to. I know you and Dad had a falling out . . ."

Peter smiled despite himself. The "falling out" had been an explosion between the two men violent enough to hurl Peter from his home and his profession and send him sailing into orbit in all the less hospitable places in the world. "You could say that," he said.

In the distance Peter saw the bride dressed in the traditional white gown. From here she looked pretty. Most things on the estate looked pretty—from a distance.

"Why did you say Thomas was getting married?"

Austin shifted nervously. He had the defensive air of a man who is under frequent attack. "I didn't think you'd come if it was just for me."

"Do you think I couldn't figure out it was for you?"

44

Austin stopped and faced his older brother. They were the same size, but Peter was leaner, harder.

"You're a cold son of a bitch," Austin said. "You always were."

"You dragged me halfway around the world by invoking Tommie's name. It had better be good."

"Tommie's the only one in the family you ever loved, wasn't he?" It wasn't true, but Peter didn't think there was much point in denying it at the moment. Austin had whipped himself into this emotional lather without much help from Peter, let him get himself out as well.

Austin paused for dramatic effect. "I need your help, Pete."

Peter watched the bride coming their way, making her way slowly through the well-wishers.

"Austin," Peter said. "I figured that out when I got your message. What kind of trouble are you in?"

Austin bristled. "I didn't say I was in trouble!" He paused, composing himself. Peter suspected he was shaping the lie he would tell, too.

"I started working for Dad, you know."

"No, I didn't know." Austin had been only nineteen when Peter left.

"In the transmission room. . . . I'm on to something. It has to do with Tommie, in part, with his death. . . ."

And then the bride was upon them. Austin stepped up his performance a notch, turning on the public face again.

"Sweetheart," he said, holding out an engulfing arm. The bride dutifully stepped into it. "Margo, this is my big brother, Pete!"

Margo smiled, but a little wearily. She had been smiling all day. "Hello," she said.

Peter took her hand and held it for a moment while he studied her. She was pretty from up close, too. Lovely fair

45

skin with raven-black hair and heavy eyebrows that could have been drawn on with a stick of charcoal. Not exactly to the Rwandan taste, he thought, but very nice.

Margo's smile weakened at the edges as Peter held her in his steady gaze. She was used to looking at the face, it was much like Austin's, but stronger, the face of an adult. She realized with a little shock that she had seen very few genuine adults in her life. A lot of grown-ups, but very few who had the internal maturity of this man.

Then suddenly Peter smiled, really smiled for the first time in days. It was as if the clouds had parted and a ray of sun shone through on his face alone, the transformation was so complete. Margo gave an involuntary gasp of pleasure and relief, then tried to cover it, looking away, embarrassed.

"She's something, isn't she?" Austin said, the pride evident in his voice.

"Hello, Margo," Peter said softly. "I'm glad to meet you."

"Isn't she pretty?" Austin said.

"I don't discuss other people in their presence, unless they want me to," Peter said. "Do you want my opinion?" he asked Margo.

"No!" she blurted. But she realized she did.

A servant approached them. "Mr. Stanhope," he said to Austin, "the orchestra would like to know when to play."

"I've got to take care of everything," said Austin. He walked off, leaving Margo and Peter alone.

"You've got a good day for the wedding," Peter said.

"You're really not going to tell me, are you?" Margo said.

"Tell you what?"

Margo laughed and touched his arm.

Sligo pulled the crumpled picture from his pocket. It was from the society pages of *The New York Times,* not a great likeness in the best of circumstances, but now there were two of them! He looked at the picture, then trained his sights on the two men standing with the bride. The picture could be of either one of them. Now what, kill them both? Then one of the men moved off. The older of the two stayed with the bride. She laughed and touched his arm. That was the groom then. Sligo steadied the gun, took a deep breath, held it, and squeezed the trigger.

The man in the scope's sights fell, clutching his side. He was hit, but Sligo couldn't tell if he was dead. There was a scream, then another. People were moving, panicking. The cops down there were already in action, scanning the perimeter.

Sligo dropped the rifle, hung from a limb, then dropped to the ground himself. For just a second he debated about the rifle. The smart thing was to leave it there. He'd been wearing surgical gloves, there was no chance of fingerprints. But he'd paid a fortune for the thing. With a little luck he could sell it back at fifty percent. He picked up the rifle and began to run. He wished he knew if the man was dead or not.

HEADLINE, *THE NEW YORK TIMES*:

# U.S. Is Willing to Assist Shah in Finding Refuge

# 4

Nardo came off the jet at Dulles International like an avenging angel. He would break Sam Bobrick's neck if there were any more slipups. The trouble was, Sam was a little too slippery to get a good hold of. All CIA people were like that; it didn't make any difference if they were supposedly in retirement like Sam or not. They never really retired, Nardo knew that. There wasn't one of them who wouldn't take on some kind of mission if offered, no matter what the official payroll at the agency said. Like old war horses staggering forth at the call, they didn't quit the agency, they just got called on less often.

He was there now, waiting to meet Nardo's flight. Close enough to the entrance to be polite, but off to one side so he could watch everyone else. Typical, typical. Old Sam with that ludicrous Marine haircut with his hair white as snow.

"Hello, Tom," said Sam, taking the overnight case from Nardo's hand as if Nardo had been carrying it all the way from California and needed instant relief.

"You screwed it up, didn't you, Sam," said Nardo.

"Did you have any bags, Tom?" Sam asked. He led

51

Nardo toward the baggage claim, walking swiftly, always one pace ahead of Nardo so he delivered his lines over his shoulder.

"No, I don't have any goddamned bags. I don't intend to be staying very long. Unless you screw it up again. . . ." Sam turned abruptly, yanking open a door marked Flight Personnel Only. Nardo scurried to catch up with him. How does an old man move so fast, Nardo wondered as he followed the former agent down a narrow corridor.

"You can always bunk in with me, if you like. I've got the spare bedroom," Sam said. "Or there's a Best Western about a mile away."

Sam opened another door and they were in the pilots' parking area, again marked Flight Personnel Only. Sam led Nardo to the plainest, dullest, most average-looking four-door sedan he had ever seen. The perfect spy's car, Nardo thought contemptuously. Put it against a background of city traffic and it would disappear completely.

But Sam walked past the sedan and opened the door of a pea-green Porsche 911. Settling behind the wheel, he pulled on a pair of very thin leather driving gloves. "It's not a great motel," said Sam. "But they have one of those water heaters in every room. You can make a cup of instant whenever you like." Nardo stood by the passenger door, gawking.

*I was on the White House staff of the President of the United States,* he thought in a rage. *You're a goddamned sixty-five-year-old spy with a kid's haircut. You're not even* employed *anymore!* How the hell did the rest of the world manage it? As he settled into the comfort of the Porsche's leather seat he took some pleasure in the realization that he'd soon be able to buy a fleet of these cars—if people like Sam didn't louse it up for him. As they drove away he hoped Sam would grind the gears.

Bobrick took them to a very ordinary Chinese restaurant in a suburban shopping center, where he insisted on paying the check. Nardo didn't pretend to argue, but got right to the business.

"I gave you two thousand dollars, Sam!" Nardo said. "Two thousand will kill somebody, won't it?"

Sam made shushing motions with his hands. "Well, won't it?"

"Usually," Sam agreed.

"Well, he isn't dead, is he, Sam?"

"It doesn't appear so."

"Why not!"

"Now, let's try to be calm," said Sam. "Tea?" He poured himself a cup.

"I'll pour the goddamned tea in your ear if you don't give me some satisfaction!"

Sam looked levelly at Nardo. A small smile of certain superiority, and contempt, played on his lips. "I don't think you will, Tom."

Nardo twitched in his seat. *That's why the little bastard keeps the Marine haircut,* he thought. *So he can think he's tough.* Nardo speared a piece of pineapple from his sweet and sour pork and jammed it into his mouth.

"So, why isn't he dead?" he said more softly.

"Good men are hard to find, Tom. A thousand dollars isn't much money these days, especially when you figure in expenses."

"I paid *two* thousand, Sam!"

"I do charge a finder's fee, Tom." Sam closed his eyes and rubbed them. "There are hired killers and there are assassins," Sam continued. "For that kind of money all you get is a hired killer."

"A dumb one, at that," said Nardo.

"It's not a line of work that attracts intelligence," said Sam.

"What is he, Mafia?" Nardo asked.

"Oh, no, they wouldn't take him. He's Irish."

Nardo laughed harshly. "Blackballed by the Mafia, there's some recommendation."

"They have their standards," Sam said.

Nardo started to laugh again until he realized Sam was serious. "Of course," said Nardo soberly. He didn't want the little spook to think he wasn't knowledgeable.

"So what do we do now, Sam? What's your best advice?"

Sam shrugged. "I sent him back."

"Back?"

"To the hospital to finish the job."

"Jesus, Sam!"

"He was paid to do a job. It would be very bad precedent to leave the job undone."

"Jesus! The man is incompetent! I don't want him shooting up a hospital. We're not looking for national publicity on this!"

"Calm down, Tom."

"Call him back. Stop him."

"I can't stop him," Sam said.

"Why not?"

"I don't know where he is. It doesn't work that way. I don't know where he is, he doesn't know where I am. We communicate by prearranged calls to public phones. It's part of the craft, Tom."

The old spook thought he was running a World War II spy ring. "Sam," Nardo said, struggling to remain calm. "Sam, I had hoped this would be fairly discreet." He was forced to laugh at the ridiculousness of the statement.

Sam saw no humor in it. "I didn't send him in with a shotgun, you know. He works better up close, so I let him do it that way this time."

Nardo shook his head, his eyes closed. Disaster. Just when he could smell the money, disaster.

"Don't worry," Sam said. "There won't be any mess this time. I told him how to do it."

"Oh. Good," said Nardo, trying to keep the sarcasm from his voice.

"There's only one thing," Sam said. "It will cost you more. We all have our expenses."

Dr. Weinberger was a big man, a former collegiate basketball player who had taken up tennis and couldn't stop talking about it. Peter had a headache and his side burned terribly and the doctor kept tugging on his mustache and talking about tennis. Peter suspected it was more for the nurse's benefit than his own.

"When can I leave?" Peter asked, interrupting.

"Ah." Weinberger paused, clearly not ready for medical talk. "Well, you were lucky. The bullet hit nothing but heavy muscle. No bones. If it hits a bone, then you get shattering, the bullet flattens out, the bones splinter—as I say, you were lucky. You should be able to get out of here in a day or two. . . . medically."

"And nonmedically?" Peter asked.

"Well . . . medically is all I deal with," said the doctor. The change of subject appeared to make him uneasy.

"What are you trying to say?" Peter asked. He shifted up on one elbow, and paid a price in pain.

"Nothing," said the doctor.

"Then what are you trying not to say?" Peter asked. Weinberger chuckled nervously. Why did they put him in these

55

positions? He was just supposed to take out foreign objects and sew them up cleanly.

"All I'm trying to say is that as far as *I'm* concerned, you'll be up and walking in a day or two, barring complications."

"That's as far as you're concerned. Who else is concerned?"

Weinberger waved his hands vaguely.

"In that case," Peter said, "I think I'll check myself out of here." Peter swung his feet to the floor, gripped the bed tightly for a moment to ward off the first wave of dizziness, then stood up. It felt as if someone had laced the wound with thorns, but he had lived with worse.

"Nurse," Weinberger said quickly. "I think you'd better go get that a . . . go get him." As the nurse hurried out Peter sat back down. Whatever they had given him for the pain had made him nauseous, and it wasn't doing much of a job on the pain either. There was probably a better way of getting what he wanted, but he wasn't thinking all that clearly, and he knew it. This was crude, but effective.

The nurse hurried back. For a moment Peter thought she was alone, then he realized a very short man was following in her wake. The man moved around from behind the nurse, impatient with her for blocking his way. His face was soft and puffy, but his eyes were hard and his mouth was set in a grim line. Peter imagined he marched through life angry at the indignity of being short.

The nurse slipped away immediately. Weinberger made an ineffectual try at bridging the situation.

"I was just saying to Mr. Stanhope that medically he's a very lucky fellow . . ."

The little man jerked his head toward the door in peremptory command. Weinberger chuckled nervously. "Well, I'll leave you to it . . ." He started out, but at the door he paused, made an assertion of authority. "Don't overtire him."

The man waited until the doctor had gone, then closed the door. "Don't try to leave until I tell you," he said without preamble.

"Who are you?"

"My name is Rimbaud." He flashed a badge at Peter, quickly returning it to its case.

"What was that? Your IRS badge? You're holding me for my back taxes?"

Rimbaud tried to smile, but it came off as a sneer. "I'm with the National Security Agency," he said. "We feel it is not in your best interests to leave the hospital just yet."

"Since when is the NSA concerned with my best interests?"

"Since you got shot."

"That must keep you busy," Peter said. "There are a couple thousand people shot in this country every week."

"Not with a 30-.06 by a man in a tree."

"That's a deer rifle. Maybe he thought I was a buck."

"Maybe he thought you were your brother." Rimbaud watched Peter's reaction, and this time he managed a genuine smile.

Peter paused. "Who shot me?" he said finally. Rimbaud shrugged.

"Ah, well, that's the big one," said Rimbaud. "Whoever it was got away."

"Clean?"

"Clean enough. The local cops are still looking around in the woods. They found the shell casing but not much else. The man was a professional. Not a very good shot, it seems, but he knows how to avoid getting caught."

"What makes you think he was after my brother?"

"Can you think of any reason anyone would want to kill you?"

"No."

"We can think of a reason someone might want to kill Austin."

Peter waited for Rimbaud to say more. The little man inspected his fingernails. *The bastard wants to be coaxed,* Peter thought.

"How many guesses do I get?" Peter asked. "Ghoubadi."

It was Rimbaud's turn to be surprised. Peter had taken a wild stab with the only shaft he had. It had apparently struck home.

"What do you know about Ghoubadi?" Rimbaud asked.

"He's very devout. He prays overtime."

"The pious hypocrite. What else?"

"Who wants to kill my brother?"

The two men stared at each other for a moment. Peter hoped that Rimbaud assumed he knew more than he really did. He had exhausted his hole cards, and the only thing left to play was a bluff.

"I don't think you know anything about Ghoubadi," Rimbaud said. He watched Peter's expression closely.

Peter smiled, big and broad, all innocence. "You're absolutely right. I just made up a name."

Rimbaud continued to study him, looking for a telltale break in his expression. Peter laughed inwardly. *He's actually looking deep into my eyes.* The first thing he had learned about interrogation techniques is that the guy who could look him straight in the eye was usually lying his head off. Peter continued to hold Rimbaud's unwavering gaze.

"You're lying," Rimbaud said eventually. Peter's smile broadened. *We took the same interrogation course,* he thought happily.

"You're the agent. You should know."

Rimbaud took the crease in his pants between thumb and

forefinger, pulling it taut. "Mr. Stanhope, let's not shit each other."

"That would be a refreshing change."

"You've been in the business," Rimbaud said. "You know how it works."

"I wasn't in the business," Peter retorted angrily. "We were an independent contractor. . . ."

Rimbaud waved away the objection. "Stanhope Security Corporation has been on the payroll of at least three government agencies for the past twenty-five years. You monitor satellite transmissions, you receive and transmit top-secret dispatches, you've got people working in both hostile and friendly nations all around the world. Hell, the course I took in evasive driving action to avoid terrorist kidnapping attempts was devised by your people. To me, that's being in the business."

Peter couldn't argue. He had devised the evasive driving technique himself. "I'm not with SSC anymore," he said lamely.

"If you're really out of the business, you're the first one I've ever heard of who made it. Once a spook, always a spook. Your brother's in the business."

Peter shook his head. "He works at the plant. I don't know what he knows about anything."

"He knows too much about at least one thing. It seems he started thinking those transmissions were intended for his personal benefit. He's an entrepreneur type, you might say."

Peter was startled. "You're not saying he's gone over."

"No," said Rimbaud. "He hasn't sold anything to the other side. He's just trying a little native American blackmail."

"Who's he blackmailing?" Peter asked. He knew he wouldn't get an answer.

"I think we can assume it was someone who resented it," said Rimbaud. "You know I couldn't tell you if I did know, but I don't. I got in on this case very late."

"That makes two of us," Peter said. "Where's my brother? I think I'd like a little talk with him."

"So would we. I hoped you'd know where he is."

"Gone?"

"Poof! Apparently he knew the bullet was meant for him."

"Did you ask his wife?"

"She's still his fiancée, I believe. The ceremony was canceled rather abruptly. Why, do you think I'll find him hiding under her bed? If he's got sense enough to bolt into a hole, he's got sense enough not to tell anyone where it is."

"So what do you want with me?"

"For the moment, just stay put. You're a lot safer here."

"He's not going to try to kill *me* again," Peter said. "He must know by now that he shot the wrong man."

"How?"

"The newspapers, for one thing. . . ." As he said it Peter knew he was in real trouble. "Don't tell me you kept it out of the papers."

"I told you I got here late," Rimbaud said. "But we did manage to make sure the media knew it was Austin Stanhope who was shot."

"Why?"

"It might make it a little safer for your brother, for one thing, if they think he's lying here in the hospital. Very few people even know you're in the country. They'll never suspect you were the one who was shot."

Peter noticed the shift from "he" to "they" when Rimbaud spoke about the killer. He knew it had to be more than one man with a gun, but it was not comforting to hear it confirmed. "And is Austin Stanhope dead?"

"Oh, no," said Rimbaud. "Your situation is serious, but stable."

The perfect description for Rimbaud's purposes, Peter thought. They could have "Austin" recover, or they could have him die, whichever suited their purposes. And the situation was iffy enough to lure the killer back to finish the job, if he were urgent enough. Which is what Rimbaud wanted. Using Peter as bait to catch the killer would give them a nice fresh trail to follow. *That's why I'm in a private room,* Peter thought. All the more tempting for the killer. Peter hoped the assassin was smart enough to smell a trap and stay home.

Sligo found the woman he wanted at midnight. She was a waitress, closing up a diner on the Greenwich Post Road. As he followed her to her car he estimated she was about five years younger than he was, which was perfect. It would give verisimilitude to his story—not that anyone was apt to be suspicious.

The waitress realized someone was behind her just as she reached the car. For an instant she thought of trying to unlock the car and jump in, but the fear of being taken from behind was too great. Instinctively protecting her back, she turned to face whoever it was. She was a tough woman who had led a tough life, and she didn't scare easily. But when she saw the gun in his hand, she could scarcely catch her breath.

"Please," she said, trying desperately to remember all the things people advised to do in a crisis. "Please, you can have my money, it's right here . . ." She offered him her purse, praying it was the right thing to do. She had no way of knowing that it would have made no difference what she did.

Sligo hit her with the butt of his .38, striking from shoulder-height down and across. The metal caught her on the forehead and ripped her skin all the way to her ear. She fell back against the car, stunned but still conscious.

Sligo turned her keys in the lock and shoved her into the front of the car, flat on the seat. *He's going to rape me,* she thought with a curious sense of detachment. *Rape me, then shoot me.* She tried to speak, but her jaw didn't seem to move. Sligo shoved up her sleeve and took a hypodermic syringe from his pocket. He found the vein in her arm and pushed in the needle.

The anesthetic reached her heart in one beat, in two it was invading the nerve centers of her brain. *He's killed me,* she thought. *I'm dying now.* But why was he moaning? Her lids fluttered and her eyeballs turned up in her head. She didn't realize she was doing the moaning.

Sligo removed the needle and replaced it in his pocket. He was pleased with how well it had gone. She was alive but unconscious for more than long enough for him to do what he had to do. And the injection had gone very well. He would do it exactly the same way next time, only then he would inject air into the vein, at least 20 ccs.

Sligo walked to the pay phone outside the diner. Sam had told him the air bubble would lodge in either the right side of the heart or the lung field, it didn't matter which, because the result would be almost instantaneous death in either case. Unless the medical examiner suspected an embolus and did the autopsy on the organs underwater to detect the escaping bubble, they'd never even know why he had died. If the guy was asleep, he'd do it that way. If he was awake and caused trouble, Sligo would put a bullet in his eye.

Sligo dialed the emergency ambulance service. When they arrived, he was beside the waitress's unconscious body, wailing about his wife who had been brutally attacked. The ambulance attendants took both man and wife to the emergency entrance of the hospital.

At twelve forty-five Rimbaud made his second inspection. The agent at the front entrance was standing unobtrusively behind the admissions desk, where he had a clear view of everyone coming and going. He had nothing to report, the hospital was very quiet, all the employees had been very cooperative. Rimbaud checked the men at the rear and side entrances. They had even less to report. He stood outside a moment, breathing the cool night air and studying the stars. He had known the constellations once. As a Boy Scout he could have navigated his way across a continent by night. Now he could identify only the Big Dipper. What happened to all that knowledge, he wondered. Was it still locked somewhere within his brain? Or was it gone forever, like the Boy Scout. An ambulance pulled into the basement entrance, past the man on guard and straight into the building. The ambulance had its lights flashing and cut the siren only as it dipped onto the entrance ramp. The agent on duty watched it go past.

Rimbaud ran up to him. "I told you to check everyone!" he cried.

"I am, I have been," replied the startled agent.

"What about that ambulance!" As he spoke Rimbaud could see the attendants wheeling the gurney into the service elevator. A worried-looking man was holding on to the woman on the stretcher. He patted her hand as the elevator door closed.

The agent turned to look. "Those are emergency patients," he said. "How am I supposed to check them out?"

Rimbaud groaned and tried to choke back his temper. "How many ambulances have gone in tonight?"

"Five or six. Hell, Rimbaud, those people are *hurt*."
Rimbaud ran into the building.

Sligo slipped away when they wheeled the waitress into the emergency ward. He took off his jacket, revealing the white doctor's smock underneath. Taking a stethoscope from one pocket, he put it around his neck, then patted the other pocket to make sure the syringe was still there. He found the stairwell and walked up two floors. The corridor was empty. He walked quickly to room 312. No one saw him.

Peter was paying a price for his decision to take no more pain-killers. If someone was stalking him, he wanted his head clear. But the price was pain in his wounded side. It hurt him every time he moved in bed, so he had given up trying to sleep, preferring insomnia to the continual jabs of fire.

He made his way to the bathroom in his private room, treading gingerly. Even sitting down was difficult. The bullet had ripped through the large muscle mass on his left side. Any movement of the left arm which jostled that muscle mass made it feel as if he were rubbing shards of glass against the skin.

Peter heard the door open in the outer room. The nurse, coming to wake him and urge more medicine that he would not take. He started to tell her to go away, when he realized the tread was heavy, the pattern irregular, as if someone were not quite sure where he was going. Peter turned off the light in the bathroom and opened the door a crack. By the night light he could see a large man in a doctor's smock, holding a syringe in his hand. The man was looking at the empty bed, puzzled.

Peter eased the door shut. Doctors do not walk around with

syringes in their hands and no ampules of medicine, he knew. Peter estimated he had thirty seconds at the most before the man thought to look in the bathroom. He quietly pushed the lock button on the door. It would not keep a determined man out for very long, but it should buy Peter a few precious seconds.

He looked hurriedly around the bathroom for a weapon of any kind. He was wearing hospital sandals and pajamas. There was nothing on the sink except a cup. Peter lifted the heavy porcelain top off the toilet water tank. It was much too heavy and unwieldy for him to swing one-handed, and at the moment two hands were out of the question. He could hear the man approach the door and give the handle a tentative tug. He figured he had fifteen seconds, if that.

The toilet was an old-fashioned one, thank God. Peter plunged his hands into the cold water and unscrewed the float ball from the ball cock assembly. On the end of the ball was a metal rod, ten inches long, ending in a rusty half-inch screw. The rod was thin and easily bent, but if it struck head on, with weight behind it, it just might do. It would have to.

The man was pulling hard on the door now. The jamb shuddered with each effort. The man was pulling rhythmically, getting all his weight behind it. Peter timed the surge, slipped off the lock, and leaned into the door the next time the man pulled.

The door flew open with all of Peter's strength behind it. Peter let his momentum carry him into Sligo, thrusting up and forward with both hands on the rod as his shoulder slammed Sligo in the chest. Peter cried out as he felt the stitches rip in his wound. At the same time Sligo screamed. The metal screw end caught him in the right armpit, stabbing an inch and a half into the tender flesh. The killer slammed against the bed waist-high. His knees buckled and the float ball, dangling down from his armpit, hit the bed, jamming the metal deeper into his body.

Sligo tried to lift his pistol, but the rod had penetrated muscle, paralyzing that arm.

Peter ran for the door, slipping in the slick-soled sandals. He kept going, half on his knees, half on his feet, as Sligo transferred the pistol to his left hand. Sligo fired twice, as much in fury as in hope of hitting anything with the wrong hand. The first shot hit the ceiling and the second tore a hole in the door as it closed behind Peter.

By the time Rimbaud reached Peter, Sligo was gone. They found the bloody float ball in the stairwell where Sligo had torn it from his arm, and not much later they found the body of the agent on duty at the emergency entrance. He had a bullet in his skull, delivered from behind at point-blank range.

While Rimbaud and the other agents were occupied with their dead comrade, Peter dressed and walked out of the hospital, into the night. Within five minutes he had vanished as completely as Sligo.

# 5

---

Sam waited for the call in his favorite booth of his favorite Chinese restaurant. Sam knew nothing about Chinese food, rarely ventured beyond the familiar blandness of Cantonese cuisine, but he liked the prices. It was still possible to get a meal for less than four dollars if you knew where to go and what to order. For a man on a pension, that was important. He was feeling a bit flusher these days, thanks to his business with Nardo. Two commissions, not very much, really, but it added up, and there were always unexpected bills for the car. The Porsche was his only extravagance, but Lord knows the maintenance was high. It was worth it, though, he thought as he remembered the look on Nardo's face when he saw the car for the first time. Oh, it was worth it.

The pay phone rang, and Sam was there in two steps. The waiters didn't even look up. They had long since ceded him rights to both booth and telephone.

"Yes," said Sam.

"Sam?" Sam winced with annoyance at the use of his name. The jerk just couldn't learn procedure.

"Go ahead," Sam said.

"This is . . ."

"I know who you are," Sam said abruptly. "Go *ahead*."

"I need some help. I'm hurt. I think it's infected."

"Were you successful?"

"I'm really hurting, Sam. They know it, and I don't think I can go to a hospital."

"Were you successful?"

"I tried, I really tried," Sligo's voice whined in Sam's ear. "He must've known I was coming. How the hell would he know that?"

Sam looked at the floor, trying to think. It was imperative that Sligo not be caught. He only knew Sam by his first name and a phone number in a Chinese restaurant, but it might be enough. Sam did not relish spending the rest of his retirement in a federal prison.

"Now, let's stay calm," said Sam, as much for his own benefit as Sligo's.

"It's red and swollen and I think it's blood poisoning. It was a thing from the *toilet!* Jesus, can you imagine the germs? I can't go home like this, how can I explain to my old lady? I can't go to a hospital, I'm sure they're looking for me . . . Sam?"

I'll get you a doctor," Sam said in soothing tones. "We'll take care of you, don't worry about a thing, we'll look after you. Now I have a place I want you to go to." Sam gave him an address in Manhattan. It was a safe house that Sam had recruited himself. To his knowledge it had been used only once, during the debriefing of a defecting Ukrainian general. It was very unlikely that it would be in use at this time. Procedure called for using a safe house no more than once a year. Anything more frequent than that would jeopardize security and anonymity. He wouldn't need it more than two days; if things were done properly, no one would ever know he had used it at all. The agency wouldn't like it if they knew he had been there, but he would have to make sure they never found out.

After he finished with Sligo, he called the girl and told her to get out. He would leave a message on her service when she could come back.

Sam got some change from the cashier, then made one more call from the pay phone. There was a hint of danger in the air now, and Sam enjoyed it. He also enjoyed the fact that he was in for another payday, a big one this time. Things would have to be very professional from now on, and that was expensive.

The Man was leading Nardo on a walk on the grounds of the estate. It was partly for exercise, but partly because Tony hadn't made a sweep for bugs in several days and the Man didn't trust the house. The Man stopped next to a towering tree.

"Tom. Tom," the Man said portentously. "Isn't that a lovely tree?"

"Yes, sir," said Nardo, to whom a tree was a tree.

The Man, however, was speaking in that ponderous voice he used when he wanted to display the depths of his soul. Nardo was convinced he had neither soul nor depth, but his voice sounded as if he were about to deliver the Ten Commandments for the first time.

"How old would you guess that tree to be, Tom? In years."

Nardo looked at the huge trunk, the great height. Who cared. "Fifty years, sir? A hundred, maybe?"

"One hundred years, Tom. Think of that." Nardo laughed inwardly. Here the old bastard was displaying his sense of history. "I wonder, Tom, if that would be a hemlock or a beech or some other sort of tree."

Nardo recognized the game now. It was an old briefing trick from the days when the Man visited foreign countries. He would memorize facts about one irrelevant topic, the history of a river or a castle, and when the time came he would disgorge it to his host. It was supposed to make him look knowledgeable and interested in the other man's country.

Nardo took a guess and hoped he was wrong. The Man would enjoy correcting him.

"Is that a beech, sir?" Oh, Christ, he'd got it right.

The older man sniffed. "I believe you're right, Tom."

It was a hell of a way to begin, but Nardo had no time to waste. "Uh, Mr. President, the thing is, we need twenty thousand dollars to do the job right . . ."

"I see, Tom."

"We need to hire . . ."

The Man interrupted him quickly. "I'm not really interested, Tom. You say to me you need twenty thousand dollars and I assume that your purpose is good and honorable. Is that correct?"

"Uh, yes, sir, that is correct," Nardo said.

"My concern is to get what is properly mine. I leave the details to you. And, of course, it is your responsibility to conduct yourself in an appropriate and lawful manner at all times. I have faith that you will do that, Tom."

*So much for the record,* thought Nardo. *It didn't work before, I don't know why you think it will work now. But then most of us are doomed to repeat our mistakes, not learn from them.* "Absolutely, sir," he said.

"In that event, I think we can arrange twenty thousand."

The blue Ford was parked on a residential street, fifty yards from the access road that led to the Man's estate. Stone was on the radio to Quigley.

"He's leaving now. They said good-bye from the front porch," said Quigley, his voice crackling slightly on the radio.

"Did you get any of the conversation?"

"Nothing when they were outside."

Very good directional mikes were available that could pick up a conversation outside from fifty yards away. But that required a trained man to operate it, and Stone's budget didn't allow for that.

"Got him," Stone said into the radio as he saw Nardo's red Camaro pull off the access road onto the street. He signed off, then drove slowly after Nardo. *Love that red car,* Stone thought. It was perfect for tailing. Very few people had taste that gaudy, it was like following a flashing light.

As Stone drove carefully in Nardo's wake he reflected bitterly that this sort of gumshoe work was really the job for a junior man. The Head of Station had had lots of praise for Stone when he delivered the news of the Man's activities, but an official commendation had not followed. At least not yet. Nor had a promotion. Of course, one never knew. The wheels of the gods and federal service were notoriously slow in their grinding.

Nardo parked the Camaro outside a Laundromat. He had gone straight to the first pay phone. Very obliging, Stone thought. He checked the notebook that lay on the seat beside him. In it Stone had listed the numbers of all the pay phones within a ten-block radius of the Man's estate. It had taken Stone the better part of a day to put the list together, and now this jerk went straight to the first one on Stone's list.

Stone spoke into the radio. "He's making a call now from 555-1389. Tell them to hurry."

Quigley alerted the contact at the phone company. It wouldn't take them long to plug into the line; it all depended on how much Nardo had to say.

\*  \*  \*

Nardo had very little to say. Sam answered by saying "Sixteen." It meant to add the number sixteen to the last digits of this phone number. That would be the number at which to contact Sam the next time. If there was a next time.

"Minus seven," said Nardo, giving him the code for the number where Sam could reach him. They had refined their technique and were operating "on full jeopardy basis," as Sam put it.

Nardo spoke again. "Go," he said. He paused for just a second to hear if Sam had a reply. When Sam hung up, Nardo did the same. The listener at the phone company caught none of it.

Open auditions were the worst part of an actress's life. They were demeaning and impersonal, treating people like cattle, judging them on their size and shape. But it was as much a part of being an actor in New York as anything else, more, and if you wanted to make it, you had to do it. And Anne Shepherd very much wanted to make it.

Along with close to twenty other hopefuls she waited in a lobby outside a rehearsal hall. Someone thrust a script in her hand ten minutes before her turn, telling her to read pages six and seven. She read them as fast as she could, trying to get some idea of the character, some sense, however fragmentary, of what the part was about, what the play was about. It was impossible to do in that time, but at least everyone else was faced with the same impossibility. The only chance of an advantage was to be a name actor, which she was not, or to know some member of the production staff who could slip you a script ahead of time. She had done that a few times, deliberately putting up with the advances of assistant stage managers just to get an edge. It hadn't worked. That is, she had got the script, but not the part. Turned down, as always, for the same unacceptable reason.

This play was something vaguely confusing about a young man called Suggs, who was apparently being derailed by city life. Well, she could identify with that easily enough, but she wasn't reading for the part of Suggs. As nearly as she could tell, she was up for a multiple role, playing a slut on one page and a sweet young thing on the next. How some of these plays got produced, she would never know.

The rehearsal hall was a large, empty room. The producer, whom she knew by reputation, was seated behind a table with two other men. One of them, chain-smoking and averting his eyes, was the director. The other, a dour, bearded young man with his arms folded tightly across his chest as if to keep himself together, she assumed was the writer.

The stage manager gave her her cue and she began to read. The trick was to act, but not too much. They didn't want a performance at this stage, but they didn't want a recital of your grocery list either. All they were looking for now was a quality, some suggestion that you were close enough to the type they wanted. The chance to act, to give an interpretation, would come in the call-back, when you had had a chance to actually read the script. If you were lucky enough to get called back. Most were not.

The writer was conferring with the director even as she read. She tried to ignore it and keep on going. The stage manager read his lines as flatly as humanly possible—which was preferable to the few who thought they were John Barrymore—and Anne responded with brightness and what she hoped they would take for charm.

"Thank you," said the director, too abruptly. She was certain it was the first time he had actually looked up.

"I could try it differently," Anne said. "With a little more emphasis on the hoyden quality." *What? Was the girl supposed to be a hoyden? What was a hoyden? Keep your mouth shut, Anne.*

"That won't be necessary." The director smiled a smile as cold as Siberia.

"It's a little hard to know exactly how to approach it, with the shift in characters and everything . . ." Anne said.

"Yes, it is difficult. Of course, we're not really after a performance now."

"I could play the first girl with a street accent, if you like," she said. *A street accent? Why not tell them you'll play her with a limp. Don't beg, Anne. Don't explain. Don't alibi.*

"No, that's all right," said the director.

*Now say thank you, Anne.* "Thank you."

"Thank *you*," said the producer, speaking for the first time. "It was very nice. You were lovely, really. We'll call you," he said with a smile. *I know that smile,* Anne thought. *If he calls, it won't be about the part.*

"I enjoyed reading your play," Anne said, startling the writer. He unfolded his arms and nodded his head. "It was very funny."

"Thank you," he muttered, surprised. *I hope it's a comedy,* Anne thought as she left.

On the way out she heard the writer say it to the director, as she had heard it so many times before, either whispered or directly. "She's too pretty."

Men seemed to think she was made for walking under parasols, sniffing handkerchiefs scented with violet, being courted on porch swings. "But I have guts," she would tell them. "I have character, I am not just my face! Give me a chance, I can be as offbeat, as lusty, as ballsy as anyone. I can *do* the part!"

"*I* believe you," they would say. "I'd believe you in the role . . ." and then the pause, the terrible pause, "but I just don't think the audience would."

Try television, they would say. Try the movies. With your looks, they'll eat you up. But Anne didn't want to be eaten up, she didn't want to be a constant close-up. She wanted to be an actress, and that meant working on the stage. All the rest was just talking heads.

Another audition was scheduled for the afternoon. After a yogurt and an apple, Anne called her service to see if there were any messages. Roy should be coming back from the dinner theater production of *The Odd Couple* any day now. He was notorious for not calling ahead of time, but you never knew. Roy was anything but the most attentive of lovers, but at this point in her life Anne didn't want that much attention. What she really wanted was work.

The answering service informed her a "Max" had called. The message was simple. "Please vacate till further notice." That meant she'd have to bunk in with Ruby for a few days. She hoped Ruby had something she could wear. She could always buy another toothbrush, but it was very inconvenient never to have any notice at all from Max. But then that was part of the arrangement, and the regular check went pretty far toward taking care of the rent.

When the telephone rang the first time, Smith made no move to answer it. He had been sitting in a rocking chair for more than an hour, rocking slowly back and forth, staring at the design on the wallpaper. In its innocent swirls and loops he saw dragons and monsters, torturers and victims, the horribly deformed and the mutilated. Each new section of the wall, each rearrangement of the arabesque pattern brought a new fantasy of the inferno to his imagination. Smith would frequently sit and rock, staring at the wall as other men sat entranced before the television screen, but Smith would conjure up a nightmare of his own imaginings. His state was not catatonic, it was willed. He was aware of everything around him, of noises on the streets below his high-rise apartment, of activities in the carpeted hallway outside his door, but his rancorous spirit was with the infernal pit his mind had carved for him out of the wall.

He did not stir to answer the phone, but he did not ignore it. The phone was an unlisted number, and Smith never received social calls. Only two kinds of people rang Smith's phone. People with the wrong number, and people with death in their hearts.

After waiting five minutes, Smith disengaged his mind from the horrors on his wall and pushed the replay button on his telephone-answering machine. A voice began the call with the proper code word, Nemesis. It gave a number to call back, the Washington, D.C., area code, and the time to call back, 5:00 P.M. It was now eight in the morning; the caller had left Smith the prescribed eight hours before returning the call. All the rules had been followed.

From a collection consisting of all the major cities in the United States and Canada, Smith took out the book for Washington. It was a reverse phone book, listing the numbers first and then the name and address. The telephone Smith was to call was in a Chinese restaurant on Seventeenth Street.

Smith caught a shuttle flight to Washington, and by three o'clock he had located the restaurant. He parked his car at a meter three blocks away, and napped. Nights were torture for him, alternating bouts of insomnia with jagged shards of sleep tormented by nightmares. Because he seldom slept well at night, he napped whenever he could during the day. For some reason the terrors of his imagination did not trouble him when the sun shone.

At four thirty he was in the restaurant, seated in a booth, with an unobstructed view of the public phone. He toyed with a plateful of fried rice, pushing it around with the fork held in his left hand, keeping the right hand free. Smith did not expect any trouble here, but he had kept alive by anticipating the unexpected.

At ten minutes to five Sam Bobrick came into the restaurant and took the back booth, facing the phone.

Smith watched from his vantage point by the door. As expected, Sam had walked right past him without noticing. Smith was glad it was Sam, he liked working with agency people. Smith liked to know what everyone was doing and was going to do, associates and prey alike. Agency people like Sam had their routines, their so-called "craft," and they stuck to it. It made them devious, but predictable. Smith was entirely unpredictable.

Sam waited impatiently. At five o'clock he started glancing at his watch every thirty seconds. At five minutes after five Smith slid into the booth beside him, and Sam nearly cried out. The agent had spent his working life among hard and dangerous people, but none of them had ever inspired fear the way Smith did.

"Hello, Sam."

"Smith."

Averting his gaze from those eyes as unfeeling as an adder's, Sam told him what he needed done, then handed him an envelope containing ten thousand dollars, the first payment.

"I keep this, regardless," Smith said.

Sam looked up angrily. "What the hell . . ."

"For my trouble," said Smith. He laid a hand on Sam's arm. From anyone else it would be a friendly gesture, but Sam stiffened as if a snake had crawled up his sleeve.

"Of course," said Sam.

The medical bag was brand new, but no one could tell it. Smith had kicked it and trod on it for ten minutes to give it the proper appearance of extensive use. He had also done some work on the black felt hat that he wore perched on the back of his head—but not as much. A hat shouldn't look as used. The addition of a plain dark suit and thick-rimmed eyeglasses completed the disguise. It was the suggestive quality of the props that made the disguise effective. It was not necessary to really alter or hide the face. Later, if anyone remembered him at all, they would recall an Orthodox Jewish doctor in his mid-forties. Smith was none of those things.

When a wary voice answered the downstairs lobby buzzer, Smith announced himself as "Dr. Shapiro." At the door of the apartment Sligo eyed him carefully through the spy hole before letting him in.

"It took you long enough," Sligo said, leading the way to the bedroom. It was a woman's apartment, that much was obvious right away. From the look of one wall of photographs, she was an actress, or someone connected with the stage. Whoever she was, she was gone, and that was all that mattered to Smith. He noticed a worn corduroy jacket in a half-open closet in the bedroom. Not at all Sligo's style, it must belong to the actress's lover. It was his only influence in the apartment, however, so Smith deduced the affair was casual, or at any rate infrequent.

Sligo had come to the door with his shirt over his shoulders. Now he shrugged it off and sat on the edge of the bed.

78

Even from a distance the angry red swelling under his arm could be seen. Smith put the medical bag on a chair, well out of Sligo's reach, then looked carefully at the wound. Crimson lines radiated from the puncture hole like a spider's web, spreading venom into the system. He certainly had blood poisoning by now, and probably an infection of the lymph nodes under the arm as well. *Just keep him away from a real doctor for two more days and he'll die on his own,* Smith thought. But of course that wasn't Smith's job. It was his task to assist nature in her elimination program.

"You have blood poisoning," Smith said. "You need an antibiotic right away." He opened his medical bag. "I'm going to give you some metocyline to begin with. If that doesn't work, we'll try something a bit stronger." He took out a syringe and an ampule of liquid.

"No needles," Sligo said. Smith looked at him blankly.

"No fucking needles." Smith proceeded to fill the syringe.

"It doesn't hurt," said Smith soothingly.

"I said no fucking needles! I've had my fill of those!" Ever since Sam had explained it, the thought of an accidental embolism had haunted him. "Give me a pill."

To emphasize his point Sligo pulled his left hand from under the pillow. The .38 pointed at Smith's chest. Smith froze. The plan had been to drug Sligo, then take him to the place of execution, somewhere far from the safe house. Now, however, he would have to improvise.

"Yes, I have a pill," he said. He put the syringe back in the medical bag. When he turned back to Sligo, he shot him once between the eyes from two feet away. The little Browning .380 with a silencer made a pop like someone exhaling forcibly. Sligo was dead before his head hit the pillow. Sligo's .38 fell to the floor with a clatter. Smith eased it to one side with his foot as he quickly wadded the bedspread and stuck it under the corpse's head to absorb the blood. Smith would have to clean up the place before he left, and he wanted to keep the mess to a minimum. He was faintly aware that something had happened during the crisis that he had missed, some noise or motion just outside his full consciousness.

He put the Browning back in his bag and elevated Sligo's head to keep the blood within the body, wrapping part of the bedspread completely around the dead man's face. When he saw the motion from the corner of his eye, he realized what he had missed earlier. As he shot Sligo there had been the sound of a key in the lock. Now a young man stood in the doorway of the bedroom, keys still dangling in one hand, a suitcase in the other, a smile frozen on his lips. *He belongs to the corduroy jacket,* Smith thought. Home from wherever, slipping in unannounced to surprise the actress. Never a good policy, nobody liked surprises in the bedroom.

The nearest gun was Sligo's on the floor beside his foot. Smith grabbed it, turned. The young man had time to say, "No," with surprising calm, as if they were two adults who could talk this over. Sligo's gun pulled slightly to the left, so Smith's shot entered through the cheekbone. This time, without a silencer, there was a loud crack that seemed to reverberate throughout the apartment for a full minute.

By the time the cop made it to the third floor of the brownstone, he was breathing hard. He was fifty years old and twenty pounds overweight, and he was scared. But when the call of "Man with a gun" comes in, you have to respond. He had his own police automatic drawn and ready, although he had never fired it except on the target range in eighteen years of service.

A doctor passed him on the stairs. "It sounded like it came

from that way," the doctor said, pointing. The cop eased aside to let him pass, then called after him.

"Hey, wait a minute," he said. The doctor turned and fired through his medical bag. As the cop hit the stairs and rolled down several steps, Smith hurried away. *To hell with it, let someone else clean up the mess.*

# 6

As the nightly news flickered greenly in the background, Peter continued to leaf through *The New York Times*. The great newspaper would be his lifeline and his means of communication. It was hard for him to imagine how any clandestine work in the country could function without the *Times*. Distributed to every major city in the world as well as the nation, it was the closest thing to a national newspaper America had. Things were much easier in other countries; in Germany, for instance, anything carried in the *Berliner Tagesblatt* could be found by anyone in the country. In America one had to be a bit more enterprising to find planted information. Still, agents managed. More messages in simple word-code appeared in the pages of the *Times* in the course of a week than went by mail, telephone, and dead drop combined.

The want ads were the busiest section, and the miscellaneous offerings the most popular there. He glanced at the column. A simple three-line slug advertising "Quantity of Orceime Avail, for immed delivery," giving an address and phone number, seemed a likely flag for an agent who knew what he was looking for. "Orceime" was probably a manufactured word, close enough to a real one to appear a simple misspelling—in this case orcein, a commercial dye—but unintelligible to the average reader. The message could be in the arrangement of letters in Orceime, or in the false address or phone number, or in any combination of the three. Sometimes the simple posting of the ad was enough to trigger preset actions.

The beauty of the scheme was that there were thousands of ads in the *Times* every day, and it was virtually impossible to check out the legitimacy of each and every one. In fact, a really top-level operation would be working through a legitimate cover anyway, running the message in one ad among a series of bona fide ones. There were dozens of ways to work it, and they were all effective if one knew the code, impenetrable if one did not.

Peter had placed his own ad immediately, paying a premium for space at the bottom of page one. It cost more, but this was a distress situation and demanded priority measures. The message, two tiny lines of pica type running the width of a column read: "Dear Bill, Bailey, All is Forgiven, please Come Home. Pearl" and giving a P.O. box at the newspaper for a response. The message was a fairly common one. The flag for Austin to be sure it was meant for him was the comma misplaced between Bill and Bailey. A second check was the uncapitalized *p* in please.

If Austin saw it, he would know how to get in touch with Peter safely. He knew to look there, of course, for it was a distress-flag system established by their father long ago. They had all used it more than once during their practice missions, and Austin knew it well. The only trick to it was to get the typesetter to write it the way Peter wanted, but a note to follow instructions precisely usually sufficed. The linotypists at the *Times* were accustomed to the peculiarities of the paying customers when it came to the ads.

Peter found what he was looking for in the obituaries. Halfway down the fifth column was the name STANHOPE— Austin Richard, of Greenwich, Conn.

Of a gunshot wound, the article stated flatly. Beloved son of Richard C. Also mourned by adoring fiancée, Margo Rynn. Funeral from the E. Cheney Funeral Home, 36 Humboldt, Greenwich. Friday, June 6, 3 P.M. In lieu of flowers, contributions may be sent to the National Foundation for Cancer Research, Bethesda, Md.

It was a neat job. No mention was made of Peter as a loving brother. If the assassin didn't know of his mistake yet, he wouldn't find out of the possibility from the obituary. The request for no flowers was a good touch too. Flowers were definitely not Stanhope style. If the assassin was looking for confirmation of his kill, here it was in black and white in *The New York Times*, the newspaper of record to the Library of Congress and every other library in the country.

He nearly missed the news story on television, cataloguing it automatically as just another murder in New York, but a few details registered after the actual item was over. Peter watched for the story on the ten o'clock news, then caught it twice more on the eleven o'clock shows by switching channels.

A policeman responding to a report of gunshots had been shot and killed by a fleeing man who had apparently already slain two other men, a James Sligo and a Roy Cantrell. Sligo was the one who caught Peter's attention. The newscasters mentioned that Sligo had been in possession of a 30-.06 Winchester. Peter knew from Rimbaud that he had been shot by a 30-.06. A festering wound in Sligo's armpit coupled with an eyewitness account of the fleeing man led the police to believe the killer was a doctor. Here, it was the wound that caught Peter's attention. There might be many men with wounds in their right side who carried hunting rifles around the city, but it didn't seem likely. Someone had executed the man who had tried to kill Peter.

The late news had an interview with a bewildered but beautiful young woman who rented the apartment in which the killings had occurred. The newscasters described her as an out-of-work actress, a phrase that had come to mean whatever the attitude of the newscaster gave it to mean. For many the term suggested a euphemism for prostitute. The fact that most actresses were out of work most of the time by the nature of their business did not alter the fact that most of the hookers in town called themselves actresses or models.

If she was indeed a hooker, Peter thought, she would never be out of work. Harried and frazzled as she was during the interview, she was one of the loveliest women he had ever seen.

# 7

Cheney was scared, but he didn't know why. For the third time in as many minutes he walked to the window and looked out into the night. The lights from the room spread a vague semicircle of yellow in the gloom, revealing the emptiness of lawn that surrounded the funeral home. There was nothing out there. At one in the morning there never was anything out there except the odd raccoon that wandered in from the wooded areas of Greenwich in search of edible garbage.

Cheney hadn't really expected to see anything. This sense of uneasiness was probably caused by some variation in atmospheric pressure working subtly on his nervous system. Or perhaps a trace of indigestion registering its effects subliminally. Cheney was a rational man who prided himself on being something of a lay scientist. He was not superstitious—he could hardly have survived in his profession if he were—nor was he given to flights of imagination. He took science on faith, putting his trust in the theories and hypothesizing of learned men. He believed in quarks and quasars and black holes in space and other concepts he didn't understand. He believed in extraterrestrial life when a consensus of scientists espoused it, and when the reaction came and other, equally lustrous, men of academe and planetarium denounced it as highly improbable, he could see the reason in that, too.

But Cheney did not believe in spooks. He did not believe in life after death—as a funeral director he had seen far too much death to believe anything could survive it—and he did not believe in ESP or any sixth sense.

He did believe the skin on his scalp was tingling, however. He did feel gooseflesh on the back of his neck, and he did feel as if his back were vulnerable. He did feel he was being watched—but he didn't believe it.

Cheney returned to the corpse he was working on, drawing the shades once again against the blackness of the night. He turned back to a room as brightly lighted as a surgical theater. His disposable paper smock and head cover heightened the similarity to a hospital. In some ways he was like a surgeon, Cheney thought. True, he was not trying to save lives, but he was preserving the integrity of the body. He was very like a plastic surgeon, he thought. No one else appreciated that fact, of course, but Cheney knew it and it gave him a certain comfort and satisfaction.

Cheney drew on his surgical gloves. He was a neat and tidy man by nature. He was a big man, his body showing the bulk and strength of a football player, but his spirit was abstemious and precise, and had become even more so because of his work. He liked what he did, but he didn't like the mess, he didn't want it touching his skin.

The cadaver lay naked on the gurney. The penis that had swollen to full tumescence at death lay limp and shrunken. The blood that filled it had long since settled in the lowest part of the body. While the top half of the corpse was almost chalky white by now, the backs of calves, thighs, and shoulders had the purplish bloated look of a blood blister. By concentrating the blood in one area, however, gravity made Cheney's work easier.

Cheney pushed the penis aside with the back of his hand and massaged the flaccid skin of the inner thigh until he found the large femoral artery. Bunching the skin with one hand so the artery would stand out, he inserted a needle the size and shape of those used to pump up basketballs. At the base of the needle was an expanded opening with a threaded interior. Cheney screwed the hose into the needle. The hose ran to the evacuator, a small electrical pump that sucked out the remaining blood from the body. The blood was pumped out and stored in a six-gallon receptable that was capable of handling the fluids of half a dozen corpses before being emptied.

As the evacuator made its familiar metronomic soughing sounds, Cheney thought he heard something else. A scrape, a click of metal, but less, something that just barely registered audibly at all, not really enough to identify. But it was a noise that Cheney was aware of on some level, just as he was aware of being watched.

He knew he was being silly, acting irrationally, but nevertheless Cheney opened the heavy wooden door leading to the storage room. The eight coffins rested on their stands, just as he knew they would. The storage room had no windows, no access other than the door Cheney had come through. Nothing else was in the room, as he knew nothing would be.

Still, it was with an effort of will that he turned and walked out of the storage room rather than retreating backward, trying to watch behind him.

The evacuator was making the discreet coughing sound it made when the pump was pulling nothing but air. As air rushed into the open cavities of the corpse to fill the vacuum in the evacuator, the dead man's chest rose and fell slightly, his cheeks sucked in and out, the lips twitched. This body a

91

day before had been a Mr. Arno Peterson. Cheney had known him vaguely, something less than a nodding acquaintance. He had worked in the produce department of a local grocery, and Cheney assumed that he had occasionally bagged some fruit for him and they had exchanged pleasantries about the weather, but he couldn't honestly remember it. He hadn't caused Cheney a moment's thought when alive, but in death he was giving him some small problems. Mr. Arno Peterson had died in his own home while trying to add a new electrical service himself, a chore he was unqualified for. The idea was to equip the spare room to accommodate a new multispeaker stereo system, a minor passion with Peterson. The result had been electrocution. Peterson had lain, twisted into the final agony, for the better part of a day before he was discovered. His limbs had rigored in their tortured positions, muscles bunched as tight as stones by the electricity, then cemented there by rigor. The knees were lifted almost to the chest, the arms crossed, fists clenched, in death's angry parody of the fetal position.

The arms caused no concern, but the legs wouldn't fit into a coffin. Cheney pulled out his retractable clamps—large, heavy-duty tools with ratchets and sprockets—not unlike a car jack. He placed two felt-covered armatures on either side of the hip joint and the tongue of the apparatus on the underside of the body. He slowly tightened the clamps. In theory the device was supposed to work like a man snapping a wishbone with a hand on either side and the center held rigid by the thumbs; but in practice the bones sometimes splintered where they shouldn't, skin tore. It took skill and practice and patience to make it work neatly, a certain touch and feel.

Cheney had the touch. The tautened adductor muscle in the rigored leg stretched, then tore. The leg swung loosely in the hip joint. Cheney snapped the knee joint in the same manner and lay the leg flat on the gurney. As he did so he paused, listening. Nothing, not a sound. He willed himself not to go and take another look.

The corpse's features were twisted into a horrible grimace caused by the electrical shock. The lips held a permanent snarl of pain. It was not a face Cheney could present to the bereaved who would come tomorrow to view the departed. His job was to change extremity into serenity. Using a surgeon's scalpel, Cheney reached inside the cadaver's open mouth and severed the muscles of the face that twisted the lips and locked the jaws open. He filled the mouth with cotton wadding to prevent the cheeks from sagging, then he closed the mouth and massaged the unattached muscles until they held the lips in the position he wanted. Just the tiniest suggestion of a smile.

Prizing up each eyelid in turn, he made tiny incisions that would allow him to pull them over the eyes, cutting off the light of the world forever.

A few veins in the face had hemorrhaged during Peterson's death scream and had not been drained by the evacuator. Using a syringe with a tiny needle, Cheney siphoned off the few drops of blood under the skin. The makeup would have covered it, but Cheney felt it was the little details that made all the difference.

Leaving the hair and the cosmetics for tomorrow, Cheney attached another hose to the needle that was still implanted in the thigh artery. This hose led to the small pump that suffused the body with embalming fluid. Moments after Cheney turned it on, Mr. Arno Peterson began to take on some of the tone and resiliency of life as his body's veins, vessels, and arteries filled with fluid again.

Cheney stifled a scream. Something was in the room, moving silently behind him. Cheney turned, instinctively grabbing the scalpel.

He saw a businessman, a commuter to New York City like the hundreds who lined the railway platform every morning. He wore a pinstriped suit and carried an attaché case. He wore tortoiseshell glasses, and his hair was neatly combed and coiffed. A lawyer, perhaps, or an executive of some kind, a banker. The man smiled slightly.

The smile helped Cheney to breathe again. His adrenaline was still pumping fast, but he relaxed a little at the smile.

"Who are you?" he asked.

"Jones," said Smith. He continued to smile. It was his only joke.

"What . . . How did you get in there?"

"I picked the lock."

Cheney chuckled involuntarily. He couldn't tell if the man was serious or not. He assumed he was not.

"What do you want?"

"Put down the scalpel."

Cheney looked at the blade in his hand. It was the first time he had been aware of it. He hesitated, taking comfort from the feel of it in his palm.

"Oh, yes," said Smith, nodding reassuringly. "It might hurt you."

"You startled me," said Cheney. He put the scalpel on the gurney, but it was still within easy reach of his hand.

"Why is that?" Smith asked.

"It's the middle of the night."

"You're working," said Smith. "I'm working."

"What did you want?"

"Show me Stanhope," said Smith.

"I . . . don't understand," said Cheney. He was very afraid that he did understand.

"You have the Stanhope body. You are burying it tomorrow, isn't that right?"

"It's not for viewing. The coffin is sealed at the family's request."

"Open it," Smith said. "At my request."

"That's not possible."

Smith smiled again, an icy twist of the lips. "Let's be friends," he said. "Let's cooperate like gentlemen and friends."

Smith stepped closer. Cheney backed against the gurney. He felt riveted by the man's eyes. Cheney had never seen such a lack of reaction before. The man was in the same room with a naked corpse, yet he hadn't once even glanced at it, much less shown the usual revulsion or fear.

"I can't show you the body, I'm sorry, Mr. Jones. You'll have to take that up with the Stanhope family."

Smith edged even closer. He was standing distastefully, uncomfortably close, almost touching Cheney with his body. Cheney craned his neck backward, away from Smith's face, which was too near his own.

"I'm asking you to leave now," said Cheney. Smith leaned into him, his chest against Cheney's.

Cheney's fear gave way to annoyance. "Get out."

Smith made a disappointed pout, his lips only inches from Cheney's face.

"Aren't you my friend?" he asked, his voice singsong, mocking.

Cheney was several inches taller and outweighed the smaller man by twenty pounds. Whatever was wrong with the intruder, Cheney was having no more of it. He put his hands on Smith's shoulders and shoved. He felt a searing pain in his knee as Smith swung the edge of the attaché case into it. Grabbing the gurney for support, Cheney's fingers touched the scalpel. Before he could lift the blade, the attaché case slammed down on his fingers with a clearly audible snap of bone.

Cheney fell to his knees, cradling the broken fingers against his chest. "You broke them," he said, amazed at the speed of the violence that had befallen him.

"I could remove them, if you'd like," Smith said. "Would you like?"

Cheney shook his head. He began to think the man intended to kill him. The taste of bile seared the back of his throat, and he felt he might throw up.

"Please," he said.

"Please yes, or please no."

"Don't kill me!" Cheney moaned.

"Oh, we haven't come to that yet," said Smith. "Now get up and show me the body."

It had finally happened to him, the random violence everyone dreaded, the sudden, senseless eruption of hate and destruction, a man knifed in the back on a crowded street for looking the wrong way, a girl shoved in front of a subway, an innocent family slaughtered in their beds. It was a curse of the times, and it had fallen at last on him. Cheney knew the man would kill him without hesitation. His only hope was to humor him, to try to dampen the murderous urge with cooperation.

Cheney pulled himself up with his good hand. When he took it away from the gurney, the fingers were wet with embalming fluid. Breaking the knee joint of the cadaver, he had torn the skin in a crease. Under pressure from the pump, the embalming fluid came out in a fine mist, like water from a punctured garden hose.

"I have to sew up that puncture," Cheney said, and even as he said it he knew he was babbling.

"He'll wait," said Smith. He tapped Cheney on the back with the edge of the attaché case. Cheney hurriedly led Smith into the public room.

A coffin rested on a crape-covered stand before a deliberately antiseptic altar arrangement that managed to suggest religion without denomination. Several straight-backed chairs were aligned in front of the coffin so the bereaved overcome with grief—or the plain weary—could sit. There were a few simple floral wreaths, but not many. The Stanhopes were not gaudy.

The lid on the coffin was closed.

"Open it," said Smith.

"I've been instructed not to. I'll get into trouble," said Cheney, remembering the short man with the French name, Rimbaud. Cheney was never certain what branch of the government the man was with, but he had been very explicit about the need for secrecy.

"You are in trouble," said Smith.

Cheney needed no further reminder. He began to unscrew the lid. The casket was the middle of his line. Cheney had argued for an expensive one, urging that Mr. Stanhope would want one, but apparently the government was paying for this one, and they economized where they could.

Cheney's hand slipped on the screwdriver, and the tool clattered to the floor. "I'm in pain, you really hurt me," he said.

Smith looked at him impassively. Cheney retrieved the screwdriver and set to work on the last screw.

"It wasn't my idea," said Cheney. A whine had taken over from his normal tone. Pain no longer motivated him, it was fear now.

"No," said Smith understandingly.

"It's not right, I didn't want to do it. They made me."

"Of course," said Smith.

Cheney removed the final screw and prepared to lift the lid. "It's empty," he said, as if to prepare Smith for the fact before showing him. Smith kept his unwavering eyes fixed on Cheney.

Despairing, Cheney lifted the lid. The casket was empty.

"I told you," said Cheney. He could feel his body quivering, but couldn't stop it.

"There's just room for you," said Smith.

"What?"

"Get in."

"Oh, God, no! Please don't kill me! I didn't want to do it."

Smith looked surprised. "Did I say I was going to kill you?"

"Please, no, please!"

"I just want to see how you look in there." Smith's tone became soothing, comforting, like a parent trying to convince a child of something harmless that only looks dangerous.

"It looks big enough, I think you'll fit. And it's all padded and comfy-looking. Just get on in."

Cheney climbed in. He didn't know why, the other man hadn't threatened him again, he had no weapon. Smith simply seemed deadly in himself.

"Oh, God," said Cheney.

Smith lowered the lid into place, and Cheney could feel his fear rise up and pound against his chest. "Don't lock it," he begged. "Leave it open." He heard the screws being screwed into place.

Smith smiled to himself as he left. Tormenting Cheney hadn't been part of the job, he had come merely to find out if Stanhope had really died. Normally he didn't mix business with pleasure, but some things were just too good to pass up.

*David Wiltse*

As Smith walked past the corpse on the gurney and out the door into the night, the bloated body of Arno Peterson began to spew forth fluid. Skin split and cavities opened and embalming fluid sprayed as the pump kept forcing it in.

# 8

When Peter reached Greenwich it was midday and the streets were vacant. Waves of heat rose off the pavement, and the back ends of air conditioners poking out of every window in every shop and home pushed more heat into the streets.

He stopped at the first public phone and dialed. A girl answered. Peter listened just long enough to hear if there was a drop in the intensity of the signal.

"Hello?" Margo said again. "Who is it?"

Peter hung up. If the phone was bugged, it was being done very professionally. A good bug was undetectable to the naked ear, but it took time to install. The quickest way was still to cut into the line directly with alligator clamps. It was not foolproof, but for someone working hurriedly and cheaply, it was expeditious.

It was a three-minute drive to Margo's condominium, hardly time for her to have left home since he called. He circled the block once, checking out all the most likely places for a shadow to park himself. A green Chevy was at the corner, windows rolled up, locks on. If anyone was using that car for a sentry post, he had a high tolerance for heat. A light blue Datsun was closer to the condominium, on the opposite side of the street. A man was sleeping in the passenger seat, a newspaper over his face. A panel truck was parked at the end of the block, the side door open for ventilation. Vivaldi played softly on a tape deck, but no passenger was in sight.

Peter picked the Datsun as the most likely choice, then the van, if someone was staking out Margo's place. And *if* anyone was trying to find his brother, it was the logical place to start. It was where Peter was starting. Peter entered the lobby of the condominium and counted very slowly to twenty, then stepped back outside. The sleeping man in the Datsun had not stirred. There was still no sign of life from the panel truck. Peter glanced up at the numbers over the door as if uncertain about the address, then went back in.

The man on the roof of the building opposite Margo's condominium put down the binoculars. They had hooded lenses to prevent a telltale flash of reflected sunlight. Smith was frying in the sun. The heat was absorbed by the tar paper on the roof beneath his feet. Every move of his shoes was met by a protesting sigh of sticky tar. Smith waited for three minutes by his watch to see if Peter would come out prematurely. He muttered to himself as he waited, a low, guttural sound just below the level of speech.

Smith had begun talking to himself in high school. A brilliant student academically, he had no gifts whatever for dealing with people. He went through his early years friendless, turning his energies inward as he mastered one skill after another, then contemptuously turned his back. He abandoned karate classes just short of gaining his black belt. In noncontact practice Smith had broken his partner's jaw with a kick. Everyone assured him it was an accident, but Smith knew it was not. He had wanted to break the boy's jaw, had

102

wanted to smash the skull and crush the windpipe under his heel. It had nothing to do with the boy—Smith rather liked him. When he saw the boy fall, clutching his face, it was all Smith could do to restrain himself from continuing the attack and finishing him off. At the age of seventeen, knowledge of the violence inherent within him frightened Smith, and he had withdrawn still further within himself.

By the time he reached college, Smith was so centered upon himself that he scarcely even noticed when others made overtures of friendship. At the age of twenty-one Smith was like a man dancing round and round in a circle with himself, arms linked, staring inward. Whatever went on outside the circle didn't interest him.

He graduated cum laude with an engineering degree. But despite his talent he lasted less than six months on his first job. When a superior urged him to do the work he was assigned—rather than a project Smith was interested in—Smith had warned the man off. The man persisted over the period of a week. At the end of a week he told Smith he was recommending his dismissal. Smith broke the man's arm in three places.

By now Smith was talking to himself most of the time. At first he had been aware of it and rationalized that he only did it when alone. Then when he began to do it in public, he told himself that he knew he was doing it, it was willed, and therefore something he could control. After he broke his superior's arm, Smith ceased to notice when he was talking aloud and when he wasn't.

He was living the secret, private life of his own mind so completely that he felt the covert life was the only sensible way to make a living for himself. He decided to be a spy. The intelligence agencies took one look at his psychological profile, his high potential for violence, and snapped him up.

He fell to the care and training of Sam Bobrick, at this point acting as a troubleshooter and specialist in "wet affairs"—the CIA euphemism for bloody business. Sam was not one to dirty his own hands, he had neither the inclination nor the stomach for it, but he was good at giving others directions. Smith was a willing subject; he soaked up the fine arts like a sponge and served Sam well until a brush with death during a minor Middle East operation.

The doctors pronounced Smith cured after three weeks in intensive care and six months in a hospital bed. When he was retested, however, his violence potential was so high and so volatile that even the agency became alarmed. Smith was released and reclassified as a part-time free-lance "occasional."

He was too good at "wet affairs" to go unused, however. There were many men who wanted his talents, men and agencies and governments, and they were willing to pay well for the service. None of them cared that Smith talked to himself. They just didn't want him talking to them.

Margo was surprised to see Peter at the door, but Peter had expected that. Her reaction contained something else, an element of nervousness that skittered along the edge of her smile and drew the corners of her eyes into a squint.

"Is anything wrong?" he asked.

Margo looked at him blankly, then laughed.

"Is that supposed to be a joke?" she said. "Austin is gone, vanished. Not so much as a word to me, not a whisper. One second I'm about to get married, the next my fiancé has disappeared. A sniper takes a shot at you—I guess you're all right. You look all right—my fiancé vanishes, and some strange little man comes to tell me I have to say Austin is dead. He doesn't tell me *why* I should say that, mind you, just that I have to, that Austin's safety depends on it. Then you disappear from the hospital. Then you show up." She waved a hand at her severely cut gray suit. "I'm off to Austin's *funeral*, for God's sake. Nobody even knows where he is, and I have to stand there while somebody blesses an empty coffin and plants it in the ground." She seemed to stop from lack of breath. "I mean what the hell," she ended lamely.

"Is there anything I can do?" Peter asked.

"How about explaining it to me."

"I don't have a clue," Peter said. It was half true, at any rate. He didn't have a clue that was strong enough to hold the weight of supposition, but he had some straws to grasp at if the need arose. He was hoping Margo could reassure him there was no need.

"Do you have any idea at all where he might have gone?" he asked.

"No. The little man went through all of that with me."

Peter walked casually around the room, stopping here and there to toy with a knickknack, to glance at a picture. "He never mentioned some place where he felt safe?"

"He used to say he felt safe with me," she said bitterly.

Peter moved around behind her, passing the bedroom door. He noticed that her nervousness increased. "I really have no idea, none at all," she said, rather too sharply, as if to pull his attention away from the bedroom door.

Peter stopped directly in front of the door, his back to it, looking at her. He crossed his arms across his chest and studied her for a moment. Margo tried very hard and almost managed to conceal her agitation.

"That's good," said Peter.

"What is?"

"If you don't know where Austin is, you can't tell anybody else." He moved back into the room, taking his seat again. "Whatever is going on, it's best for you just to go along with it. No sense in struggling unless you know what you're fighting against. You might do yourself more harm than good."

"That doesn't sound much like you from what Austin told me."

Peter smiled. "It's my advice to you. Not to me."

"Do you really think he's all right?" she asked.

"Yes. Of course," Peter lied. He really didn't know what to think until the other side made their next move. If they didn't make a move, that might well mean that Austin had been quietly disposed of, along with whatever problem he represented.

Margo seemed to be reassured. "Meanwhile, all my friends are calling to say how sorry they are. I have to answer condolence cards. I can't tell you how idiotic and bizarre it is."

"It must be difficult for you," Peter said. "Who's in the bedroom?"

"What?" she asked, her voice unnaturally high. She forced a chuckle. "What do you mean?"

Peter rose again and crossed to the window. The panel truck had moved away. The man asleep in the Datsun had twisted his head, knocking the newspaper off. His mouth was open and Peter could imagine him snoring.

"It's none of my business, of course," Peter said. "You don't have to tell me."

Margo was about to speak again when the bedroom door opened. Peter's father stepped out.

"Your instincts are still good," said Mr. Stanhope.

"Yes."

"But you shouldn't be here."

"It was safer to come than to call."

"Safest of all to do nothing."

"Was it your idea to make me the lightning rod?" Peter asked.

"I don't know any more about this than you do," said Stanhope.

Peter couldn't suppress a smile. His father always knew more about everything. That was his job, his career, his entire character.

"Do you know where he is?" Peter asked.

The older man shook his head.

"Then I can't help him, can I? I put the ad in the *Times*."

"Yes, I saw it," said Stanhope.

"I'll give him two more days. If I don't hear from him, I'll assume he doesn't need me. Then I'll leave."

Stanhope snorted contemptuously. "Yes, you leave. You do that well."

Peter fought down his angry response. He would not fight with the old man, he vowed. He wouldn't give him the satisfaction.

"Is there any way I can help?" he asked, struggling to keep his voice calm.

Mr. Stanhope turned his back to Peter. Instead of answering he poured himself a drink. Peter noticed the old man's hand was still steady as he poured, but it was rather more bourbon than it used to be, and rather earlier in the day. He quelled the surge of sympathy as strongly as he had the anger. He wanted to feel nothing toward his father, nothing at all.

Margo stiffened as Peter turned to her. She was still smarting about being caught in a lie and angry about being caught in the middle of these two stony men. They spoke to each other as if issuing commandments from their respective mountaintops, cold and aloof.

But when Peter spoke to her, his tone was soft and caring. "Can I help you?" he asked.

"Well . . ."

"I'll take care of her," Stanhope said sharply. "She's family, she'll be cared for. You decided that family matters didn't concern you any more, as I recall." The old man's tone was bitter, surprisingly angry and hurt.

"I didn't decide that. I've done what I could for him," Peter said.

Stanhope lifted his glass in a mock toast to Peter. "Of course."

"I got shot in his place."

"A beau geste," said Stanhope.

"What would you like me to do?" Peter persisted. "If there's something more, tell me."

"As you say, you've done all you could. I would hardly expect you to do more for your brother."

The elder Stanhope stood with his back to the window, his chin raised imperiously. The sunlight hit him from behind and before he moved, Peter could see the clear outline of his skull under the thinning hair. His father looked suddenly twenty years older, skeletal, a prefiguration of death. Despite his resolve, Peter felt a surge of sympathy well up and overpower him.

"Dad," said Peter, "can't we make it up? I don't care whose fault it was anymore . . ."

"It was yours," said his father curtly.

"All right, it was mine, I don't care, it doesn't matter. Let's just forgive and forget about it all."

For a second Peter thought his father was softening. Five years of bitterness and ill will seemed about to be swept aside in a moment. But the old man stiffened, his voice turned flintier than ever.

"You expect my blessings before you desert us again, do you?"

"I didn't desert. I resigned. I'll stay if you tell me how I can help. . . . Dad, Tom is dead, you couldn't have grieved more than I did—but he's dead. Can't we try to get over it?"

The older man's voice came like rocks striking boulders. "When you lose a son, then tell me about grief. Until then, have the decency to assume a parent suffers more than you can know."

Peter looked at the floor, defeated. "Do I have to die for Austin to make up to you for Tom?"

Stanhope remained silent.

"He doesn't want that," Margo interceded. "Tell him . . ."

She turned to the older Stanhope, touched his arm. He turned his eyes to her, as blank as if she weren't there, then glared once more at his son.

"Austin and I did not *quit*," he spat. "We never stopped trying to find out why Tom was killed. *You* left."

"I left because Tom's death was so senseless! How could I keep playing security games for the corporation when those games had killed my brother!"

"They are—not—games," said Stanhope frigidly. "Austin stayed. I stayed. We have been finding out."

Peter paused. "What have you found out?"

"The *corporation* has been working on it," said Stanhope. "You quit the corporation. Your brother called you back, I did not. He felt he needed you, I did not. Ask Austin."

Peter walked to the door.

"He knows how to get in touch with me if he wants me," Peter said. He paused at the door, hoping to find the right words to somehow lessen the damage he and his father had already done to each other. "Dad," he said slowly. "I'm trying . . ."

"Go," said Stanhope. He said it as a curse. "Go!"

\*     \*     \*

For the first few minutes after leaving Greenwich, Peter was able to shut off his mind completely. He didn't think of his father, he didn't think of the events that had so changed their lives, made them enemies. He concentrated on his driving, checking in the mirror now and again from habit to see if he were being followed.

Then he passed the SSC building again and suddenly he was back five years in time, joking with his brother Thomas as they walked to their father's office in the Stanhope building for a briefing on their next assignment.

# 9

From the beginning Peter had thought it was a strange operation. Too many unanswered questions, too many equivocations, too much risk, too little reason. Peter had voiced his doubts to his father, but the older man had paid scant attention.

"The plan is simple enough," Mr. Stanhope had said. "We are to determine the feasibility of an attack on the Iranian oil fields. You've done this sort of thing dozens of times."

"But always in this country," Peter said. "We've always done it for defensive purposes."

"No one is asking you to attack the oil fields," the older man said impatiently. "Just study the possibility. Just find out if it's possible."

"But who wants to know?" Peter insisted.

"The government has asked us to take on this assignment," his father said flatly. Stanhope had linked his career with the government for thirty years. It was not a connection he questioned, or one he allowed anyone else to question. "We are rendering our nation this service."

Peter knew it was impossible to penetrate the cloak of patriotism once his father put it on. It was the one unalterable, unassailable given for all of their operations. Stanhope had a rock-hard faith in his country's justice that had been born in the Manichaean conflict of World War II. His values had been shaped in that struggle and had changed little since.

"If you're uncomfortable with the assignment, you can stay home," Stanhope said. "I'll take your place. Thomas and I can manage."

From behind their father, Thomas winked. They all knew it was no idle boast; the older man was capable of just about anything his sons could do, but there was nevertheless a tinge of the parental martyr in his tone. For a moment Peter considered withdrawing. He felt he was going into the project blind; there was not necessarily anything to worry about, but he hated not being able to see the end.

Thomas saved the moment with his infectious laugh.

"Come on, Pete," he said, eyes twinkling. "It's a chance to travel. We'll get away from the old man for a while."

Stanhope grinned. There was virtually nothing Thomas could say that displeased him. He took ribbings and friendly insults from Thomas that no one else on earth could get away with. In their own way they were almost as much brothers as were Peter and Thomas.

"You won't find anything to do I haven't done," Stanhope said.

"But we'll do it so much better," Thomas said. "After all, there're two of us."

"It would take two of you," Stanhope said, his gruffness only partially masking his affection.

Thomas touched Peter's arm. "Come on, Pete," he said. "It'll be fun. I'm looking forward to it." Thomas was always looking forward to excitement, he thrived on it, and when his sense of adventure was stirred, it carried everyone with it.

"Sure," Peter said finally. "It'll be fun."

They received their briefing in a small hotel in Paris's Thirteenth Arrondissement from a man in Western clothes. He spoke with the clipped accent of an English boarding school, but he was not English. Peter guessed he was an Arab, but he could have been anything from Moroccan to Yemenite. They left Paris with instructions on their mission but no more knowledge of their employers than when they began.

The orders themselves were too explicit, with a timetable established for every move. Again Peter was uncomfortable. "If they're going to lay it all out for us like that, what's the point in hiring SSC? They're not using our expertise."

"They're experts in this region," Thomas said. "They can set things up that would take us months to figure out. I'm glad for the help."

"I like to pick my own time and place," Peter said, but he saw it was useless to argue. Thomas was excited by the idea of a midnight penetration across a border, more excited still by the prospect of a two-week dalliance in the Middle East after the mission was over.

"And I like to know who I'm working for," Peter added in one last attempt to bring his brother to his side.

"You're working for Dad," Thomas said. "That's good enough for me."

In the end Peter had to admit it was good enough for him, too.

They flew into Riyadh and were hustled immediately into a waiting limousine. They drove without pause to the coast of the gulf that was known as the Arabian Gulf to the Arab world and as the Persian Gulf to the West. The driver appeared to speak only Arabic.

"This is service," Thomas said, luxuriating in the back seat of the Mercedes. "Just lie back and enjoy the view." He glanced out the window. The same flat desert landscape they had been seeing for over an hour greeted him. "If there was a view."

"We're absolutely helpless right now," Peter said. "You realize that, don't you? We don't know where we are, we can't communicate, we're totally at the mercy of this driver. . . ."

"He seems a very competent driver," Thomas said, grinning. "He's only gone off the shoulder twice. That's not bad, considering there isn't any shoulder."

"Doesn't anything about this bother you?" Peter asked.

"I like it. We don't have to think, for once."

"I prefer to do my own thinking," said Peter.

"That's because you do it so well. Now me, I'm just a magnificently trained physical specimen."

"Sure," said Peter. "You're dumb as a post."

"There you have me. Keep me fed and well oiled and point me in the right direction."

"Doesn't anything about this operation strike you as peculiar?"

Thomas rolled down the window, letting in a gust of dry, hot air that felt as if it had come from a blast furnace in the air-conditioned car. "Peter, my lad," Thomas said, "I think it stinks to high heaven. I thought it stunk from the moment we first heard about it."

"Then why in hell are we doing it?"

"You know why. Dad wants to do it."

"Do we have to agree with him even if he's wrong?"

"We have the right to disagree," Thomas said. "You argued against it, didn't you? He listened to you. He just didn't change his mind."

"It might have helped if you'd joined me instead of acting like it was an invitation to a picnic. He listens to you."

"He values your analysis," Thomas said. "You've got a better mind for that than I do, and we all know it."

"He may value my analysis," Peter argued, "but he values your *opinion*. If you thought this mission was a bad one, why didn't you tell him?"

Thomas paused. When he spoke it was with a degree of seriousness Peter seldom heard in his brother's voice.

"Pete, he's sixty years old. He built SSC from nothing, he's been in charge all of his adult life. It won't be very long before you and I are running the firm. He knows that, we know that. But I don't want to be the one to tell him it's time to move over. He's entitled to some mistakes. I'm only thirty. I can wait for him to decide to step aside. . . . I love him too much to push him out."

Peter nodded, acquiescing silently to the special bond that existed between Stanhope and Thomas, his firstborn. Stanhope had always been scrupulously fair as a father, bending over backward to spend as much time with one son as the other, measuring his time and his praise and his affection with an equal hand for each of them. But there had always been a special intensity in Stanhope's time with Thomas, a hint of duty in his dealings with Peter. In the end Peter had come to accept the specialness of Thomas's relationship with his father, just as he had come to accept the inevitability of their present mission—because there was nothing he could do about either without hurting his father.

The driver took them to an empty stretch of beach, pulling off the road and driving across the sand to within fifteen yards of the water. Smiling and nodding, he indicated with gestures that Peter and Thomas were to stay on the beach. As he re-fueled the Mercedes from jerry cans stored in the trunk, the driver fielded all of Peter's questions with shrugs of incomprehension. At last he drove off the way he had come, leaving the brothers alone on the beach to watch the car's cloud of dust slowly settle onto the barren desert.

"Exciting, isn't it?" Thomas said. "Lost and alone in a strange land. Prey to the elements. It's like Robinson Crusoe."

"Doesn't anything depress you?" Peter asked. He knew in fact that virtually nothing did. Thomas always seemed to be happy, even in adversity.

"Think of it as a challenge," Thomas said. Which was the way Thomas generally viewed matters. He always looked for the way to wring joy, or at least interest, out of any situation. He had a knack for turning the worst drudgery into a game that Peter could only marvel at. To Peter drudgery was drudgery, and the only sensible thing was to find the most efficient way to get it over with. Austin, still young, was displaying a talent for getting out of it.

In the distance Peter could see freighters and oil tankers sailing up and down the Gulf, forming a sort of haphazard parade of nautical commerce. The Gulf was a very busy waterway. They had been waiting less than half an hour when one of the silhouettes on the horizon left the flow of traffic and headed toward the shore.

The brothers could soon make out the shape of a dhow, the wooden sailing ship of ancient design that was little changed since the voyages of Sinbad. The dhow was the basic vessel of all local commerce, used for fishing, for ferrying coolie labor from India and Pakistan to the labor markets of the sheikdoms of the Gulf, and for hauling everything from television sets to gold from port to port.

This dhow was chipped and peeling paint and looked as if she had been kicked and butted out of port by all the sleeker vessels in the Gulf. But Peter could tell that the mangy appearance was calculated and carefully maintained. The mainmast that once held a triangular lateen sail was now rigged with a block and tackle, as a freighter should have been, but atop the mast was a sophisticated antenna for the most advanced electronic systems. Beneath the deck two huge diesel engines purred in tandem, sending ripples of vibration through the hull even when the ship was stationary. A thick carpet of indifferent design and machine manufacture that covered most of the main deck where cargo would normally be lashed was barely worn by use. This dhow was no routine transporter of vegetables and refrigerators. Ugly and commonplace enough to avoid suspicion from a distance, fast enough to outrun the Coast Guard when necessary, sophisticated enough to slip between patrols at night, she was used to smuggle gold into India.

The captain was a short, smiling Arab in the traditional flowing white robe and headdress. He squinted at the brothers through his wire-rimmed glasses, looking more like a clerk in some remote branch of government service than a modernday brigand. The only other crew member, a lascar who looked as if he'd stepped from the pages of a robust Kipling tale, was an Afghani whose travels had brought him from the mountain fastness of his homeland to the rocking deck of a ship. He wore dull tan pajama bottoms that billowed out from his legs, then nipped in at his ankles, where they were tied with a bit of twine. His face was seamed and dark and rugged, his eyes as unforgiving as those of a hawk, but his fingernails and toenails were brightly painted with henna in accordance with local superstition.

Neither captain nor lascar spoke English, French, German, or Spanish, the languages the brothers had between them, but again verbal communication did not seem necessary. The captain knew what he was doing and set out immediately across the Gulf as the sun dipped below the horizon at their backs.

The lascar served them first small cups of very strong coffee heavily spiced with cardamom, hovering close by with the pot in case they should want more than the few swallows that barely covered the bottom of the cup. When they had finished the coffee, he served them again, this time with Czech-made Skorpion submachine guns. The compact gun with its collapsible wire butt was more of a machine pistol, capable of being fired with one hand on the wooden pistol-grip. It was a cheap, nasty, dangerous weapon up close, virtually useless beyond forty yards.

"What the hell is this for?" Peter demanded. The lascar nodded and withdrew.

"Why Czech weapons?" Peter asked Thomas. "Why any weapons at all?"

Thomas didn't answer because he was standing by the rail, mouth half-open, breathing deeply and slowly. His hands gripped the wooden railing, knuckles white with pressure.

"For God's sake, don't get seasick on me now," Peter said.

"Doing my best not to," Thomas muttered, trying to smile.

As the ship reached the center of the Gulf the captain consulted his watch, then put the engines in neutral. They wallowed in the swell worse than ever, bouncing on the waves like a cork without any forward motion from their engines. The sun had vanished completely, and their only light was from their running lights and the occasional tanker passing in the distance.

When Peter gestured for the captain to get on with it, the Arab pointed to his watch. They were sticking to a timetable, the same timetable Peter had objected to from the start.

Peter returned to his brother and found him on the platform that stuck out from the stern of the boat and passed for a latrine. It was nothing more than a jut of timber, slightly larger than a man's body, with a hole in the middle that emptied into the sea below. It was enclosed by a barrel-shaped railing, high enough to hide a squatting man's body so that his head would be visible on one end, his feet on the other. Thomas was not squatting, however, he was leaning far out over the railing, moaning with each roll of the boat.

Peter found a life jacket in the cramped hold and managed to tie it around his brother. Beyond that there was nothing he could do for him. The continued pitching of the ship was making him queasy himself. He tried to concentrate on the mission, the pointless appearance of the submachine guns. There was no need for them, they had no intention of using them. Peter knew from experience that guns had a tendency to get fired, whether they should be or not, and the best way to avoid using them was to avoid having them.

The captain consulted his watch once more, then the ship moved forward again. The forward motion reduced their pitch and roll, and Peter felt relieved enough to check on Thomas, who was still in the open-air latrine.

"We should be there soon," Peter said, although he had no idea if that were true. Thomas could only moan and nod in reply.

Eventually Peter began to sense the presence of land. The scent of salt water and diesel fumes was penetrated by something dry and acrid. The blackness of the horizon seemed to have a different quality, a different darkness. A shimmering light appeared at the edge of the water, then slowly rose skyward as the ship steamed forward. Peter recognized it as the flame of natural gas being burned off atop an exhaust stack. They were close to the oil fields, closer still to the shore.

"Turn off the running lights!" Peter ordered the captain. The man shrugged, uncomprehending. Peter pointed to one

119

of the lights and said again, "Turn off the lights! We can be seen for miles!"

Again the captain shrugged, pointed to his ear. Peter smashed one of the lights with the Skorpion muzzle. Expressing alarm, the captain reluctantly cut the lights.

"We'll go in from here on our own," Peter said. "Kill the engine." He reached past the captain and shut off the engine himself. As the motors died, Peter kept his attention on the shore, ignoring the captain and his gesticulating lascar. Without the interference of the running lights, Peter could see more clearly. He thought he detected shapes rising above the sand, shapes of indeterminate form but the height of a man, that were possible to see only when they moved. As the motors died, there was a great deal of movement, then everything on shore froze.

Another sound attracted Peter's attention away from the shore. To the rear and off to his right Peter saw the running lights of another dhow. It glided up to them and reversed engines, coming to a stop in the water not twenty feet away, holding there, as if waiting for Peter's dhow to move.

Peter turned to the captain, whose face had gone tense and blank. *He looks like a man who's about to jump ship*, Peter thought, *but doesn't want anyone else to know it.*

"What is this?" Peter demanded, gesturing with the Skorpion, then wheeling it back toward the captain. The captain took a deep breath, as if resigning himself to his fate. A sound of frightened voices came from the other dhow. In the gloom Peter could make out the forms of many men on the dhow. As his eyes grew accustomed to the shifting lights on the rocking ship, he realized the deck was crammed with people, all of them in some kind of military uniform. From this distance it was impossible to make out the nationality of the army the men belonged to, but most of them appeared to be wounded or ill. Many of them lay or half-reclined on the deck and against the rails. Others stood with the peculiar stance of the injured, curling themselves protectively around their wounds. It looked like a hospital ship, but there was no sign of doctor or nurse or comforts of any kind, only the uniformed wounded.

There was a babble of voices speaking Farsee, the language of Persia. Peter was unable to pick out the few words he knew from the rising call of distress. One voice sang out in French. Peter saw one man leaning out over the railing of the dhow, stretching his arms toward him in a gesture of supplication.

"*Au secours!*" the man called to Peter. "*Au secours!*" Then he switched to German, "*Hilfe! Hilfe!*" and finally to English, like the radioman on a sinking ship beating out distress signals on every available channel.

"Help!" he cried, reaching toward Peter. "Help! We are prisoners!" The rest of the men picked up the cue and rushed to the side of the dhow, like beggars who have found a bene-factor, all of them stretching their supplicating hands toward Peter. Their voices cried out in Farsee and English, over-lapping and drowning each other out so that Peter could distinguish no individual words. But the meaning was clear enough.

"We'll go in from here on our own," Peter announced. "Help me with the dinghy." The lascar did not move. Peter raised the Skorpion, suddenly glad he had it. The lascar's hawklike eyes moved from Peter to the weapon, and back to Peter's face, judging his determination. The captain spoke finally, and the lascar moved forward reluctantly. Peter and the lascar lowered the dinghy into the sea. With difficulty Peter maneuvered his brother into the smaller boat. Thomas

121

was still sick and the pronounced roll in the dinghy only made him worse.

Peter rowed off at a right angle from the ship, parallel to the shore. The captain yelled down to him in Arabic, clearly disturbed, indicating he should go straight ahead to the shore.

Peter didn't know what was awaiting him and the boatload of wounded on the shore, but he knew he didn't want to find out. He rowed steadily away from the stark whiteness of the captain's robe, putting the bulk of his own dhow between himself and the boatload of men. Their voices were going from distress to panic now, and Peter rowed faster. The captain was gesturing frantically to someone on the other dhow. When Peter could scarcely make out the shape of the dhow's hull and only the snowy robe of the captain was visible, the dhow's engines started up again.

The running lights came on and both ships started to move. Peter's dhow backed up, heading quickly for deeper water. The captain was in a hurry to get out of there, Peter noted. But the dhowload of prisoners headed straight for shore. As the dhow approached the strand of barren beach, bodies started to fall from it and splash into the water as if a giant were walking randomly down the deck, kicking and pushing the prisoners overboard.

Suddenly everything seemed to happen at once. Powerful spotlights snapped on from the shore, illuminating the beach and water where Peter would have been if he had gone straight from the ship. At the same time, lights came on at sea. Two Iranian patrol boats which had been lying in the darkness converged on the escaping dhow. There was a flurry of movement behind the lights on shore and Peter could make out running soldiers, trucks, jeeps, the paraphernalia of two patrols of men.

A loudspeaker screeched electronically on shore. There was

a shout, an adjustment was made, and a voice came over the speaker in English.

"You are under arrest!" the voice said. "Do not resist. Stay where you are!"

The prisoners in the water froze where they were, shielding their eyes from the light. After a moment's hesitation they moved toward the beach again, those who could walk supporting those who could not.

The loudspeaker screeched again and a different voice boomed out, giving the same harsh orders in Farsee. Again the prisoners froze. Even from this distance Peter could see how poorly the uniforms fit most of them, as if they had been outfitted very hastily with the expectation that they would not need the uniforms long. There was no telltale insignia of any kind on the unadorned khaki. Except for their language, they could have belonged to any army in the world, official or unofficial.

The English-speaking voice came back over the loudspeaker. "Thomas Stanhope! Peter Stanhope! Make yourselves known to us! No harm will come to you! I repeat, you will not be hurt! Make yourselves known to us!"

"We were set up," Peter hissed fiercely in the dark. "They were waiting for us."

"Head into shore," Thomas said. "Get behind their line and we'll be okay, they'll expect us to go away from them." Thomas was still sick and weak, but Peter could see his adrenaline was working in the emergency.

The patrol boats seemed to understand the situation sooner and started stabbing their lights in the direction of Peter and Thomas. After a moment the spotlights on land joined them and together all beams formed a cone of light, methodically searching.

Peter grabbed Thomas under the arm and flung the both of

them into the sea. Their momentum drove the dinghy farther out to sea as Peter clung to the life jacket and towed Thomas to shore. With the weight of two bodies pulling on it, the jacket's buoyancy was barely enough to keep their chins above water. Riding so low, they weren't visible between the waves as they made their way to the beach.

The bewildered prisoners moved once more to the shore now that the lights were off them. Some of the searching lights seemed to give up hope of finding the dinghy and as if on signal they swiveled back to the prisoners who were dragging themselves out of the water.

One shot rang out alone, and a prisoner crumpled to the sand, clutching his neck. There was a long pause that seemed to stretch into minutes. The other prisoners looked toward their fallen comrade as if he had done something embarrassing to them all, breaking some mutual pact by dying on his knees clawing at the bullet hole in his throat. Finally the silence was broken by another shot. It seemed deliberate, as if the same gun were firing, taking leisurely target practice. Another prisoner fell, spinning backward and landing facedown in the sand where the water lapped at his hair.

The spell was broken, the prisoners realized what was in store for them. They began to scream with one voice just before the entire fusillade hit them. Everyone was firing and the prisoners fell in clumps and clusters, most of them hit several times. The shots came from different directions and drove them first to one side and then the other before gravity pulled them down. The man who had called out to Peter lasted the longest. Amazingly none of the hail of bullets hit him, as if by mutual agreement to save him for the last. He stood amid his dying comrades, yelling out in all the languages he knew as if the entire massacre was just a problem in com-

124

munications that could be solved if only he found the right tongue.

The shooting stopped and still the man stood there, screeching in Farsee now. There was a long pause, as long as the one that had held everyone between the first murder and the second. Finally, as an afterthought, one of the submachine guns loosed a burst and the linguist joined his comrades in a heap. Their blood flowed into the sand and was washed away by the waves. It was a very clean massacre.

Thomas had been right. Once onto land and through the line of patrol, Peter lost them easily as they continued to focus on the sea. Helping Thomas to run on legs still weakened by the seasickness, Peter led them to the rear of the patrol. They flopped onto the sand, gasping for breath.

Looking back at the stretch of beach bathed in harsh spotlights, Peter saw a bizarre aftermath to the massacre. Iranian soldiers passed among the fallen prisoners, distributing weapons. Each of the dead had a Czech-made Skorpion or machine pistol pressed into his inert hand or dropped nearby in the sand. Three officers crisscrossed the mounds of bodies, looking for signs of life. An occasional pop of a revolver marked the discovery of another prisoner still breathing. There would be no survivors to tell this tale. Except for Peter and his brother.

Some of the spotlights again began to search the waters, stabbing through the dark for Peter's dinghy. Segments of the patrol split off like amoebas, searching the shoreline for Peter and Thomas.

One man left the others and walked into the darkness of the desert. Backlighted by the spotlights, he moved in silhouette against the horizon, a lone wolf stalking his prey. As if guided by scent, he came toward Peter and Thomas, pressed into the sand. Peter moved the Skorpion out in front of him, but knew that he dared not use it. The firing had stopped and a single shot now might bring the others.

Peter gave the Skorpion to Thomas. "Don't use it unless you have to," he whispered, then crawled off, hoping to circle around behind the man.

One of the spotlights finally found the dinghy bobbing high on the waves fifty yards out. There was a shout, then a burst of excited voices. The other spotlights swiveled to concentrate on the dinghy. The arc of one of them swept across the man, lighting his face for a fraction of a second so that Peter could make out his features. The same light also fell on Thomas before it swept out to sea. The man saw Thomas lying in the sand and turned, raising his rifle. Peter and Thomas leapt at the same time, but Peter was too far and Thomas too slow. The man fired reflexively, hitting Thomas in the chest, then whirled immediately to face Peter. Peter ducked beneath the gun, clawing out at the man in the darkness. The strength of his rush bore them both to the sand. Peter rammed one hand upward, catching the man between the legs. He squeezed and yanked, feeling something soft yield to his fingers. He pulled again with all his might and something tore. The man dropped the rifle and screamed and screamed.

The shot that hit Thomas saved Peter's life. It was mistaken by the soldiers during the confusion over the dinghy as a signal to fire. A scattered volley of shots splattered around the dinghy before the officers could bring it under control. The volley of shots covered the man's screams and by the time it stopped, Peter had silenced him with a blow of the rifle butt to the head.

The soldiers were further distracted by the drama of the patrol boat sweeping down on the dinghy. By the time everyone finally understood that Peter and Thomas were drowned or vanished, the brothers were far down the coast in the darkness.

Peter carried Thomas on his back until dawn, making his way down the shore. At first light he found a fishing boat and bribed his passage to Dubai on the other side of the gulf.

The fishermen took him on and accepted the two wristwatches as payment. They looked curiously at the corpse the American cradled in his lap the whole way, but none of them dared to point out that the man was dead.

Peter roused from his painful reverie with the taste of copper in his mouth, as if he had just relived the fear and sorrow of the doomed, treacherous expedition in the desert. A car in his rearview mirror had been nagging him for some time.

The green Chevy was nearly two hundred yards back, and had been holding that position for ten minutes. Peter couldn't make out the license plate at that distance and couldn't be sure it was the same car that had stood locked and sealed in front of Margo's place. He played with his speed, going faster for a few minutes, then dropping back to an irritating slowness that had other cars passing with annoyed blasts on the horn. The green Chevy kept its distance, hanging back, sometimes fading out of sight entirely behind hills.

When the Thruway snaked through The Bronx, Peter pulled off on Dyre Avenue. He drove one block then turned to his right and stopped just past the corner. In less than a minute the green Chevy rounded the corner and drove past Peter. The driver didn't so much as glance at Peter's car. Peter got a glimpse of a bland face, a face hard to pin down as to ancestry or region. It could have been Slavic or English or northern Italian. The man's lips were moving as if he were singing along with the radio.

Peter reversed his car and backed into the intersection. He spun the wheel and headed back the way he had come, leaving his pursuer on a one-way street with traffic behind him.

Peter returned to the Thruway, driving steadily, making no further attempts at evasion. At this point he didn't want to lose the tail, he wanted to learn how good the man was. It was always best to have a test of skill before it really counted. Knowing the opponent's strength before an encounter was crucial.

There was no further sign of the green Chevy until Peter turned off at his Manhattan exit. Just a glimpse of green in the rearview mirror before the traffic swallowed it up was enough to let Peter know what he needed. He entered his hotel with the knowledge that whoever was after him was damned good. He was working alone, which meant that if the man was government, his case had a low priority. Or it meant the man wasn't government at all, which was the possibility Peter didn't like.

The man who answered the phone at the National Security Agency was evasive, as he had been taught to be.

"I'm not sure we have an agent Rimbaud, sir," he said. "It will take me some time to check our files. If you'd leave a number where we could reach you."

"Tell Rimbaud that Peter Stanhope is calling," he said impatiently. "I'll call back just once, in fifteen minutes. If he's not there, I won't call again."

"But sir, I can't . . ." Peter hung up on the earnest young voice. He took a short walk on the streets close to his hotel, trying to spot his tail. He didn't really expect to catch anyone good in that short a distance, and he didn't. After sixteen minutes he called again from a pay phone on the street.

Rimbaud was there. "Where in hell are you?" he demanded. "How do you expect us to give you protection if we don't know where you are?"

"Your protection nearly killed me last time," Peter said. "If they bought your story that Austin is dead, I shouldn't need protection anyway."

There was a pause from Rimbaud, and Peter's heart sank. "Tell me where you are," Rimbaud demanded again, but this time with less energy.

"They didn't buy it, did they?" asked Peter.

Rimbaud paused again, then spoke reluctantly. "We found the mortician in one of his caskets this morning. He wasn't really hurt except for some broken fingers, but he'd had the daylights scared out of him. Whoever did it to him was asking to see the Stanhope body."

"Did you get a description?"

"Not much of one. The mortician was too scared to make much sense, but he said his visitor was named Jones."

Peter asked, "What did he look like?"

"The guy said he looked like a lawyer. That's all we could get out of him, but we're still working."

Peter turned and scanned the pedestrians around him. He could see at least two hundred people, none of them paying any attention to him.

"Are you having me tailed?" Peter asked.

"How the hell could I have you tailed if I don't know where you are. . . . Do you have one?"

"Give me some good news," Peter said. "At least tell me you had my brother's fiancée's place staked out."

"Goddamn it," Rimbaud muttered. "This is serious. If you've got a tail, let me know where you are so we can help."

"Can you think of any good reason he won't assume I'm Austin, just like the first one did?" Peter asked.

"We'll catch the son of a bitch if you cooperate," Rimbaud said.

"All right," said Peter. "I can use a chaperon tonight. I have a date."

HEADLINE, *THE NEW YORK TIMES*:

# Former President Flies To Mexico to Meet Shah

# 10

Anne Shepherd moved through her apartment as if it were haunted by ghosts. The horror of the triple murders seemed to infuse the air long after the blood had been washed away, the sheets and pillowcases burned. Roy's corduroy jacket still hung in the open closet, suggesting a cozy intimacy that had never existed. They had been lovers, sporadically, through inertia and convenience, substituting the shared vicissitudes of a common profession for passion. Anne knew she should have given the jacket to Roy's parents when they arrived, stunned and bewildered, pleading for some hint, any suggestion that would give meaning to the death of their son. But somehow giving them the jacket would have seemed like the final indignity, as if Anne were not willing to keep his memory alive for any longer than they were in the apartment. She knew they wanted her to have loved Roy, to have cared and mourned for him as deeply as they did, as a justification for them, as a vindication for him. Because they wanted it so much, Anne wanted it too, and while they were with her she had wept with them, remembering only the good, projecting his future success, keening at her own misery. And through it all she had been forced to act only a little.

She was, quite literally, at a loss how to behave. She was not so bereft that she couldn't continue with her daily life, but the very magnitude of the crime seemed to demand a period of something, if not mourning then perhaps just horror. It didn't seem appropriate to go out, to work, to see friends, to entertain herself in the hundred ways available in the city, as if the wing of the Angel of Death had not swooped down and grazed the earth where she stood. But she certainly couldn't spend her days in the apartment while it still reverberated with the screams of ghosts.

When the man she had met at the police station came for her, she left eagerly. She didn't know what he wanted exactly, it seemed official but without the oppressive quality of the dreary men who had grilled her at the police station, and then the second set of inquisitors, somewhat better dressed than the police, who had grilled her in her apartment. It had been easy to deal with the police. She knew nothing and had told them so. The second set of men, the ones who had whisked her away from the police—government men, she knew, but what branch or capacity she wasn't certain—had had different questions on their minds. It took them a while, but they finally got around to asking about Sam—not by name; she didn't know his name. He was simply Max to her, and she hadn't believed it was his name when he told her. She had told them the truth, all she knew about Max, which was very little. The checks had come regularly for nothing more on her part than a little inconvenience now and again. She had never known, suspected, or even speculated very long on what purpose Max had for the apartment. Whatever it was, there had never been any trace afterward except a few glasses returned to the wrong cabinet and cigarette ashes in the garbage.

The other man had approached her as she was leaving the police station, and if he was a cop, he was certainly an improvement over the previous models she had seen. He was attractive and polite as he explained that he would like a few minutes with her when she had had some time to recover from the shock. This show of consideration had swung her to his side immediately. She had just come from a lengthy grilling at the mercy of cops who were clearly enraged at the death of one of their associates and seemed too willing to believe that she was somehow responsible. But this man was considerate and pleasant, and when he suggested they meet for dinner, she was so surprised that she said yes.

Peter was surprised at the eagerness with which the girl met him. She positively jumped at his suggestion that they go out to eat, and chatted brightly in the elevator like a sorority coed on her way to the cotillion. A heavyset man with a suit much too warm for the weather stepped into the elevator just as the doors were closing. He made eye contact briefly with Peter, but Anne didn't notice.

The bodyguard stayed ahead of Peter by a steady ten yards, his eyes constantly rolling over everyone and everything. A second agent followed them by twenty yards. Smith noted them both, and their positions. They weren't very subtle, designed as much to scare off any attackers as to actually foil an attempt.

Smith paid for a lottery ticket at the corner newsstand, then laboriously selected two magazines while he waited. As he fussed with the lottery ticket he watched the pedestrians following in Peter's wake. There he was now, a third agent, trailing the others on the opposite side of the street, staying well back to observe anyone who might be following the main party.

Smith sneered, muttering to himself. It was very standard

government procedure, effective against amateurs. What did they expect, a fusillade of machine-gun bullets from a speeding limousine? A kamikaze attack from close range with a handgun? Of course, the Sligo killing had been a bit flamboyant, not at all Smith's style. He was actually embarrassed by it, but it could very well work to his advantage. They were looking for a blunderbuss; he would give them a stiletto.

Smith waited for Peter and his entourage to pass completely out of sight, then walked to Anne's apartment building. She had had a good lock installed since he'd been here, and it took Smith the better part of two minutes to work it open. No one passed him in the hall as he worked. He let himself in and eased the door shut and reset the lock. After waiting for his eyes to adjust to the dark, Smith began to look for the best place to wait.

Peter took her to a restaurant called Hisae's, where English ladies and gentlemen of the early eighteenth century strode and posed in faded murals of pink and black. The banquettes were decorated in soft purple and pink, with throw pillows for the customers to toy with or cuddle. The menu had an Oriental bias, but an exotic one, a far cry from the noodle dishes and stir-fry bean curd Anne treated herself to on a weekly basis. She had heard of the restaurant, knew that several Broadway stars dined there regularly, but she could never afford it.

Two of the agents waited outside and the third stood next to the nervous maître d'hotel.

"Do you know anything about wines?" Peter asked.

"A little," Anne said, surprised. "I've been reading about them. I can't afford any of the good ones, but I think I understand the spirit that infuses them." *Oh God, Anne, she* thought, horrified by herself. *The spirit that infuses them? What are you talking about?*

He smiled sympathetically. "That's the main thing," he said. "Would you like to order for us?" He handed the heavy leatherbound wine list to her.

For a moment she didn't understand. The entire elaborate pretense of ordering and tasting the wine was a male prerogative that her escorts had never given up, no matter how ill-prepared they were—or how cheap the restaurant. There was something in the ritual of wine selection that reeked of the male right, and no one had ever handed it over to her any more than he would have handed over the absolute right to discuss finance.

Anne took the heavy wine list and nearly dropped it, then buried her nose in it for several minutes to get over her embarrassment. When she told him she knew a little about wines, she had exaggerated. What was this need to impress the man anyway?

"My father is an oenophile," Peter was saying. "I think that's why I've deliberately avoided learning much about wine." It took Anne a moment to realize that an oenophile was not a sexual fetishist of some kind. "I've gotten used to rice wines and palm wines and maté and native beer they let ferment in a huge gourd in the full sun. It comes out tasting like zucchini, but it will curl your toes."

She glanced up from the wine list with a flustered look. There were far too many wines, too many châteaux, too many *appellations contrôlées*. "What?" she asked.

He was looking at her with a peculiar intensity.

"I'm sorry, I didn't hear you."

"You're a beautiful woman," Peter said. "I don't mean to embarrass you by saying that."

Anne blushed to the roots of her hair. Her face felt as if someone had poured warm sauce on her head and the heat was trickling down. She was used to hearing it, but from him it sounded different, and altogether better. "How could that be embarrassing?" she said.

"I won't mention it again," he said. "But I had to let you know. I mean, you look extraordinary."

"Now that is getting embarrassing," said Anne. She hoped it was dark enough in the restaurant to cover her burning face.

Suddenly the sommelier was standing at their table. Anne picked the second cheapest wine that had a half bottle.

"The Liebfraumilch," she said. "A half bottle."

"That's all right," Peter said. "It's on an expense account. We can go for a full bottle."

Anne looked at the wine list again, wondering if he was trying to tell her to pick another wine. She had only taken the Liebfraumilch out of desperation anyway. It was the only name she recognized and felt confident of pronouncing. *To hell with it*, she thought, *if you're going to make a fool of yourself, do it with conviction.*

"Very well," she said. "Make it a full bottle of Liebfraumilch."

The sommelier sniffed as if he noticed an offensive odor she couldn't detect. He glanced at Peter for confirmation. But Peter ignored the waiter.

"There's a tribe of Pygmies that makes a drink out of honeycombs, not just the honey, but the combs, the young larvae, everything. . . . They don't ferment it, they bury it for about a month. It has a—distinctive—taste." He smiled at her. He seemed to have been smiling at her all evening.

The waiter moved off to fetch his wine without a protest. *God bless your heart*, Anne thought of Peter. *I don't know what on earth you're talking about, but God bless you anyway.*

He told her about the crocodiles, and she listened, rapt, awed and fascinated. She told him about the difficulties of the acting profession, and he seemed genuinely interested. He asked intelligent questions, understood her frustrations, sympathized with her depressions, encouraged her ambitions. For once she didn't feel as if she were just alibiing for her lack of success. In a way it was like talking to another actor who knew the problems.

They drank the whole bottle of wine. It was wrong for the meal, much too fruity, but he didn't seem to notice, and Anne silently thanked him for that and didn't compound her mistake by apologizing for it.

It was the first time Peter had relaxed since leaving Africa. Partly it was the wine, he knew. Partly the security of three government agents standing guard. But mostly it was this beautiful girl, the way her eyes lit up with interest when he told her some of his adventures, the way she watched his face as if she were learning something. She was shy and bold at the same time, part gamine, part sophisticated beauty. Some day the two parts of her personality would weld together, and then look out, she would be one hell of a person. She was one hell of a person now. It took Peter somewhat by surprise to realize that he liked the girl as herself, on her own confused terms, not just as someone to make love to, or someone to work with, or someone to pry information from. And Lord, but she was good to look at.

When he finally asked about the murders in her apartment, she told him everything, including the part about Max. He seemed particularly interested in Max, and when she told him all she knew, he was quiet for a moment. She didn't mind, she liked watching him as he thought. She didn't mind that they had had this dinner just so she could answer his questions. Her nerves had long since vanished, and she was just glad to be with him. She knew that deserved some investigation, but introspection could come later. Right now she just wanted to enjoy what was left of the evening.

"They were using your apartment as a safe house," he said at last. "A place to meet in emergencies, a place very few knew about, probably this Max and his superior and no one else. Every spy network has at least one."

Anne came to full attention with a start. "Spies! I thought he was cheating on his wife or something."

"Let's say agents. CIA, maybe. They would need a safe house in New York since they have no license to run operations inside the United States. They may have been using your place to hide from FBI surveillance."

"The FBI is watching the CIA?"

Peter didn't bother to answer. "It could be the FBI, of course, but it doesn't sound quite their style. There are more than half a dozen other intelligence agencies that operate in New York, American agencies, I mean. Of course it could have been a foreign agent. God knows how many of those there are."

"Russians?" she croaked.

"Russians, East Germans, Czechs, Chinese, West Germans, French, British, South Americans, Ghanians, Senegalese . . . I don't know what all these days. I've been out of the business for a while."

Anne was feeling light-headed, and she knew it wasn't the wine. In the course of a minute he had matter-of-factly lifted her from her world into a realm of shadows, a kingdom of cloak and dagger that was built on unreality. The brutal murders in her apartment had been horrible enough, but within the context of modern urban reality, of random violence and suddenly erupting homicide, she had been able to comprehend it. Things happened, they filled the newscasts. But espionage was different. By its very nature it was unknown, existing for her only in novels that she didn't bother to read.

"Are you some kind of spy?" she asked, feeling very silly. "Not that I would expect you to tell me the truth if you were."

"Will you be disappointed if I am—or if I'm not?"

Anne blushed again. She was becoming transparent.

"I think it would be hard to truly know a spy," she said. She forced herself to look into his eyes as she said it.

Peter held her gaze for a moment before answering. Then he told her the truth because there was no reason not to.

"I've never known a spy who liked the word," Peter said. "Spies, after all, are those people who get caught out of uniform during a war and are lined up against a wall and shot. The other side uses spies. We use agents. Agents qualify for health insurance and pension benefits and expect to die in bed with their wills brought up to date. A good agent doesn't crawl under barbed wire fences to smuggle out the secret plans. He hires a local spy to do that for him. A really good agent never leaves his desk at all except to attend diplomatic receptions. I'm at least about half serious about that. No one wants to risk a good, intelligent man by sending him to the other side to photograph the plans or send messages in invisible ink. It's not that an agent doesn't know how to do those things, it's just that he hopes to hell he'll never have to.

"Most of the actual dirty work of intelligence gathering is done by rather desperate people who are working for greed or fear of blackmail or sexual favor or ideological hatred. Or stupidity."

He paused, regretting that he said it.

"Like me?" she asked.

"I don't mean that," he said lamely.

She nodded. "Like me. That's all right," she added with a laugh, noting his discomfort. "I don't mind being stupid. I'm not crazy about being used, but I figure I can't help being dumb. What I really want to avoid is being mean. . . . God, that sounds noble, doesn't it?"

"A little," he agreed.

"I take it back," she said, smiling. "I hate being stupid."

"Let's just say you were gullible. There are worse ways of being taken in. You didn't do any spying, after all. The worst kind of gullibility is called false-flag recruitment. That's when someone convinces you you are working for your own government, appealing to your patriotism."

"And you're actually working against them?" she asked.

Peter nodded. "It happens all the time. Even to people who should know better." He paused. "Like me."

She looked at him in astonishment. "You?"

"Only it wasn't for my government—it was for my father."

In the silence that followed Anne struggled against her impulse to urge him to continue. She could tell that what he had just said came out with difficulty, as if the admission had been forced through a door long sealed. Impatience on her part could easily force the door closed again—but she was so curious.

Peter needed no prompting, however. He was talking about it for the first time in five years, telling a stranger, always the best kind of confidant, but a stranger toward whom he felt a strong and surprising affinity.

"All of the intelligence agencies in this country job out a great deal of work that they are too busy or unqualified to handle themselves," he said at last. "My father's company is in effect a government subcontractor. We—they now, but it used to be we—develop programs for training agents for certain kinds of specialized situations. A simulated attack by terrorists on a nuclear plant, for instance. We would do a study to figure out the best way for terrorist groups of varying sizes and capabilities to attack a nuclear facility—to take it intact, to take it regardless of destruction, to hold it indefinitely, to hold it for a few hours, to blow it up—any number of possibilities. I would put myself in the position of a terrorist leader, get inside his head as much as possible, and work out my plans for taking the facility. Then I would reverse positions, knowing the logical ways of attacking, and work out a defense. After we'd refined both attack and defense and run them through the computer several thousand times, we would take a class of appropriate federal agents and teach them how to defend against such an attack, and how to rout it once it had occurred."

"Did you ever teach our agents how to do the attacking, in another country, for instance?" Anne asked.

Peter grinned. He liked her mind, it was quick and perceptive.

"Well, as I say, we were subcontractors. We did what we were hired to do—provided it was in the best interest of the United States—and us."

"What kind of answer is that?"

"That's what is known, technically, as an evasive answer," said Peter. "There's a lot I can't tell you. It's classified in the first place, and it wouldn't do you any good to know it in the second. Would you like some more wine?"

"Oh, yes," she said quickly, not because she wanted the wine but because she wanted to stay where they were and keep talking.

He ordered the wine this time, without referring to the wine list, a bottle of vintage Château Margaux. The sommelier seemed much relieved.

"The government agencies also farm out most of their radio-transmissions work. There are several hundred space satellites in need of constant monitoring, sending back scientific information, relaying ground-to-ground and ground-to-air communications, things like that."

"You mean private contractors are involved in that?" she said incredulously. "Shouldn't the government do it?"

"Qualified men are hard to find, hard to train, and they don't like working for government pay if they can get twice as much working for themselves. But mostly it's just the American way. The government doesn't manufacture our weapons, you know. They are all made under contract by private firms. The space shots have been overseen by the government, but private industry built all the components and did much of the training of the astronauts.

"One of our briefs was the Middle East, for instance," Peter explained. "We monitored radio communications from there."

"You mean you have an office in the Middle East?"

"It's not necessary. All you need is the right antenna—which is not as simple as it sounds—and a knowledge of the right frequencies. It took us ten years just to discover the frequencies used by all the scheduled airlines, the military channels, the government channels, the commercial radio and television channels, and so on."

"Do you mean you can sit in New York and eavesdrop on television in—I don't know—Syria or someplace?"

"Television is easy, at least the audio portion. I know of a listener who picked up the Secret Service communications during the Pope's visit to New York. The listener was in Israel at the time, but he knew when the motorcade was going to turn left before people lining Fifth Avenue knew."

"It all sounds kind of indecent somehow," said Anne.

"I agree," Peter said. "But it took me a while to come around to your point of view. You see, I was raised to believe service to my country was the highest duty. My brothers and

I were brought up to be in the business. Just like a man in the hardware business hopes for his sons to join him, my father taught us to think like agents, dream like spies. By the time I was sixteen I could fire just about any portable weapon known, from a bazooka to a close-range assassin's camera that shoots one hollow-head .38 slug. I could also take them apart and put them together again. By the time I was twenty I could send and decipher more than a dozen types of code. Give me enough time with a computer and I could break most codes except the very best. When most kids were playing football or basketball, my brother Tom and I were practicing self-defense on each other. God how we used to fight, all dressed up in padded protective clothing, thank God, or we would have killed each other once a week. My other brother, Austin, was ten years younger than I was, and he used to sit on the sidelines and cry whenever it looked like one or the other of us was dead, which was pretty often."

"It sounds ghastly," she said.

"Yes. It sounds that way. But it wasn't. I had Tom, you see. And my father. I loved Tom without reservation, and he loved me. There was none of the jealousy you normally see between brothers. Maybe we worked all that out during our self-defense sessions, or maybe it was because we had a sense of working for a common goal, I really don't know. But our love for each other was the one fixed star in my universe. Tom and my father . . ."

Peter paused, picking his words with care. "I don't know what my father felt for me. I say this with hindsight. At the time, I suppose I assumed he loved me. Fathers are supposed to love their children, aren't they? I don't know what I felt for him, either, to be honest. I suppose I loved him too. I do know that I had tremendous respect for him. He was the toughest, brightest, most determined man I'd ever known. I think I can still say that. He could do everything he taught us to do and better, and a lot more besides. And, do you know, it sounds terribly Spartan now, but it was fun."

"What happened?" Anne asked.

"What do you mean?"

"Why aren't you still with your father and your brothers?"

"My brother died," he said abruptly. He drained his glass with a conclusive air.

His voice sounded so sad that Anne reached out to comfort him, covering his hand with her own. The contact stirred him from his memories. He looked at her lovely face and smiled. He wasn't living five years ago, he was living now.

"Let's go," he said.

# 11

---

After thoroughly investigating the girl's apartment, Smith prepared his escape route. The agents protecting Stanhope would be out in front of the building, or, in the worst of circumstances, right outside the door in the hallway. That fact established some strict requirements for the job. One, it had to be silent, which ruled out the Browning. Even with the silencer the gun gave out a quite audible cough that might be recognized by an experienced man in the hall.

The second requirement was for a very fast getaway. The kitchen window offered the best prospects. The brownstone was an old one, built when ornamentation was not only fashionable but financially feasible. The broad windowsill gave a foothold from which he could reach the cornice running over the windows. From there it was an easy climb, not much more difficult than climbing stairs, really, to the roof. Smith knew from experience that access to a rooftop in New York was like a gift of keys to the city. He could go virtually anywhere, fast and undetected.

The kitchen window was barred by an iron grill, effective at keeping someone out, but of no use in keeping someone in.

Smith removed the screws holding the wrought-iron grill in the wall and replaced them with kitchen matches he found over the stove. The matches were strong enough to hold the static weight of the grill, but could be removed with a yank when the time came. To ensure that his tampering would not be noticed, he unscrewed the kitchen light bulb, leaving it loose in its socket.

His escape route secured, he decided on a weapon. He rummaged through kitchen drawers until he found the knives. Testing each one on his thumb, he selected a stainless steel boning knife, long and lean as a stiletto. For security he took a smaller knife and tucked it in his belt. If everything went at its smoothest, he would be able to kill the man, leave the knife behind, and have the girl blamed for the murder.

They probably wouldn't believe the girl killed him, but it might raise enough doubts to cause some confusion, and any confusion was a bonus for Smith.

His preparation complete, Smith removed the ballast from the fluorescent bulbs in the bathroom, then stepped into the bathtub and pulled the shower curtain closed. He settled down to wait. Stanhope would come in to say good night, or he would not. If he did not, nothing was lost, Smith would kill him another time. But if he did come in, Smith would take a particular relish in killing him under the noses of the agents. Smith did not mind waiting. He had the patience of a serpent when his prey was in sight.

Peter and Anne walked home together. After the cathartic conversation at the restaurant Peter felt completely at ease with her. He could not remember when he had last had such a total feeling of comfort with another person. He wasn't hiding anything for once, he wasn't playing a role, pretending to be a man who came from nowhere with no past, no family. He had not realized how very weary he had become of acting like a man who had invented himself, sprung as it were from his own imagination. He had hidden his past not because of any need for secrecy but because he had wanted to deny it, and by denying it to rub it out, erase it entirely. Being home again, confronting his father's steely unforgiveness, had forced him to realize he could not dismiss his past. And talking to Anne about it had made him realize he no longer had to.

They walked side by side. Anne had not noticed the agents that bracketed them front and back—indeed, none but a trained eye would have—and in fact she noticed very little around her except the man at her side. It seemed that all of her senses strained to be aware of his every move, his every change of mood, nuance of inflection, the rhythm of his breathing. As they walked, the sidewalk seemed to roll beneath them like the deck of a ship. Inadvertently they swayed, now and then bumping lightly into each other. The contact was no more than a brush, but as their hands touched, Anne jerked away, embarrassed. She had wanted him to touch her so strongly that she was afraid he had sensed it. She continued to talk, laughing lightly, playing the role of the charming innocent ingenue, trying to disguise the fact that her mind was racing through a headier scene in which she ripped his clothes off and threw herself on his body.

When he casually put a hand on her shoulder she thought she would scream. He did it so easily that it seemed the most natural gesture in the world, but she could feel the weight of his hand burning through her clothing like a hot iron. *You've got to stop this*, she thought frantically. *You're just building up for a terrible letdown. The man has shown no interest in you at all, he's footloose, a rambler, worse than an actor, a trained James Bond. You'll see him tonight and that's an end to it . . . although he did say you were beautiful. . . . But you've heard that before,* she thought harshly, *and it's never prevented anyone from behaving like a snake. Not that I mean he's a snake. He's fascinating, he looks terrific, he's probably even sweet if he'd give himself a chance—stop it!*

She led him to her apartment in a state of fierce confusion. As they approached the stoop of her brownstone a man suddenly materialized at Peter's elbow.

"Will you be long, sir?" he asked.

Peter looked at him curiously. "No," he said finally.

"It's just that I'm due to go off shift," the man said.

"Don't worry, Haley," Peter said. "I'll be right back and you can go home."

"I wasn't suggesting that you hurry, sir. I just wondered whether to call my wife."

Peter smiled and took Anne's elbow, leading her into the building.

"Who was that?" she asked.

Peter smiled at her but didn't answer. It was the most maddening thing about him, this ability to not answer when he didn't want to, as if he had conveniently gone deaf. Anne would at least bother to think up a lie, but he seemed to assume a right to unexplained silence. *Well, thank God I've found something about him I don't like,* Anne thought. *I'll try to concentrate on that.* As she nursed her small annoyance they walked to her door.

Smith heard the footsteps in the hallway and immediately roused himself to full consciousness. He ran his thumb again along the cutting edge of the boning knife as he heard voices coming from the entry.

150

Straddling the doorway, the key still in her hand, the door ajar, Anne hesitated. "Well, you're leaving the country, then, are you?" she asked, but she thought, *Quit being polite and unbutton his shirt, that will give him the idea.*

"Back to Africa, I guess," Peter said. "There's nothing I can do here."

*I know something you can do, and right now, too,* Anne thought.

"Well," she said with undue heartiness. "It was nice meeting you. Thank you for dinner."

As he kept looking at her in that maddening silence of his, Anne felt her smile beginning to weaken. *Do something,* she screamed at him in her head. *Do something or go away, but don't leave me standing here, worrying that my desire shows like a bad rash. Beautiful girls don't make the first move,* she thought, *we don't have to. Why doesn't he know that? What if I just sort of tugged at his belt? Would that seem forward?* With a playfulness that astonished her, she slowly reached out her hand. The next thing she knew he was shaking hands.

"Good night," he said.

Anne hurried inside and closed the door. *I almost did it!* she thought, aghast. *What on earth is the matter with me! Am I suddenly so lustful, or is it really just this man?* She walked toward the kitchen, filled with a kind of nervous excitement that burst forth in sound.

"Ay, ay, ay, ay, ay, oh, oh, oh, oh," she yelled, pursing her lips to form each sound perfectly, projecting from the diaphragm in a makeshift version of her daily vocal exercises. It sounded stupid, but was a lot less harmful than jumping up and down beating her head against the wall, which was what she felt like doing.

The light in the kitchen was out. She crossed the familiar

151

room in the dark and opened the refrigerator. The interior light was all she needed to pour the glass of soda she wanted to counteract the harsh aftertaste of dinner and wine.

She stood next to the grilled window. Something gnawed at the edge of her awareness, something different, something not quite right. She glanced around, her eyes playing over the matchsticks in the screwholes of the window grill, but with her mind not registering. Then she heard a sound, somewhere out of the kitchen, faint, but it made her catch her breath.

She heard it again, a footstep, moving in her direction. It was in the hallway, and she moved quickly through the dark rooms toward the door. *My God,* she thought, *I forgot to lock the door!* She passed within three feet of the bathroom door but did not see the form that slipped back from the doorway into deeper darkness.

There was a single knock just as she reached the entry door. She quickly slipped the chain into place before speaking.

"Who is it?" she said as she automatically raced through the possibilities, knowing full well that a crazed ax murderer was only one of them, and not the most likely.

"Peter Stanhope."

In the bathroom Smith smiled to himself as he slipped silently back behind the shower curtains. He had willed Stanhope to come in.

Peter stood in the doorway, unsmiling, his dark brown eyes staring intently at Anne. She thought he seemed to have grown taller, and his presence was almost overwhelming. She struggled for something brittle and witty to say, but her throat was dry and her mind was blank. Peter touched her shoulders, pulled her to him, and kissed her.

For just a second Anne was stunned. She had wanted it, but she hadn't expected it. Then she responded with an energy that surprised her.

Sexual desire struck them both at once like a tidal wave. As soon as their lips touched they seemed to be beyond thought, beyond reason, responding completely to each other. As if some huge reservoir of excitement that hadn't existed until they came together had suddenly burst, inundating them both, sweeping them away, they clung to each other.

They were in the doorway for less than a minute, but in that time they swept upward through all the stages of growing desire. Anne pulled away, gasping from the intensity of her emotion. She felt she would suffocate, felt her heart would burst; but even as she pulled away she held onto him, pulling him toward her, tearing at his shirt.

Peter put his arm around her waist and it was like a ring of fire, searing her flesh with an irresistible heat. He pulled her to him again, pressing his pelvis against hers. She came to him, grinding her body against his, gripping his head in her hands, and pulling his mouth to hers again.

And then there was no time left, no time, no need for the dalliance of gentle lovemaking. Their mutual desire had sprung up without warning and could wait no longer. Peter lifted her and carried her toward the bedroom, their lips still locked together.

They clawed at each other, pulling off their clothes, tearing at the flesh itself in their intense desire to get at each other. They were both moaning, sighing their impatience in long, low shuddering falls, as if they might expire before consummation.

Smith listened to the noises of their lovemaking from his hiding place in the bathroom. Perfect, he thought. He couldn't have planned a better distraction. A knife in the back as the man mounted the girl would look like a crime of passion, the classical defense against rape. The girl's fingerprints were already on the knife, of course. It was dark enough in the apartment so that she would probably never even see Smith. All she would notice would be one last and premature spasm from her lover, then she would open her eyes to find a dead man atop her. If things were going as passionately as they sounded, she might even be confused enough to half believe she did it herself without knowing.

As Smith eased out of the tub one foot slipped slightly on the smooth porcelain surface. The tub was old and uneven. Tiny pools of moisture were held in chips and pockmarks. Smith's shoe caught one of the little puddles. He lurched forward unsteadily, putting all his weight too suddenly on the one foot that stood on the bathroom floor. Instinctively Smith grabbed for the shower curtain. The strength of the curtain was enough to slow him, and he put the other hand forward to where he knew the bathroom sink was. The plastic shower curtain tore soundlessly off one of the rings that held it in place. The sudden slackening just as he had regained his balance and started to relax was enough to make him take another step forward. He hit the sink, the wooden handle of the knife in his belt colliding with the porcelain with a thud muffled by his body.

In the bedroom Peter froze atop Anne. Even before the sound he had sensed the flurry of sudden motion from the other room. It gave off emanations below the level of conscious hearing, but some primeval part of the brain heard it and recognized it just as a shark can sense the disturbed patterns in the ocean that are given off by a fish in distress.

Anne heard the sound too, but what alarmed her more was the sudden tension in Peter's body. She couldn't see him, but she knew his body was poised, ready to move, ready to flee or attack. She didn't know why, but in the space of less than a second she had gone from lustful excitement to terror. She was scared as hell, and all because of the way the man atop her was suddenly as still and ready as a panther.

It took a few fractions of a second more for her to realize she had heard a sound coming from the bathroom. When it came to her, she could feel the hair on her neck and scalp suddenly tingle, and her heart, already racing, threatened to tear loose in her chest. One tiny sound in the darkness and she was suddenly transformed from a woman making passionate love to a terrified animal, crouching in the dark, naked, alone, and hunted.

She started to speak, but before she could, Peter was on the floor, moving in a crouch toward the noise. She could see the shape of his broad back, strangely pale, almost luminescent up close, but as he moved away from her it faded and disappeared in the enveloping darkness. Anne sat up in bed, straining to see him, then quickly scooted against the headboard, protecting her back.

When Peter heard her move on the bed behind him, he stopped. "No lights!" he hissed. Any light shining behind him now would make him a perfect target for whoever was out there. And he was not absolutely sure someone was there. His mind had already raced over all the other possibilities of creaking floorboards and mice and things falling by themselves. The sound, the barely perceptible intake of breath, the total cessation of movement all had a human quality to them. He knew he might be overreacting, but Peter had spent years of his life making such distinctions and acting upon them immediately.

He sensed the floor move under his bare feet and then the disturbance of something large moving quickly away from him. He still had seen nothing and heard nothing beyond the first muffled thud, but he sensed where the thing was and he sensed it was a man.

A lamp had been on in the living room when Peter had come in from the hallway only minutes before, but now the room was dark. One thin shaft of light came through the living room window from outside and slashed diagonally across the room. Peter froze, just beyond the fringe of illumination. He eased himself into a squat, pressed against the wall, offering as small a target as possible. On the other side of the spear of light was the blackness of the bathroom. Peter scanned the area, not trying to look at anything directly but using the keener nighttime sight of his peripheral vision. After a moment's adjustment he could make out the bulk of the kitchen cabinets, the thrust of the stove, the slightly eerie ghostly glow of the off-white refrigerator. And there, in the middle of the floor, low to the ground, a dark shape somehow darker than the surrounding blackness. Did he really see it? Peter looked around the shape, never directly at it, letting the corners of his eyes see for him. Did he recognize the shape of a man in a kneeling firing position? Peter soundlessly eased himself onto his stomach on the floor, giving the man virtually no target at all in the dark.

The two men were immobile, facing each other from within their caves of darkness across the barrier of light. Neither moved, but soon Peter thought he could detect the sound of the other man, breathing shallowly, as if frightened, or excited.

From this angle Peter could see something he had missed before. Lying just on the fringe of the light was a knife, a kitchen knife with a wooden handle and a long, thin blade. The man must have dropped it when he took out the gun. Peter thought of his chances of reaching the knife before the man fired. They were suicidally low.

Smith could just make out Peter's bulk. He held the Browning .380 in both hands, the right elbow supported on the right knee. He didn't want to use the pistol, but now it seemed he had no choice. If the man moved across the shaft of light, tried for the knife, he would kill him. He had no desire to try for anything different at close range in the dark. One shot in the heart, then out the window and over the rooftops. But only if the man came into the light. Lying down, Stanhope presented almost no target at all, and with the agents outside, Smith could not afford to miss. He would have to do something quickly in any event. The woman was still in the bedroom. She might do anything at any moment, run to the window and scream for help, walk into his line of fire, anything. Perhaps he would have to risk a shot at the man in the darkness anyway.

Anne nearly screamed when the phone rang. She had been listening for sounds from the other room where Peter was, and the absolute silence frightened her more than any noise could have. She was trying to think what to do, but everything had happened so fast, his return, the first burning kiss, the rush of emotion, the passion that had virtually flung them into the bedroom, the noise from the bathroom, Peter's instant reaction, disappearing into the dark like an animal after its prey. Then the telephone, close to her ear, screaming at her. She fumbled for it, knocking the receiver to the night table before she got it up to her ear.

"This is Haley, Miss," said an unfamiliar voice. "Is Mr. Stanhope there, please?"

At the sound of the phone Smith stood upright to get a better angle to shoot downward where he thought the man's back would be. But Peter snaked backward immediately, pulling around the corner and out of sight. Peter scrambled to his feet once around the safety of the hallway corner and ran to the bedroom, still bent half over, moving now with surety through the dark apartment as if it were his own.

He slammed the bedroom door deliberately, making as much a point of it as he could. The man with the gun in the kitchen was a desperate, trapped animal. It was sometimes best to let a cornered animal get away, because they were at their most dangerous with their backs to the wall. And despite his instincts to protect himself by attacking and taking the initiative, Peter had not forgotten that he was naked and without a weapon, or that he might jeopardize Anne.

"He says it's Haley," Anne whispered, her throat nearly closed with fright.

Peter felt across the bed until he touched her, then found the telephone. "Haley!" he said.

"I didn't mean to disturb you, but you said you were coming right out. I thought if there's nothing wrong, I should just call the wife . . ."

"Come up!" Peter ordered. "Come in armed and low and send someone around to the back entrance if there is one." Even as he said it he knew it was too late. The intruder was probably gone already. He had been in the apartment waiting for them, Peter was sure of that, which meant he had had plenty of time to plan an escape. And under the circumstances Peter was more than happy to let him escape. He was clearly a professional, and Peter had seen nothing to convince him of the competence of the men on his side. The intruder had not panicked, he had switched from attack to defense without a mistake and had been prepared to wait for his chance. Even if they took him, someone would probably die in the process. Better to let him go.

Smith was out the kitchen window before Peter spoke into the telephone. A light mist had started to fall, coating the ledges with a fine residue of moisture. Smith had made it to the cornice above the window and was reaching for the roof when his foot went out from under him. Before he had time to realize what was happening, he fell, hitting the flagstones of the little courtyard with a force that tore the ligaments in his ankle. Smith felt the searing pain in his leg even as he tumbled onto his shoulder, protecting his head from the impact. He was conscious throughout and knew that he had to move immediately, but for several seconds he couldn't breathe. The fall had knocked the wind out of him, and he gasped like a man emerging from great depths. When he finally filled his lungs with a series of short, jagged breaths, he turned over and shoved himself to his knees. He got to one foot, but when he touched the ankle to the ground, the pain knocked him to his knees again. Flight was out of the question. He couldn't hobble, much less walk. There was no possibility of pulling himself over the high wooden fence that encircled the courtyard.

Clasping the Browning, he glanced up at the window from which he had fallen, three stories above him. No face peered out, no hand pointed down at him, no strident yell of "There he is!" He had only seconds, a minute at most, before they discovered the iron grill lying on the kitchen floor under the window.

Desperately he searched the little courtyard. Someone was growing a garden, surprisingly lush in this harsh city environment. Cabbage, tomatoes, and beans were surrounded by borders of marigolds, petunias, and geraniums, all bursting with health. Smith saw the reason in one corner, under the kitchen window on the ground floor—a compost heap. The gardener had created his own compost within a three-foot square enclosed in chicken-wire mesh. Kitchen refuse and dirt had been mixed with ashes, old newspapers, and cow manure, doused with water, and left to brew and rot itself into rich fertilizer. The mound of moldering debris was four feet high, deep enough to hide a man.

Wincing at every move of his ankle, Smith dragged himself to the compost heap. With one last glance up at the window, Smith burrowed under the rotting refuse. The interior of the pile was steaming hot. Smith pulled the mess of kitchen slops and manure over his head, scrunching down as far as his ankle would permit. The pile itself gave off an odor of fermentation, a heady, sweet scent, but it was the smell of fresh manure, only recently applied to the top layer and not yet chemically broken down, that assailed his nostrils. Smith fought the urge to retch. Something wet and slippery moved across his face in jerky movements. It took him several horrified moments before he realized it was an earthworm.

His eyes pressed tight against contamination by the refuse, scarcely breathing because of the stench, his ankle now pulsing with pain with every beat of his heart, his body tensed against the urge to flee the repulsive mess into which he had burrowed, Smith's only sense open to the world was his hearing. He waited for them to come, and then waited with increasing incredulity that they did not come. The agents were audible at the kitchen window from which he had fallen. They checked the handholds leading to the roof, then one of them went to to roof and Smith could hear the man conferring with another agent at the window, reasoning that their quarry must have long since vanished over the rooftops. Still Smith waited as one of the agents searched the courtyard, just to make sure. He could see the beam of the man's flashlight filtered through the several inches of compost that covered his face. Smith lay absolutely still until his muscles were on the verge of cramp, screaming with the urge to flee. The agent stood next to the compost heap, resting an arm on the chicken wire as he conferred with the tenant of the ground floor apartment, the gardener, about ways out of the courtyard.

Smith could hear neither the voice of the man he had come to kill nor that of the woman. They would have been whisked to safety as soon as the agents arrived. It would make his job all the harder, he knew, but as he lay covered by ordure, his foot in agony, his skin crawling, Smith kept himself calm by plotting the ways he would find Stanhope and kill him. Oh, yes, if he never did anything else again, he would find and kill him.

At four in the morning Smith finally dragged himself out of the mound of garbage. Every step was torture, and by the time he could hail a cab to take him to the hospital, his teeth were stained with blood seeping from the inside of his mouth where he had bitten down to keep from crying out. His heart was ablaze with hatred for Stanhope. This was the second time Stanhope had nearly killed him.

# 12

Peter had insisted that the government relocate Anne. They said good-bye in the hotel where Rimbaud would keep her until a suitable apartment could be found.

The parting was as awkward as if two strangers at an orgy, groping ecstatically in the dark, had suddenly been tugged naked into the spotlight and introduced to each other. The fierce flame of passion that had overwhelmed them had been dampened by the strange interlude of fear, then totally doused by the bureaucratic aftermath of Rimbaud and hotel clerks and arrangements for lodging and plans for retrieving her possessions from the apartment. She would never return there now, no matter how thoroughly exorcised of ghosts and cleansed of midnight prowlers.

Rimbaud left them alone for a moment. Peter had been in enough hotel rooms over the years to find almost all of them automatically depressing, fairly shimmering with the spectral emanations of countless lonely nights. Anne was still young enough to find a hotel room faintly erotic; the bed, so prominently displayed, so obviously the sole purpose for the existence of the room, was something to be consciously ignored like the open trouser-fly of a forgetful older gentleman. Under the circumstances, however, Anne found the presence of the bed just another embarrassing reminder of the frustrated and still inexplicable scene in her apartment. She didn't know what wellspring in her spirit had been so drastically tapped by this man. She had known a bit of casual sex, not enough to qualify her as promiscuous, but rather more than she would care to admit to. It seemed to be a concomitant of her youth and her beauty and the acting profession. But she had always known why she was doing it with this particular person at that particular time in this particular place, and consequently her ardor had always been tempered with a strong sense of reason, with a knowledge that she had willed the act, or at least willingly consented, with full consideration of the implications. With Peter it had been as if all of her will and reason had been erased, not just tamped down and conveniently tucked away for the duration, but entirely expunged, as if they had been the first fuel for the fire that started the conflagration.

"It seems all right," Peter said in a slightly formal tone. He seemed to be having trouble knowing where to put his hands.

"Yes," said Anne. She looked around the room, pretending her eyes registered anything.

"If it's not all right, I'll have him find you another one," Peter said.

"No, no, this one is fine," Anne said, smiling and waving a hand vaguely. "It seems to be very nice." For a moment her eyes focused on a print that dominated the wall opposite the bed, bold, broad wavy lines of red, white, and black ascending vertically with one perfectly round red circle placed in the lower right-hand corner with what the artist must have considered artistic panache. Anne vowed to turn the painting to the wall as soon as Peter left.

Peter gave up the struggle to find a casual position for his hands and crossed his arms over his chest, an attitude he associated with a censorious schoolteacher squinting disapprovingly at homework. One good thing about the Rwundi tribal squat was that your options were drastically reduced. You kept your arms in front of you and low or you overbalanced and fell down.

"If you need anything . . ."

"Yes, I know, thank you," she said hurriedly. She seemed as eager to have him gone as he was to go.

He could just shake her hand, say good-bye, and turn and go, recovering from his unease in the solitude of Rimbaud's company. Walk out of her life and forget all about her. He had done it before, many times before. But he was reluctant to do it now.

He cleared his throat, suddenly feeling like a pompous ass. "About what happened . . ." he started.

Anne broke in, laughing too brightly. "Yes, wasn't that strange?"

Peter said, "I may have been a little rough . . ."

"Oh?" said Anne, thinking she had been the one who had been rough.

"Not rough exactly, but I sort of forced myself on you." He paused, the sentence ending in a slight upward lilt as if he were asking a question, asking for confirmation.

Anne forced herself to look at him, smiling slightly, wearing a mask of polite interest. If he had forced himself on her, it was the first she knew of it, but she wasn't going to make a fool of herself again by contradicting him or embarrassedly avoiding his gaze.

165

"I don't usually act like that," Peter said, pausing again.

*Good God,* thought Anne, *does he think I do?*

"These things happen," she said. "Not to me, but they do happen."

"I think I'm trying to apologize," Peter said. He smiled at last, and the scar by his eye stood out against the darker skin.

"Not at all, not at all," Anne said, wondering what play she had cribbed that line-reading from. "It was interesting."

Peter laughed. "Yes. It was that."

They both continued to fend off the issue, turning the heat and passion into something curious and mildly amusing but having nothing to do with them, a story heard secondhand that could be appreciated as the unrelated oddity it was.

"You'll be safe enough now," he said, moving toward the door. "If anyone was really there, and I'm not certain there was, he would have been after me. This man Max who was using your place will probably disappear. I doubt that you'll hear from him again. If you do, contact Rimbaud."

"As you say, he'll probably disappear. I've already determined that I'm going to treat the entire experience as something very bizarre that happened to someone else." Peter knew that he was being lumped into the same category. Something disposable.

Anne followed him to the door to see him out, playing the good hostess.

"I don't believe I ever thanked you for the lovely dinner," said Anne, determinedly plastering yet another layer of formality over their discomfort.

"My pleasure," he said. He extended his hand.

"Good-bye," she said. She took his hand, then found herself in his arms, not knowing which of them had put her there and not caring.

They made love with the lights on, but neither of them saw

anything. The first time, they were silent, as if in awe and shock. The second time, which followed the first almost immediately, they were like a pair of panthers, groaning and howling as if in pain. Even Rimbaud, waiting impatiently outside the door, was surprised by the noise of their passion. For an instant he considered breaking in to be sure what he heard was ardor and not a mugging, but discretion won out and he retired several yards farther down the hallway, and when the maid came he engaged her in conversation until the tumult subsided.

Once outside her hotel Peter was still stunned. If that hadn't been rape, it had been the nearest thing to it. He didn't know how to assess it, didn't know what it meant. He didn't even know the girl, had spent one evening with her, knew very little about her, but when they touched, his reaction was so strong he wanted to scream, wanted her so badly he almost fell to the floor with weakness. Why? And why had he left her? And why were they both so embarrassed afterward when they had both obviously wanted it so much? He was fairly certain that he would have made love to her in a darkened doorway on the street if that had been the only place available. So why had he left her? And why was her face already fading from his memory? And why the hell had he left her?

# 13

Austin Stanhope came out of hiding in New York City. It was the easiest city in the country to hide in if you knew the districts. Most people moved within tight circles, limiting their activities to the areas where they lived and worked. Few habitués of Madison Avenue spent their idle moments kicking around in the converted lofts of Soho, for instance. Bankers did not come up from Wall Street during their lunch hours to eat in an Egyptian restaurant in the nineties on the West Side. In fact, those who lived on the East Side seldom went to the West Side for any reason whatsoever. Austin knew many people in New York, but he also knew the circles in which they moved, and he avoided them.

He emerged from the single room occupancy hotel on Ninety-sixth Street just off of Broadway dressed like the welfare recipients who occupied most of the hotel. After the shooting at his wedding that had felled his brother instead of himself, Austin had fled to New York in a panic, still dressed in his wedding tux. He borrowed money on both of his credit cards while still looking ultra respectable in his tuxedo. His first purchase had been in a discount store, where he bought a cheap brown suit. Leaving the tux in the changing room, he walked out wearing the suit, the cuffs turned up in a broad band, until he found a tailor who fixed the trousers while he waited. The first night in the hotel he slept in the suit. With a two-days' growth of stubble on his chin and the crumpled suit, he became a part of his background, a nondescript man in an army of similar men, out of work, strung out, edging toward desperation in a meek and browbeaten way, men to be ignored in the daytime, avoided in the dark.

The IRT subway took him past Greenwich Village, bypassing the swath of midtown where he might meet someone he knew, and he walked aimlessly for a few minutes on Delancey Street, finally picking a public phone at random. He intended a rather lengthy conversation, one long enough to be traced, and he wanted a phone far enough from his hiding place to be safe but close enough to public transport for him to leave the area quickly.

He dialed the operator, then the California number. When the operator came on the line, he gave her a phony credit-card number and name. The only thing that mattered was to have the sequence of numbers right, and the operator would duly log them in. It wouldn't turn up as bogus till next month's bill. Austin had thought of the irony of reversing the charges but didn't want to take the chance that his party might not accept.

A woman answered on the other end, sounding professionally annoyed. Austin switched on the pocket-sized Philips tape recorder, his second purchase in the city.

"Five five five, seven oh five one," said Martha Sawyer.

"I want to talk to him," Austin said. "Tell him it's about his money."

"Who is this?"

"Just tell him it's about his money," Austin repeated.

"I can't do that," said the woman. She sounded offended.

Austin waited, letting the silence work on the discomfort of the listener. His father had long since briefed him in the uses of the telephone. It was a very formal instrument, demanding a regular, metronomic pattern of responses. You could not pause, think things over, offer a smile or a nod instead of a grunt. You had to take your turn in the conversation or things didn't work at all. People got very uncomfortable with silence on the phone, and many rushed to fill it with their own voices, often volunteering information they had not intended to give.

"Hello?" Sawyer said at last. "Are you there?"

"Tell him it's about his money," Austin said again. And then, hearing her consider his demand, "You don't want to be the one who didn't tell him."

The Man gestured frantically for Nardo to lift the extension. "I don't want to talk to him," he said in a premature whisper, since neither man had yet picked up the phone.

Nardo spoke into the extension. "Who is this speaking?" he demanded in a voice deep and firm enough to command respect, he hoped.

"I want to talk to your boss," said Austin. "It's personal."

"He's not here," said Nardo. His boss nodded encouragement as he listened in at the phone on his desk. "I'm authorized to take any messages. You said something about money."

Austin paused. Nardo studied the floor so he wouldn't have to watch his employer.

"First of all, I'm alive," Austin said.

"Congratulations. Who are you?"

"The man you tried to kill," said Austin. "That was very annoying, it caused me a great deal of inconvenience."

171

The Man was talking at Nardo, his palm pressed over the mouthpiece. "How can he be alive, Tom? You told me it was all arranged."

Jesus H. Christ, thought Nardo. Twenty thousand dollars down the toilet and he still wasn't dead.

"What?" he asked. He had missed the caller's last sentence.

Austin said, "If you want your sixty-eight million dollars, you're going to have to up my fee. I want two million now. I've had expenses."

Nardo winced. The Man had told him it was only twenty-five million. *Only* twenty-five million? And of course he had believed him. *Well,* he thought, *if I still believe the old bastard after all these years, I probably deserve what I get.*

The Man was waving silently, trying to attract Nardo's attention from across the room. Out of annoyance Nardo waited a second longer than necessary before raising his eyes. His employer was nodding his head and mouthing the word "yes."

Nardo covered the phone. "Do you mean pay him, sir?" he asked incredulously. "Two million dollars?"

"Tell the little shitpot we'll pay," said the Man.

Nardo spoke into the phone. "How do you want the money?" he asked.

"In cash. No bill larger than a fifty. In a black attaché case. Put the attaché case in a locker in Grand Central Station. . . ."

"New York?" Nardo said. "You're in New York?"

Austin snorted with laughter. "Good, sleuth, good. Very clever."

For some reason that Nardo didn't fully understand, the Man was smiling. *It might be because he enjoys hearing the bastard make fun of me,* Nardo realized. But he didn't think that was it. The Man looked actually gratified at something.

"I hope you're taking notes," Austin continued. "Or are

you taping this? You people are good at taping things. Of course, just what good it will do you I don't know, you can't very well go to the Feds with it, can you? You're not exactly on the side of the angels in this business, are you? But I can go to the Feds or the papers, and I am taping it."

The Man was nodding rhythmically to all of this as if it were just what he wanted to hear. He glanced at Nardo and gave him an excited wink. Nardo nearly dropped the phone.

"Or are you doing it for 'historical' reasons?" Austin continued. "It will look very good in the next volume of memoirs. How I was outsmarted in my quest for sixty-eight million tax-free dollars."

Nardo made a mental note. He had said sixty-eight million again. The old man had been prepared to cheat Nardo, his only loyal associate in the last ten years, out of his share of the difference between twenty-five and sixty-eight million. *My time will come,* Nardo thought grimly, looking at his boss, who didn't seem to notice the forty-three-million-dollar difference, probably didn't even remember lying to Nardo about it. He just lied as a matter of course.

"Not that I intend to deprive you of all of it," Austin said, then immediately wondered if he should have said it. That was indeed his plan, to deprive them of all of it, to bleed them of two million of the Man's own money, more, if they'd stand for it, while tantalizing them with the key to more. But he would never give them the key, never. They had to suffer, that was the whole purpose. The money wasn't important, except that it would hurt them to lose it, hurt them very much. Nothing could hurt them enough, Austin realized, but at least this was a start. After all these years it was a good beginning.

Still, talking too much was rotten field craft. It was time to put an end to it. "If you want the numbers, come up with the money. Put the attaché case in a locker in Grand Central

173

Station and put the key inside the signboard of track 15. Do it within forty-eight hours."

"Two days!" Nardo exploded. "There's no way we can raise that kind of money in two days!" He didn't in fact know if time was any difficulty or not, but he felt an attitude of objection and delay was the right one. Again the Man overruled him.

"Two days is all right, Tom," he whispered, pressing the mouthpiece against his chest.

"Oh, you've got some nice laundered cash lying around," Austin crooned. "Sure you do."

Nardo was beginning to hate this son of a bitch and his self-satisfied air. He also hated the fact that the bastard was going to make two million in cash while Nardo had yet to see a penny.

"But, sir," Nardo protested to his boss, "should we make it so damned easy for him?"

"The easier the better, eh, Tom?" the Man answered, favoring Nardo with another of those winks that was so studied it made Nardo cringe in embarrassment.

"All right," Nardo said into the phone, struggling to keep the sullen tone from his voice, "we'll have it in two days, but it won't be easy."

It took both Nardo and his employer a moment to realize the line had gone dead.

"I hate that guy's insides," Nardo said, hanging up the lifeless phone.

The Man's laugh was like a sharp bark. It was an entirely different sound from the one he used to feign amusement.

"That's very appropriate, Tom. Our friend is cocky, very, very cocky, and not nearly as smart as he thinks. We have the code word. I don't think we need his numbers at all. We have friends, after all, don't we? We'll get the money without the numbers. And you just might get a chance to look at his insides." His shoulders shook with mirth and he barked three times, like a seal at feeding time.

Austin walked quickly to the subway, checking only cursorily to be sure he wasn't followed. He knew he was in no real danger yet. The moments of jeopardy would come in Grand Central when he tried to retrieve the money. That would be the time for them to make their play, if they were going to make one, but Austin was ready for it. He had a plan to get the money safely and get away without anyone larger than a flea following him. He grinned as he stepped into the subway car and started back uptown. They had made a try to get him and missed; now he had the upper hand and would keep it.

After the first hour of blind panic when someone tried to shoot him at the wedding, Austin had been enjoying himself thoroughly. It was really the first time in his life he had been completely out from under the wing of his father, and the sense of freedom was exhilarating. From the moment he had abandoned his traceable car in The Bronx and begun his bus and subway journey to midtown Manhattan, he had felt in control. The nearly incapacitating terror that had shaken him from the moment Peter fell amid the screams of the guests had slowly seeped away during the furiously fast drive to The Bronx and been replaced by a resolve to carry on with his plan.

There was no need to dispose of the car. By leaving it unlocked he ensured that local talent would have it off the street within an hour or so, and within a day or two at the most it would be repainted, the serial number obscured—or changed completely and perfectly if it fell into the best of professional hands—and hours later it would have a new owner, very pleased with himself for having gotten such a deal on a practically new Datsun.

Once safely hidden in his welfare hotel Austin had the time

and security to lean back and savor the headiness of his new-found liberty. He saw the two-line advertisement on the front page of *The New York Times,* and took comfort from the knowledge that he had a pipeline to help if he needed it. Contacting his father directly had too much inherent risk, the older man was too well known, too easy to stake out and wiretap. Not that he intended to call for help. He had his prey right where he wanted it, zeroed on the cross hairs of his sights. He would consider this blooding as a maturity rite, a ceremonial act of independence.

At first he had regretted not having told Peter what was going on, but now he was glad. This action was his own, had been from the start, even if he had weakened temporarily and summoned Peter back from Africa. Austin felt that he had suffered more than anyone by Thomas's death. He had been nineteen, the favored and coddled youngest son. In a way it was like having three fathers, all of them vying with each other to see who could lavish the most attention on him. He had loved all three, admired them all too, his real father and his two big brothers, ironclad men.

Stanhope was looser and freer with Austin than he had been with Thomas and Peter; Austin was the child of Stanhope's middle years, the change-of-life surprise. His mother had died shortly after Austin was born, and his father became an unexpected font of love for Austin, giving him a double dose of affection to make up for what he feared the boy would miss from his mother. The iron rules the older boys had been forced to follow were relaxed for Austin. He was made to feel like a young prince inheriting a kingdom held in trust for him by faithful regents.

Thomas was Austin's favorite, always happy, always smiling, showing Austin how to make life a game. But it was Peter he turned to in trouble, Peter the practical one, the born teacher who loved to spend hours with Austin, showing him how to solve problems.

He loved all three, and then his world was shattered and he lost all three. Thomas died. Peter left following a raging battle of mutual recrimination with his father that lasted for days, each man blaming the other for what had actually been an act of betrayal by their own government. Stanhope had trusted his government, and Peter had trusted his father. Stanhope had not realized that the administration of the Man was capable of such deceit and treachery. Peter had not fully realized that his father could be wrong. In the crushing despair of the moment, they blamed each other.

After Peter left, resigning from SSC and disappearing into the darker corners of the earth, Stanhope withdrew within himself, pulling away from Austin as if afraid to love too much again. Austin's life, which had been sheltered, now became cloistered. On the verge of becoming an operative like his brothers, Austin was suddenly wrapped in gauze, restricted to school and his studies. The SSC corporation was closed to him for years until he graduated from college and begged his father to take him on. Even then he was shunted into communications, desk work—all the safe jobs.

Until now. Until he had found a way to get revenge for his shattered world. When the routine monitoring of satellite signals had turned up the communication to the Man, he couldn't believe his luck. Because of Austin's lack of field experience, Stanhope was reluctant to give him the chance, but when he finally did, Austin seized the opportunity.

In the listening post in the old gas station, agent Stone had to restrain himself from whooping with delight that he had been on duty to hear this and not Quigley. His fellow agent had been bitterly resentful that the Man was handing Stone his career on a platter. After Stone had reported his first blockbuster, the Head of Station had upgraded the priority of his unit. Stone was now privy to a direct line for reporting anything that he deemed urgent. Stone had been very careful not to abuse the privilege, waiting with growing impatience for the Man or that bungler Nardo to overstep themselves again. It had been worth the wait.

Stone dialed the direct line to Head of Station, and learned from his secretary that the HOS was gone for an extended weekend. The ostensible reason was to get his son reinstated in school—the boy had managed to get thrown out of three so far—but Stone suspected that the HOS had really gone to Washington again to nose his way around his superiors. The man was frightfully obvious the way he sucked up to anyone who could advance his career. That was the reason, Stone was convinced, that he was Head of Station although only two years senior in service to Stone, and that Stone, who was a better agent coming and going, was still stuck in a converted garage with Quigley and his ubiquitous bags of potato chips.

The opportunity was simply too big to pass up. If HOS wasn't around when he should be, if he was off tending to private business on company time, then Stone had no choice but to go over his head. If Stone got all the credit, which he certainly deserved, and HOS wound up looking like an absentee landlord, well, that was too damned bad.

Stone called the district head directly and told him that Nardo, former White House aide, former deputy press secretary and full-time toady, was about to blow off the head of a blackmailer. And if that wasn't worth a promotion, nothing was.

Rimbaud was made to wait half an hour while the great and august Director of Operations of the National Security

Agency did whatever it was he did in his private toilet. Rimbaud assumed either he suffered from persistent constipation or else the man was setting records for self-abuse. Director Levy was a gaunt, austere-looking man with a grayish pallor to his skin that resisted the sun, the wind, booze, or anything else that tried to redden it. Rimbaud thought of him as devoid of sexual desires. It was as impossible for Rimbaud to imagine Levy in the throes of lust as it was to picture an oyster copulating. And even that was giving Levy the benefit of the doubt. Which left constipation, and Rimbaud could well believe it. He had thought Levy was full of shit from the moment he was appointed director.

When Rimbaud was finally ushered into the presence, Levy was still drying his hands on a paper towel. He waited until he had finished drying, then carefully folded the disposable towel as if it were a napkin before dropping it into the wastebasket. Only then did he gesture Rimbaud to sit down.

"Just what exactly were you trying to accomplish by this inquiry?" Levy asked at last. He flicked a paper on his desk as if it were a speck of lint on his suit.

"Sir?" said Rimbaud.

Levy was still standing behind his desk as if he expected this interview to be over at any second.

"I mean, Mr. Rimbaud, just what particular can of worms are you trying to open? And why are you attempting to deposit said can of worms on my plate?"

Rimbaud paused a moment before answering. "My memo, sir, is asking for instructions for the disposition of certain alleged conspirators whose alleged conspiracy is . . ."

Levy looked wearily at the dull green wall. It reminded him vaguely of nausea, someone else's nausea—not at all pleasant, but not personally discomforting.

"This isn't the police force, Rimbaud. Speak English."

"I heard there's been another blackmail threat in the— Stanhope business and that they're going to kill him. Do we move in or not?"

Levy thrust both thumbs in his belt and hitched his pants. The waistline was at least two inches too large on his gaunt form. He looked to Rimbaud as if he had lost weight suddenly due to a severe illness and was not expected to recover. Unfortunately, however, Rimbaud thought, the truth was that they just don't make clothes to fit men with concave torsos. Levy's hipbones jutted out farther in front of him than his stomach did. Rimbaud himself was given to flesh and had to diet continually to stay slim. Otherwise, because of his short stature the slightest sign of a paunch would make him look like a jelly doughnut. He didn't get the respect he deserved because he was so short anyway, and could ill afford to add overweight or he'd be a laughingstock. Which was just another reason to dislike Levy. Not that the guy needed any extras, he was dislikable enough on his own merits.

"Have you heard who is going to be killed?" Levy asked.

"Stanhope."

"And do you know where he is?"

"No, sir."

Levy sniffed. "Then one assumes you can't afford him protection, can you? . . . Can you?"

"No, sir," Rimbaud said reluctantly.

"And have you heard who is going to do the actual killing?"

Rimbaud twitched in his seat. He knew he shouldn't have sent the memo. He should have simply acted on his own—and ended with his ass in a sling if anything went wrong and Levy found out about it.

"No, sir."

"Then you cannot prevent him, can you?" Levy studied the ceiling for a moment, rubbing his throat. Rimbaud was reminded of a stork that had swallowed too large a fish and was trying to massage it down.

"Mr. Rimbaud," Levy said, "what is the source of your information?"

"I just heard it around," said Rimbaud.

"Around."

"It's in the pipeline."

"Ah," said Levy, sounding greatly pleased. "The pipeline. The scuttlebutt. The poop. The word. . . . Have you received any *official* word, Mr. Rimbaud?"

"No."

"Have you received any direction from your immediate superior about action in this matter?"

"You are my immediate superior . . . sir," said Rimbaud.

"That," said Levy, "is what I thought. I was under the distinct impression that you were employed by this agency as a directed employee—not as a free-lancer who tries to find trouble wherever he can. Tell me where I've gone wrong, Mr. Rimbaud."

Rimbaud was trying to decide what to do with the body if he killed Levy where he stood.

"I assume I have not gone wrong," Levy continued. "You are not an undercover cop who is supposed to sniff out rumors, you have no official directive to do anything in this matter, you don't know where the supposed victim is, and you don't know who the would-be killer is. Just what in hell did you intend to do!"

*I intended to arrest Nardo on a conspiracy charge,* Rimbaud thought, *pump him to find out the rest, and haul the whole bunch in, ass over elbows, including the Man. And you know it, you constipated scarecrow.*

"I didn't have a clear plan in mind, sir," he said aloud. "The purpose of the memo was to elicit one."

Levy seemed suddenly impatient, as if the interview had already gone on much too long. "Your diligence is commendable. However, in a word, the agency doesn't know what you're talking about."

Rimbaud knew he wasn't going any higher in the agency. The cold fish like Levy who ran things had never taken him completely seriously because of his size. He cut a slightly comic figure for them, no matter what he was doing nor how excellently. They were like Prussian Junkers, looking down their aristocratic noses at the upstart peasant in their midst, someone to be tolerated because of his usefulness but never to be admitted to the privileged class of the normal-sized.

But being barred from higher positions didn't mean that Rimbaud didn't want to hang on to the one he had. He had a nice pension to look forward to in six years. Not enough to live on, of course, but a pleasant supplement to whatever other salary he could earn. As a man still in his forties with twenty years of agency experience, he should have no problem getting work with a security group in private enterprise, one of the many that did business with the government—provided he came armed with the proper recommendations. Recommendations given by men like Levy, who also doled out the government contracts.

The only workable assumption was that the people Levy took orders from would not object at all if Stanhope were dead.

Levy tapped Rimbaud's memo. "The first time you were involved with this Stanhope case, an attempt was made on the life of Peter Stanhope despite the fact that you had half a dozen men trying to prevent it. The second time you had Mr. Stanhope under protective surveillance—extremely close and cooperative surveillance, at that—there was an event."

"A false alarm," Rimbaud corrected. He had carefully

worded his report on the incident in Anne's apartment to make it sound as if his men had been on top of things from the beginning rather than reacting after the fact. Apparently he had done less of a job of glossing over than he hoped.

"An event," Levy repeated. "An alarm, false or otherwise, would hardly have been expected under the circumstances. You have a very—interesting—record in this case so far. More noteworthy for excitement than for success. Rather more excitement than we like when protecting people, Mr. Rimbaud. And now you'd like to intercede again, this time on your own initiative—and it would be entirely on your own initiative— or have you had second thoughts in the matter?"

Rimbaud nodded, very slowly. "I'm glad you have put matters in a different light for me, sir." If they wanted Austin Stanhope dead, they could have him dead.

Levy smiled, a stretching to the gray skin that never revealed any teeth. "That's my job. Would you like this— memo—included in the file?" Levy lifted the paper and dangled it between thumb and forefinger.

Rimbaud knew what he meant. *Would I like it on my record as an instance of troublemaking.* The little agent delicately took it from Levy's fingers. He carefully tore the paper in two.

"No, sir, I think not. Thank you."

"If that's all, then," Levy said, dismissing him. Rimbaud wadded the torn memo in his hand and walked out.

Back in his own office Rimbaud flattened out the wrinkled memo, carefully taped it together, and then made two copies. He was off the hook with Levy and his superiors, but if this thing blew up in everyone's face, Rimbaud would have evidence that he, at least, had tried to do the right thing. And if that put Levy on a skewer, Rimbaud could think of no one except Levy who would complain.

# 14

---

The telephone rang, activating the answering machine. Smith lay on his bed, ankle encased in a plastic splint, his eyes closed. He was not asleep, his mind was racing, but he had found that it was easier to ignore the pain in his leg with his eyes closed. Several bottles of medication were stacked on the night table, unused. When the pain was at its worst, on the second night, he had taken one pill. The experience had been terrible, the mild narcotic had stirred his already feverish imagination, goading it into pathways he had never experienced before. Feeling helpless and paralyzed, Smith had been forced to endure nightmarish visions that overwhelmed his highly developed resistance and left him ravaged with terror. His world was already surrounded by demons, but the pain-killer had allowed them to penetrate the very innermost sanctum, the one inviolate crevice in his mind where the real Smith, Smith the observer, Smith the intellect that could ultimately distinguish between reality and self-induced fear, was hiding.

He suffered the pain. And each minute he suffered, his

hatred for the man who had caused it, Stanhope, grew. When he turned on the message machine, he expected little of use. He had already turned down two offers because of his ankle, one to eliminate quietly and without suspicion a known international terrorist who had entered the country legally and presented a political embarrassment to many, and the other from a mobster who wanted an inconvenient trial-witness to suffer an accident. Smith would have refused the second commission even if he'd been healthy, because he did not associate with criminal elements as a matter of principle. He disapproved of them.

With surprise, then growing excitement, he recognized the voice on the tape as Sam's. Sam meant Stanhope, and that was whom he wanted, broken ankle or not.

Sam stipulated United Airlines gate 35 at JFK Airport as a meeting place. His reason was clear. Smith could not pass through the metal detectors to get to the gate while carrying a gun, and Sam wanted him unarmed. Smith was amused. Sam must be getting frightened and stupid in his old age. Normally Smith had no qualms about meeting a client unarmed. They had as much to lose as he by betraying him to the authorities. However, he didn't want Sam to think he had outsmarted him. Smith might be temporarily crippled, but he was no less cunning.

Smith spent the day in preparation. His final stop was a fish store where he bought a pint of shucked oysters in a plastic container. With mild revulsion he picked out one of the slippery gray mollusks and slipped it into a plastic sandwich bag that he put in his shirt pocket, then handed the rest of the pint back to the clerk, who shrugged and put it aside to take home for his family.

With his paraphernalia gathered around him and the oyster

in his pocket, Smith waited on the corner for a taxi to take him to the airport.

The cabdriver, Ephraim Pincus, an Israeli who had come to America to study industrial design and had found battling the city's traffic preferable to dodging Palestinian bullets, listened aghast to the assortment of regurgitating noises in the backseat of his taxi. When they had first started, he had pulled the cab to the side, ordering the man to throw up outside the car.

Before Pincus could turn entirely around in the seat, the man had evaded the protective shield and grabbed his neck with a grip that made the driver's eyes water.

"Drive the car, schmuck," the man had ordered in a voice that sounded anything but frail. "Unless I puke on you, you've got nothing to worry about."

Pincus drove, catching a glimpse of the bland face now and again in the rearview mirror. He would sit calmly, features composed, then explode without warning into a huge gagging reflex, eyes popping, cheeks bulging with the effort to keep the vomitus in. But nothing ever actually happened. It was as if the man had the dry heaves, but he seemed to be perfectly comfortable when he wasn't gagging. The most peculiar aspect of the performance, Pincus realized after it had been going on for half an hour, was that the man seemed to be practicing, as if learning how to throw up if the need ever arose. Still, it was preferable to being blown up while on a bus crossing the Negev, as one of his cousins had been.

Wheeling through the traffic and never checking the cars behind him, Pincus slid the cab in front of the airport cop and into the space that had just been vacated by a limousine on its way to Connecticut. Pincus was in a hurry to get rid of this fare. Listening to all that dry puking had begun to make

him sick to his stomach. He opened the collapsible wheelchair and steadied it as the man lowered himself into it, holding onto the roof of the cab. Pincus handed him the two
metallic crutches and put the blanket across his lap.

Inside the terminal an airlines employee hurried to relieve
Pincus.

"Hope you feel better, mister," Pincus said.

"Thank you," the man said, his voice weak and quavery.
He thrust a ten-dollar tip into Pincus's hand. "You've been
very patient."

Pincus watched, puzzled, as the airlines woman wheeled
the man away. Despite all that heaving the guy had looked
perfectly healthy in the cab. Now suddenly he looked like he
was at death's door. Pincus had seen malaria attacks come that
quickly, but malaria didn't cause the heaves. Whatever his
problem was, he wasn't Pincus's problem anymore, and remembering the strength of the man's grip on his neck, Pincus
was damned glad of that.

Smith leaned back in the wheelchair, moaning softly as the
woman wheeled him toward the inspection barrier.

"Are you all right, Mr. Parker?" she asked, stopping the
wheelchair and leaning over him solicitously.

Smith spoke in a tiny voice, "Oh, yes. Thank you. It's the
radiation treatments." He smiled weakly, bravely, as the ill
do to comfort the healthy.

The woman stood up, backing off involuntarily from the
presence of radiation, even twice-removed. "Oh," she said, not
knowing what else to say.

As they approached the arched metal detector the woman
went forward to have a quiet word with the guard, an intense
young man whose nameplate read "R. Salter." Smith leaned
back, eyes half-closed, moaning softly, but he took in the uniformed New York City cop standing by twenty feet away, idly

watching. Smith noted the loop of leather holding the police-man's gun securely in his holster, estimated how long it would take him to flip off the loop and pull out the gun. Much too long for the cop's welfare if Smith had had a healthy leg, but under the circumstances Smith was not sure.

R. Salter gestured to the woman with his portable metal detector. He wanted to oblige, but he felt a need to perform his duty, too, especially with a cop watching. As they talked Smith surreptitiously slipped the oyster from the plastic bag in his pocket and into his mouth, covering his actions with a handkerchief with which he dabbed at his lips. He tucked the oyster in the side of his cheek where he could dislodge it with his tongue when he needed to.

Brandishing the metal detector like a dousing switch, R. Salter approached Smith. The woman employee took the crutches off his lap and held them while Salter ran the ex-truded tube of the metal detector over Smith's body. The light flashed and the alarm crackled like radio static during a thunderstorm.

"It's the wheelchair," said Salter to Smith, a note of apology in his voice. "I'll just take a look manually, if that's all right, Mr. Parker."

"Do your job, son," Smith said faintly.

The uniformed cop looked on, edging a step or two closer. Salter knelt down, fingering the wheel of the chair. He didn't really know what he was looking for, but he was determined to make it look authentic now that he'd gone this far.

"May I remove this, sir?" Salter asked, already lifting the robe from Smith's lap. Smith coughed once, lips pursed.

"Is this necessary?" the woman asked impatiently.

It was the wrong thing to say to someone already insecure and determined not to show it. Salter stiffened his back. "Help him stand up," he said to the woman. "Just for a second."

191

Smith coughed again in warning, then suddenly with an explosive noise vomited into his handkerchief. The oyster, fat, amorphous, and trailing mucus, plopped into his hand. Smith quickly covered it with the handkerchief, but not before everyone had seen it.

The cop turned away, rolling his eyes, unaware that Smith's whole attention was on him. Salter backed off, feeling very foolish. Wordlessly he nodded to the angry woman, who was glaring at him. She returned the crutches to Smith's lap and wheeled him toward the gate as he dabbed at his lips and smiled bravely.

Fifteen minutes later Smith was alone in the men's room, where he locked himself in the stall designed for the handicapped. He eased himself gratefully off the seat of the wheelchair. For the past twenty minutes he had been sitting on the firing assembly of a Uzi submachine gun, and it was not comfortable. Unscrewing one of the metal crutches, he removed the barrel of the gun from the hollow leg. The T-shaped metal butt was in the armpiece of the other crutch.

The fully assembled submachine gun fit barrel-first into the inner pocket of Smith's raincoat, the barrel held in place by a Velcro strap that could be torn off in a fraction of a second. The gun snuggled neatly under his armpit, and, if he had chosen to, by keeping one hand in his pocket he could have freed the weapon and sprayed the entire lobby with a clip of thirty-five .32 shells in less than seven seconds. But he had no intention of shooting anyone. The gun was just a bravura performance, a bit of theatrics to impress Sam.

As Smith came toward them on crutches Nardo grabbed Sam's arm.

"Why, he's a gimp!" he exclaimed. "You never told me that, Sam. I didn't pay good money to hire the handicapped."

"It's a job-related accident," Sam said wryly. "Line of duty, and I wouldn't joke about it to him, if I were you."

Smith clomped closer to them on his aluminum crutches. Nardo was surprised the man looked so average. If Sam hadn't pointed him out, Nardo would never have guessed this one to be a hired killer. He wasn't naïve enough to expect a scowling Mafia hood, or someone with his teeth filed to a point, but he had anticipated something exceptional, some fire in the eye or a prepossessing show of strength—or even something negative, a milquetoast, a midget, anything to set him apart from the herd. But this man was exceptional only for looking so unexceptional.

They sat three abreast in the waiting room chairs, Sam in the middle.

"You made it without incident, I hope," said Sam.

Smith smiled, a dry, humorless look that was almost a sneer.

"Why not? Can you think of anything that would have caused me trouble?"

"No. It wouldn't be to our interest to cause you trouble."

"He just likes airports, is that it?" Smith asked, eyeing Nardo, who twitched uneasily on his seat.

"It's more convenient here," Sam said soothingly. "He's just gotten in, and he'll fly out again right after this. He just wants to impress the importance of this assignment on you."

Nardo nodded. "Very important."

"It usually is," said Smith. He was slowly unbuttoning his coat, taking unusual care with it. Nardo wondered if his hand was partially paralyzed, he toyed with each button so long before undoing it.

"Tom here thought maybe I hadn't conveyed the proper sense of urgency to you," said Sam.

"Frankly, we thought you'd have finished up by now," Nardo said. "What's the delay?"

193

Smith's fingers froze on the button. His face went dead calm, losing all animation. He looked almost as if he were sleeping with his eyes open. His voice, too, was totally flat.

"I've been—hurt," he said.

"Yes, well, we're sorry to hear that, of course, but that brings up the next point. I'm not at all sure a crippled man is right for this job . . ."

Smith undid the last button and the coat fell open, revealing the Uzi strapped inside. Nardo nearly choked.

"Jesus Christ," he muttered. "Put that away. What the hell is that? Jesus Christ." He glanced at Sam. To his surprise the old agent was smiling slightly, nodding to Smith like a teacher indicating approval to an enterprising student.

"On the other hand," Sam said smoothly, "we're not asking him to run a footrace, are we, Tom?"

"No! No, we're not!" Nardo blurted quickly.

"If he assesses his capabilities as adequate to the task—and I daresay they are—then we'll accept that assessment, won't we, Tom?"

Nardo nodded, trying to swallow. He couldn't take his eyes off the evil-looking weapon.

"I didn't hear you," said Smith.

"Yes," said Nardo. "You're the man for the job."

"There's more than one way to do it," Smith said. "And besides, I'm going to do it, whether you like it or not. If you get in my way . . . don't get in my way."

"No," said Nardo. "No, no, I won't."

"Perhaps you should tell him what you came to say, Tom, while he buttons his coat."

And so Nardo told Smith where to find Austin Stanhope and when to kill him.

# 15

Austin walked across the nearly deserted grand concourse of Grand Central carrying a large paper bag. With his clothes and five-day growth of beard he looked like a man who might carry things in a paper bag, perhaps all he owned. It was nearly midnight and the station, an anthill of activity by day, was winding down. The gates to many of the tracks were locked; only a few sleepy commuter runs, the last of the day, were still waiting to depart into the night. Austin waited until the cop on duty in the station made his periodic round of the waiting room, whacking his nightstick against the long wooden pews to shock the sleeping derelicts awake before he rousted them out of the building for the night.

Furtive, hunted-looking men were routed from the men's room, where they spent the day cruising constantly for partners in their own brand of sex, negotiating quickly for the price of a blowjob at the urinals while stunned commuters tried to ignore what they saw and hurried away.

As the cop swept the detritus of city life out to the streets where it would redistribute itself, Austin slipped through an open gate and made his way to track 13. A few yards away from the track was a hole in the wall. Beside the hole the word "here" was scratched onto the concrete siding in yellow chalk, a guide to station maintenance workers and derelicts alike. He climbed down a shaky fourteen-foot ladder, walked down another stairway, and entered a passageway beneath the tracks of the terminal's lower level. The oppressively hot passageway had been nicknamed the Burma Road long ago by a maintenance worker with a sense of wartime history. Austin shed his suit coat as he walked, knowing the heat would only get worse.

At the mouth of the tunnel he stopped. In front of him was the entrance of a network of cavernous tunnels housing the steam pipes that heat and power the terminal and many surrounding buildings. One can enter as Austin did from the station itself, or from a variety of more elegant doorways, such as the embossed metal door on the ground floor of the Waldorf-Astoria, or at the moneyed portals of the Chemical Bank building on Forty-seventh Street. But once inside, all pathways lead down and down to a depth of six levels below Park Avenue.

The tunnels were, as Austin knew, a sort of hell on earth, with heat as stifling as a sauna bath, an area as devoid of natural light as the tomb, with huge, emboldened rats and, lurking in corners like monsters in a fairy tale, the wild-eyed, desperate men, thirty to forty at a time, who made the filth-encrusted tunnels their homes by night. They were men who had all but severed their ties with society, too proud to accept the blandishments of welfare or Salvation Army handouts, too blasted and burned-out to do anything positive to help themselves. Respecting one another's privacy as much as they needed their own, they spread throughout the tunnels, sometimes coming together to share a meal, then retreating to their own corners to savor the total distance from friends, family, society, that their natures demanded.

Austin took a flashlight from the paper bag and switched it on. Once he entered the tunnels, light would be intermittent, coming from the infrequent bare bulbs hanging from the ceiling, many of them burned-out or stolen and relocated by the tramps. The flashlight had brand-new batteries, and Austin had another set in his pocket, along with a spare bulb. The prospect of going into the tunnels alone was frightening enough, but the possibility of being down there without light was more than he wanted to contemplate.

He was ready, but still he hesitated, running rapidly over the details of his plan, trying to think if there wasn't an easier, safer way. But he knew there was not. Tomorrow the delivery of the attaché case full of money would be made. From that point on he had to expect that every entrance and exit to the station would be watched. The only safe way to get to the locker would be if he were already in the station, or at least under it. Very few people, except for the railroad personnel and the derelict community, knew of the existence of the tunnels. The police knew, of course, but by and large they gave the tunnels a wide berth. The derelicts knew the catacombs much better than the police, and, after a lifetime of harassment by the authorities, they were not apt to give any cop a very cordial welcome.

But the Man would not be using the police, of course. He could hardly afford to go public with his problems, and it was very doubtful that any outside help he used would know of the tunnels or their many exits. Austin could come up from the tunnels like a mole in a garden, take his money, and disappear the way he had come. Anyone trying to follow him underground wouldn't have a chance. Once he was sure he was alone, Austin could come up for air again several blocks away, unnoticed, unremarked, and safe.

No, it was still the best plan; all it required was a bit of courage. He switched the light off and on several times to re-assure himself it would work when he needed it, then with a deep breath he entered the tunnels.

The darkness was absolute. It seemed to swallow the beam of the flashlight, to suck it in voraciously, so that the pathetic trickle of white light only served to accentuate the pitch-blackness around it. For the first few minutes Austin felt the dark as a physical force, something so solid he had to lean forward to force his way through it. It seemed to resist him, making every step a physical and mental effort. The flashlight was too small for the job. He had selected a small, tubular model that took two nine-volt batteries, because it was small enough to handle easily and not be conspicuous in his clothing or the bag. But now it seemed as inadequate as a candle in a cemetery. If he kept the beam pointed down toward his feet so he could see where he was stepping, he could see nothing at head level or to either side.

Within the first few hundred yards he stepped headlong into a low-hanging beam, the blow knocking him back and down. He landed hard on the base of his spine and dropped the flashlight. The flashlight rolled away and went out. For a second he was just stunned, then panic took over. He couldn't see a thing, not a thing, but noise seemed to be all around him, a whirring, scuttling, scraping mixture of sounds as if all the thousands of denizens of the dark, temporarily stilled by the presence of man and his light, had come to pulsating life again. He sensed movement all around him and instinctively jumped to his feet so that whatever it was couldn't crawl over him. His body demanded flight, his muscles screamed with the urgency, but there was nowhere to go, and the wrong way would take him deeper into the darkness.

Every breath was loud, almost a gasp that seemed to resonate in his chest with the moan of a man in a nightmare. He had to have the flashlight. If it was broken, he had a spare bulb and batteries in his pocket. Touching them through the fabric of his suit coat, he realized with surprise that he still clutched the paper bag and the contents had not been disturbed. He had kept safe the things that were essential to his plan but had lost the one thing, the flashlight, that was essential to his life.

Austin eased himself to his knees. Putting the paper bag between his legs so he could feel it at all times, he began to grope along the floor with both hands. The concrete surface was gritty against his fingertips, dotted with chips of masonry that had fallen from the walls, all partially covered with a film of dust. Something warm and moist slithered against his hand, then recoiled away as Austin gasped. It had felt like a large moving tongue, but when he calmed down he realized it had probably been a blind salamander, a heat-loving, lizard-like animal that made its living off the insects that teemed in the tunnels. As he paused, trying to steady his breathing, something with bristly fur started to crawl up his trouser leg. Austin kicked out and heard a sharp protesting squeal, then the scuttle of claws on concrete.

The sudden movement of his leg knocked over the bag, which fell on the concrete with a clink of glass. The bottle in the bag rolled slightly, and Austin just barely had the presence of mind to grab at the sound and stop it. Securing the bag again between his legs, he resumed his search with groping hands, keeping up a loud, wailing *ahhhhh,* as much to comfort himself as to frighten off whatever lurked in the darkness around him.

It took three minutes to find the flashlight, but it seemed to Austin as if he'd been there on his knees for half a day.

The light came on immediately when he tested it. As the beam played in front of him it caught the fiery glow of two red eyes, shining like the orbs of Satan. The eyes were almost on a level with Austin's own as he knelt on the floor, and his entire face prickled with vulnerability. If the thing chose to leap at him, there would be very little he could do to defend himself. Austin screamed. The eyes switched off as the thing turned its head from the beam. As it crossed the ray of light and ran off, Austin could just make out the shape of a body, silver-gray in the dark, as large as a man's foot, with a tail, naked and scaly, half again as long.

He stood, shivering, for more than a minute, playing the beam around him in rapid, frantic jerks. He located the low concrete beam on which he had banged his head, the concrete wall on one side, and the asbestos-covered steampipe, nearly wide enough for a man to crawl into, eight feet away on the other side. Forward and behind him the light was swallowed up by darkness that seemed to have no end.

Finally he started forward again, now moving the light all around as he walked, like the flashing beam of a lighthouse. He climbed over giant water pipes, scaled steep ladders, crouched under low beams. Occasionally he would come to a pool of brightness in the dark, light spreading for yards in either direction from an overhead bare bulb. In these pools of light he found signs of human occupation, old newspapers spread out on the dirt-laden floor as a mattress, a plastic drinking cup, discarded and crumpled aluminum plates from frozen dinners. But nowhere did he see a definite sight or sound of man. Occasionally the air would seem to pulsate as if something had just departed quickly, withdrawing into the dark. Austin would stop, call out softly, "Hello." The sound would echo through the tunnel, coming back to him from the surrounding silence as a mockery of his attempts to communicate.

He pressed on, looking for the right circumstances. He had been in the tunnels before, during one of the counterinsurgency exercises his father would take them on. But he had been just a boy then, surrounded by the protective bulk of his father and two older brothers. It had all seemed safe enough then, just pleasantly frightening, like the haunted house at the amusement park. He knew it was not real, nothing could actually hurt him with his father at his side, and there was an end to it all, they would reemerge when his father was ready to have a good meal and go to a show. Now there seemed no end to it, it was as far to travel backward as forward, the hellish quality of the place was no longer make-believe, no longer just a part of an exciting weekend exercise.

After forty minutes Austin found the man he needed. He was asleep, lying just at the edge of a pool of light, in a cramped gully behind a double set of pipes. The man was wearing a waist-length winter jacket with a heavy wool collar, despite the heat. His mouth was open and he was snoring slightly, the newspaper mattress close to his mouth waving with each exhalation.

Austin sank with relief to the floor. It had been a long walk, made more difficult by the tension in his muscles caused by fear and caution. His head throbbed where he had struck the beam, and he was dripping with sweat. He made no special effort to be quiet as he positioned himself with his side to the sleeper, not facing him directly but still watching him from the corner of his eye.

From the bag he drew out the treasure, a gallon jug of cheap red table wine. It was not a good wine, but good enough so Austin could stomach it, and he knew he would be drinking a lot of it.

The bottle made a solid clink on the concrete, and the sleeper snapped awake. Austin could sense the tension in the other man's body even though he didn't move. Austin continued to act as if he weren't aware of the sleeper's presence, reaching into his brown bag and producing a can of sliced peaches, a can of beans, half a dozen sticks of dried, hard sausage. It wasn't much, but Austin knew he could live comfortably enough on it for a day and a half, even if he shared it, and it looked cheap enough to be the legitimate scroungings of a derelict.

Turning his head as if to scratch his neck, Austin sneaked a closer glance at the other man, his eyes cast down at the floor and flicking upward only for half a second. It was too much for the sleeper. He scuttled back farther into his cave behind the pipes like a frightened animal. Austin returned to his business as if he hadn't noticed.

He unscrewed the top of the wine bottle, letting the raw, slightly acrid smell of the wine act as his lure. He lifted the bottle to his lips and drank, spilling a bit on his chin and taking his time about dabbing it off. He put the bottle down an arm's length away from himself, an arm's length closer to the man watching him from the shadows, leaving the top off so the smell would permeate the cone of light and beyond.

It was like luring a frightened dog out of hiding. First put down the bait, sit very still a distance away so the dog can see you mean it no harm, then let it come out and sniff you and the bait, being careful not to make any sudden movements.

After a few minutes Austin's human dog came out.

"This is my place," the man said. His voice was husky, as if he had not used it much lately.

Austin turned as if noticing him for the first time. He gestured toward the bottle.

"There's enough for two," Austin said.

The man sat up, and Austin studied his face directly. His lips and mouth seemed loose and curiously unformed, as if they had been transplanted from an old man onto the face of one much younger. Judging by the eyes and relatively smooth brow, Austin's target was about thirty years old, but his lower face seemed that of a man of sixty or seventy. A piece of gauze was taped to his forehead, the result of some blow that reminded Austin of his own encounter with the overhanging beam.

The man looked steadily at Austin, who turned away and rummaged in his paper bag again. This was the crucial moment. The important thing was to avoid direct eye-contact that could be interpreted as a challenge or a threat. Austin tried to appear as harmless as possible, but meanwhile his right hand on the side out of the man's view crept to his jacket pocket and the nickel-plated .22 caliber Saturday night special. The gun was not powerful enough to stop a charging man, he would have needed a .45 Magnum for that, but it had cost only sixty dollars and had been easy to get.

The man's gaze wandered down from Austin's face to the bottle of wine on the floor. He sniffed once and twisted his lips.

"I don't mind," he said at last. Moving forward, he squatted by the bottle and took a long drink. He smiled, twisting his sunken cheeks into deep creases and nudging the bottle back toward Austin. After taking a drink, Austin held out one of the shriveled sausages. *And now let him lick my hand*, Austin thought. *Scratch him behind the ears and he's mine.*

The man took the sausage rather daintily between thumb and forefinger. He paused for a moment as if uncertain what to do with it, then reached into his shirt pocket and pulled out a full set of false teeth. He blew on them fastidiously to remove any lint and slipped them into his mouth. His face immediately looked thirty years younger.

"Got 'em in the Army," he said, noticing Austin's surprise.

"Figured it was a chance to get some free dental work, so I had 'em yank all my teeth." The man winked, making Austin a fellow conspirator against the Army. "Got my money's worth there."

The man reached into his other shirt pocket and drew out a pair of wire-rimmed glasses. "Got these in the Army, too," he said, a note of pride in his voice at having done so well by himself in the service. He looked at the glasses for a moment, mildly puzzled, as if they brought back a memory but he was uncertain if it was a pleasant one or not. Finally he breathed on the lenses and, with the same air of fastidiousness, cleaned them against his shirt, then put them on. All his parts in working order, he looked at Austin once more and smiled like a host welcoming an unexpected but cherished guest.

Waving his hand toward the wall as if he were a man showing off his newest acquisition, he said, "I sit over here." He crossed to the wall and stood there, waiting politely for Austin to join him. Only after Austin sat and leaned back against the concrete wall did the man sit himself.

His name was Whitey, a sobriquet that stemmed from being a towhead for the first six years of his life. The hair had long since faded to a lackluster brown, but the name had stuck. Along with the mention of the Army, it was the only reference to his past he made in the day and a half that Austin spent with him.

Eventually he showed Austin the rest of his treasures, the broom with the abbreviated handle that he used to keep his living area reasonably clean. The stick of roll-on deodorant he used regularly. He didn't often have the opportunity to bathe, but he had a loathing of body odor and prided himself on not having sunk to the level of a bum so far gone as to stink. The most curious of his treasures was a jar of skin cream that he

204

used to lubricate his hands every night before sleep. He was not even certain himself about the purpose of the cream except that it was a link with a more civilized past, a remnant of breeding that showed he still knew how to behave even if he did live six levels below the city streets.

Whitey also owned a ball-point pen he never had occasion to use, although he spoke once of the possibility of sending a postcard home to say he was all right. From his accent Austin guessed "home" was somewhere in the hill country of the South, Tennessee or Arkansas perhaps, but Austin didn't ask and Whitey didn't say.

To his surprise Austin found he liked Whitey. Despite their having nothing in common. There was something so elemental in the shared appreciation of the wine, the spicy sausage, the tomatoey beans, the slippery wet peaches, that it was impossible not to feel a fellowship with his companion, two men seated against a wall in a cone of light in the vast darkness of the tunnels.

Whitey awoke the next day while Austin slept. Although it was impossible to tell night or day in the tunnels, Whitey knew it to be night outside. He lighted his candle and left Austin to sleep off the effects of the wine. Hours later Whitey returned with three potatoes and put them on an aluminum plate on the pipe. From another pocket he took out a large plastic produce bag with the name of a supermarket chain written across it. The bag was filled with water and tied at the top with a twist of wire. Whitey poured some of the water into the plastic cup, and Austin drank it greedily. Dropping the potatoes into the water, Whitey resealed the bag and placed the plastic directly on the bare steampipe, where the asbestos had been scraped away.

The water kept the plastic from burning, and in minutes it

was boiling, cooking the potatoes. After he had eaten, Austin felt better. He comforted himself with the knowledge that within a few hours he would be out of the tunnels, safe and rich.

Whitey produced a bottle of plum wine that made Austin fight back his gag reflex and his stomach twist in protest. He declined a second drink, and when the bottle was offered a third time he held it to his lips but only pretended to swallow.

"Whitey, I need you to do something for me," he said at last. "I got a bag up in the terminal in a locker. It's got everything I own in it. I need you to get that bag for me."

Whitey loosened his dentures with his tongue, then snapped them back into place, waiting for Austin to continue. "I'd get it myself but there's a guy up there I don't want to see."

Whitey nodded. He could understand paranoia, having spent most of his adult life avoiding guys he didn't want to see. The very vagueness of Austin's situation vouched for its authenticity to Whitey. It was exactly how he would have worded a similar situation. Too many details would have been unwanted, an intrusion on the privacy of both men.

"There's a bottle of rum in it," Austin said, throwing in his clincher. Whitey sucked on his dentures again, snapping them back into place with an audibly moist slap.

"You'll be moving on then, I guess," Whitey said. It was the closest thing to a personal question he had asked.

Austin had guessed that he had already outstayed his welcome, but the host was simply too polite to suggest it.

"Soon as I get my bag. You can have the rum, it doesn't agree with me."

"Whatever's right," Whitey said, rising to his feet.

Leading the way with his red candle, Whitey led them out of the tunnels in surprisingly short order. He moved with an ease and certainty born of months in the darkness, and it was all Austin could do to keep up with him. Whitey brought them into the terminal via a different route than Austin had used on his way in, and they emerged by track 7.

It was 4:00 A.M., and the great terminal was deserted. Austin stood behind the cloudy glass door of the track gates. Pressing his eyes against the crack where the doors met, he could clearly see the bank of lockers where the attaché case would be. There was no sight of any other human, no sound at all. Of course that didn't mean that someone wasn't sitting with a rifle in any one of dozens of hiding places. Still, Austin doubted it, doubted they would try anything that foolish again. But on the other hand he didn't plan to expose his back and find out.

Whitey walked across the marble terminal floor, his footsteps sounding exaggeratedly loud in the silent hall. He put his hand in the signboard announcing trains leaving from track 15 and felt around for a moment. His fingers touched the key, and he held it up for Austin to see.

From his hiding place Austin watched Whitey approach the bank of lockers, key in hand. The whole thing had been ridiculously easy, Austin gloated, forgetting his time of terror in the tunnels. Whitey had proved as good and obedient a dog as he had hoped. Austin thought perhaps he would give the man fifty dollars, no, make it a hundred, to ease his disappointment over there being no bottle of rum. He would prefer the rum, most likely. Austin smiled and almost started to whistle, he was so pleased with his success.

Whitey found the locker and opened it. He looked around once, half expecting to see the man Austin was trying to avoid. He saw no one. The attaché case was in the locker. Whitey pulled it out and lifted it high for Austin to see. The case was heavy, but it didn't feel as if it had a bottle in it. It might be the wrong case, of course, the wrong locker. Whitey opened it to make sure. He snapped the locks back with his thumb, lifted the lid. His eyes had just enough time to register the sticks of dynamite and the wires running to the battery connected to the latch. His eyes had time enough to see them, but his brain didn't have time enough to register them before the bomb exploded.

Austin saw Whitey lifted off the ground by the force of the explosion before he heard the noise. Whitey took the brunt of the blast in the face and neck. The bomb had been loaded with heavy-duty staples that flew into him like a rain of metal driven by the force of a hurricane. They were taking no chances on missing. The explosion alone would have killed him. The flying shrapnel sliced him apart like meat in a food processor. His face was hamburger by the time he hit the floor, his neck and throat completely open. Blood pumped out of his terrified heart and streamed through the severed carotid artery like a gusher, flying across the marble floor and splashing up against the wall bordering the stairs ten yards away.

Austin was sick against the gateway window but was on the run almost immediately, fleeing for the safety of the tunnel. He vomited again as he ran, insanely trying to kick his shoes clean, before he stumbled down the ladder and into the darkness. He careened through the tunnels, sobbing uncontrollably, trying to forget the sight of a man being torn to shreds in less than a second. Waving his flashlight crazily, he tripped over a pipe and fell. The flashlight slammed against a wall and shattered. He stumbled on for a while, blind, until he fell again. After that he continued on his hands and knees in the dark. He finally came out into the light from the entrance in the Greenwich Savings Bank at Forty-third Street. He had stopped weeping, his eyes were dry but hugely wide and staring until they cringed with pain against the sunlight. His clothes were covered with his own spewings, and his breath came in shallow whimpers. He staggered away from the tunnels like a man released from hell.

# Swiss Will Study Assets of Shah, Freezing His Accounts

# 16

Herr Frischel sipped his cocoa, then dabbed at his lips delicately. He loved his hot chocolate topped with a mound of Schlagsahne, the irresistible Swiss whipped cream, but it always left him with a creamy mustache and sometimes a white dot on his nose as well. It was not fitting for the head of special accounts of the Zuricher Gesellamt Bank to appear comical. Not even if the client was a bit of a clown.

Frischel looked at the nervous American sitting across the desk, sipping his coffee rather loudly. The man was nervous and not very bright, but that was none of Frischel's concern. What was Frischel's concern was that the man claimed some of Frischel's money—that is to say, the bank's money—and he wasn't entitled to it. It probably was intended for him, Frischel didn't dispute that. But he wasn't entitled to it.

"You must have the entire code sequence, you understand," Frischel said patiently. He had explained all of this before.

"No, damn it, I don't understand," Nardo said. "Are you trying to tell me I can't get at the money? I have the password, Sanctuary. That's the password, isn't it, Sanctuary?"

Frischel smiled politely, neither confirming nor denying.

"I told you, the rest of the message was garbled, we didn't get the rest of it."

"If you could ask those who sent you the message to repeat it, perhaps."

"They're dead!" Nardo exclaimed angrily. "Let me explain to you, there's a revolution going on there. Do you read the papers? Do you know what a revolution is in this country? People get killed. Okay? So here's the situation. The man who was in charge of this operation, the deputy minister of finance, had his head shot off. Okay?"

Frischel sniffed. For all their vaunted efficiency, it was amazing how irrelevant the Americans could be.

"The clerk who actually sent the message got killed too. Okay? The chief minister of finance has disappeared, we don't know if he's dead or imprisoned or hiding or what. Nobody else knows the code. Who am I supposed to ask?"

"Was there no other principal involved?" Frischel asked. He knew very well, of course, that the money was the Shah's, because it had been withdrawn from one of the imperial family's accounts in Frischel's bank less than a month ago. Since then the money had probably gone through three or four banks in as many countries until it was laundered as clean as could be. The service fees, commissions, exchange-rate differences and a probable gratuity or two had whittled and shaved the original sixty-nine million down to sixty-eight million and change, but Frischel had no doubt that it was the same money. He had no trouble believing that the money was intended for the former President. He could easily imagine the purposes. As an officer of the bank, however, he did not know any such thing. The world of Swiss banking is elaborately Byzantine, deliberately so, and for just such occasions. Not only was Frischel's right hand not to know what his left hand was doing, his ignorance was officially approved. Officially he knew only that the account had been established by a correspondent bank in Mexico with very specific instructions as to how access could be gained. Which made it very hard to get your hands on if you didn't know the magic words.

"Of course there was a principal," Nardo said angrily. "Do you think he bothers himself with details like code words?"

"It might have facilitated matters if he had," said Frischel. "You see, Mr. Nardo, we have our procedures. Our bank's reputation, the reputation of the entire Swiss banking community, depends on reliability in following procedures the client stipulates. If you would like an account where a thumbprint is required instead of a signature, that is possible. If you would like an account with no names whatever, only numbers, this is possible. We once had an account wherein the only identification for withdrawal was the matching half of a torn ten-deutsche-mark note. Our clients need but stipulate the conditions they desire—and we abide by them, to the letter. If we did not, the institution of Swiss banking would cease to exist as an international convenience."

"You know who I represent, don't you?" Nardo asked. "I explained that to you very carefully."

Frischel glanced at his hot chocolate. The Schlagsahne was slowly dissolving. Frischel liked it fresh and puffy so he could take some in his mouth and feel the texture.

"It is not a question of doubting your identity, Mr. Nardo. Your identity, in fact, is quite beside the point. Our instructions on this account are very clear. The money is to be delivered to anyone possessing the code. If no one comes forward to claim the money within three months of the date of establishment of the account, the account is sealed."

"Does that mean we can't get it if we have the password a day late?"

*What it means,* Frischel thought, *is that the bank will have*

215

*use of sixty-eight million dollars until the Mexican bank takes the proper legal steps to retrieve it. Since that amount of money can earn the bank well over nine million dollars a year in interest at current rates, the retrieval procedure will take a very long time indeed. And my standing within the bank will hardly be diminished,* Frischel added. The beauty of accommodating clandestine operations such as this one was that they so often went awry for the participants—but never for the bank.

"It means the account will be sealed. Apparently the other party to this transaction had some reason to put a time limit on it. We can only accommodate him."

*The son of a bitch put a time limit on it because he knows if it doesn't work quickly it won't do him any good,* Nardo thought. *Who wants to spend his exile in Honduras or Guam or someplace like that?*

Nardo sighed. "You're telling me I got to have the numbers."

"The numbers are part of the necessary key."

"How many of them are there? You can tell me that much, just tell me how many."

Frischel frowned. Politeness only seemed to encourage the American. "I do not in fact know," he said. "You provide the numbers and I will verify them with my instructions. I can do nothing more to help you. Procedures. You see my problem."

"How much time do I have left?"

Frischel debated whether to tell him. Ultimately there seemed no harm in it.

"Two weeks," he said. "You must have the entire code within fourteen days."

# 17

Nardo was so agitated that Sam thought he might do damage to himself. He was trying to conceal it, but as he lifted the teacup to his mouth, his hand shook. The chopsticks proved impossible to handle, and after a moment Nardo gave up any attempt at eating.

"Have you ever dealt with a Swiss banker?" he demanded of Sam.

Sam continued to eat. In his day he had established more than one blind Swiss account and had found the Swiss as hard to pin down as an earthworm in loose dirt. The banking game was entirely theirs, they owned it, and if you cared to play, you had to do it at their price and with their rules. They were also frequently the only bankers willing to accommodate some of the rather bizarre arrangements that Sam sometimes required. He did not see any point in mentioning this to Nardo, however.

"The Man seemed to think I could just waltz in there and get the money," Nardo whined. "He seemed to think his name was enough, all I had to do was give the code word and say it was for him and that would be enough."

"It wasn't enough," said Sam.

"No, it wasn't enough! What do you think I'm trying to tell you? Do I look like I got the money?"

Sam took some pleasure in watching Nardo's distress. Nardo was the type of man whom others could not stand to see happy for very long.

"We need all of the code to get the money, that means all of it, the numbers, too. Christ, the old man should have realized that. How important does he think his name still is? Tell you the truth, Sam, I think he's past it. I'm not sure he's playing with a full deck anymore."

"The dumplings are a real treat," said Sam.

"Yeah, they're an unbelievable goddamned treat! What's the matter with you, Sam, aren't you listening? I'm this close to being a rich man and I can't get hold of the money!"

"Keep your voice down," said Sam calmly. "I'd like to come back here sometime." Sam reached toward the dumpling dish in the center of the table.

"This one is really yours, if you want it," he said, gesturing with his chopsticks. "I've already had three."

Nardo shoved the dish toward Sam. "We've got to find that blackmailing little pecker, Sam! It's a good thing you didn't manage to kill him."

"Some Chinese waiters do speak English, believe it or not."

Nardo stopped and looked around. Half of the restaurant staff was watching him. With an effort he eased back in his seat. Without realizing it he had been half-standing in the cramped booth, leaning toward Sam and speaking louder and louder in his agitation. He rolled his shoulders to get rid of the tension.

"Maybe this mess has all worked out for the best," said Nardo. "I wouldn't want to have a thing like that on my conscience."

David Wiltse

"No, no one would," Sam said, wondering idly what conscience Nardo was talking about. Sam dipped the remaining dumpling in the hot sauce and swallowed it like an oyster.

"What do you want me to do this time?" Sam asked.

"Call off your boy. Tell him to stop trying to—uh—eliminate our blackmailer. We want him alive so we can talk to him."

"Is that a joke?"

"What joke? Am I laughing? What's so hard about not killing him? So far you've shot the wrong man and blown up a derelict and destroyed public property and slaughtered a few innocent bystanders. I imagine you could stop, couldn't you?"

"Fine," said Sam. He dabbed at his lips with a napkin to give himself time to gain his composure. He didn't like being upbraided by an excitable toad like Nardo, even if he was paying the bills. Nardo had gotten good value for his money. These things did not always run smoothly, but you couldn't expect a civilian to appreciate that.

"Fine. You tell 'my boy,' as you call him. You tell him to stop."

"What's so hard about that?"

"He won't want to stop," Sam explained. "He wants to kill Stanhope. He hates him."

"How can he hate him? He doesn't even know him."

"Oh, he knows about him," Sam said. "He's known about him for years. He wants to kill him very badly, I think."

"But he can't do that!" Nardo exclaimed. "We have to have him alive, we have to get the rest of the message. . . . Well, I mean we have to have him alive for a while. I don't suppose he has to stay alive forever."

"Fine. You tell him."

"Why won't you tell him?"

219

"Because if he doesn't get to kill Stanhope, he just might want to kill somebody else."

Nardo started to laugh. "Come on, Sam."

"He's not exactly stable. Of course, you do stand to make a couple million dollars. Maybe you can think of a way of putting it that he'll understand."

"A commission, maybe?"

"He doesn't want money," Sam said. "He wants blood."

*Well, I want money,* Nardo thought. *And no antiquated CIA spook is going to talk me out of it.*

"What's his phone number?"

"Yes, well, there's the problem," said Sam. "He isn't answering his phone, he isn't returning messages."

"Maybe he's sick."

"Oh, he's sick, all right. And frustrated and very, very dangerous. If you want to call him off, you're going to have to go tell him in person."

Nardo swallowed. Why did everything have to be so goddamned complicated?

Debating whether to have another or not, Nardo watched his reflection in the mirror behind the bar. He was, he had to conclude, a pretty damned good-looking guy—at least when seen from the proper angle. Viewed head on, the face he saw when he shaved, he was ruggedly attractive. That was the term. Not perfect, not your classic good looks, but virile, with a good broad mouth and eyebrows that nearly met in the middle. Why he had never had more luck with the opposite sex he just never understood. His profile, whenever he saw it in a photograph or in the proper combination of several mirrors, was a disappointment to him. It was the face of a stranger with a disastrously weak chin and a nose that came to a point.

Even his mouth, his good broad mouth, had a tremulous appearance when viewed in profile. It was the face of a man he didn't like very much. But now he was viewing himself head on just over the pouring spouts of Cutty Sark and Glenlivet, and what he saw inspired him with confidence. What the hell, he was a man who could handle anything. He was about to come into a fortune and had had to handle a host of problems to do it. There was only one more hurdle, a tiny one, and he could take that as easily as he could take another drink. He signaled for the bartender to do it again.

Approaching Smith's apartment, Nardo felt very sure of himself. The alcohol had warmed him and dissolved his last doubts. He would be firm with this man Smith, let him know who was calling the shots. He was even prepared to offer a bit more money out of his own pocket if necessary. It would all be paid back with astronomical interest as soon as the last barrier was removed and the Shah's money poured in. The Man's share of the sixty-eight million—or at least the share he admitted to—was five million. Nardo had been promised a fifth of that, a cool million, right off the top. He could do a lot worse than fire a man for that.

He paused just outside of the door of Smith's apartment. From within came a sound that sent a chill down Nardo's spine, a high, shuddering sigh, like an animal in pain and terror. The sound stopped for a second, and Nardo pushed the buzzer. There was no corresponding ring inside the apartment, but again he heard the sound, a whining whimper. Now it sounded not like an animal but like a child.

Nardo tried to open the door, carefully. It moved a few inches, then stopped as the chain lock tautened. Through the crack Nardo could feel a wave of oppressive heat mingled with the fetid odor of musk, like the inside of an animal's cage.

221

His eye caught motion, and he looked up to see the chrome surface of a gooseneck lamp. The curved top of the lamp reflected light like a distorting mirror. As if looking through the fisheye lens of a camera, Nardo saw a man standing naked in the middle of the room, somewhere behind the door. He had an erection, and he was hitting himself on the chest and thighs with a metal-bristled dog's brush, hitting himself, then slowly dragging the talons of the brush across his skin, leaving a trail of red lines where the blood welled to the surface. The man's eyes were exaggeratedly wide and staring, fixed on the wallpaper across the room. His head was thrown back, his teeth bared, and the high-pitched moan, that mixture of fear and pain, issued from his throat with every blow of the brush.

Nardo pulled back, horrified, disgusted, shocked. He closed the door, trying to do so quietly, but the last thing he saw in the fisheye of the chrome lamp was the head of the naked man as it swiveled toward the door. As he turned and walked quickly back down the hallway, Nardo heard the chain lock being torn out of its groove, heard the door swing open. He turned in time to see the naked man running at him, his penis still hugely swollen. Nardo started to speak, but before the words could come out he was lying on the cold marble floor, on his back, the breath knocked out of him. Smith dragged him back to his apartment by his heels. Nardo's head bumped once as it was dragged over the doorsill, then his feet were dropped and he lay on his back in the middle of the room. Smith stood over him, the Browning in his hand pointed at Nardo's eyes.

Nardo tried not to look at the man's penis or the welts on his chest and thighs, but if he looked directly at his face, he could see only the barrel of the gun. He was so frightened he couldn't breathe. He thought he was going to soil his pants.

222

Smith was trembling, but Nardo didn't know if it was from cold, rage, or the residual effects of whatever orgiastic activity Nardo had interrupted. It took Smith some time to get control of his voice, as if he had been dragged abruptly from some other world where a different tongue was spoken, and he had to get used to the feel and shape of human words once again. Nardo was amazed that someone who had reacted so fast physically should still appear to be in some sort of mental daze. He did not realize that Smith was struggling with all his might against an urge to blow Nardo's head off.

After several moments Smith's breathing eased and the tremor left his hand and arm. He backed up slowly until the backs of his calves touched the edge of the bed. He sank down slowly onto the rumpled bedclothes. The sheets were as ridged and rutted as a contour map, as if they had not been changed, or indeed even stretched flat, in weeks. Smith was on the very edge of the bed, the pistol held between his knees in both hands, his forearms resting atop his thighs. His penis, still turgidly erect, thrust upward between his arms, nudging the skin just below his navel. Nardo had the sense of being in the lair of an animal in rut. Smith eyed him like a beast that didn't know whether to mate with him or kill him.

Smith finally managed to maneuver his tongue around some words. "I think you came to the wrong place," he said in a voice thick and hesitant with disuse.

"We . . ." Nardo had trouble with his own voice, it was several registers too high and his throat felt as if it were being squeezed shut. "We've met," he said. "At the airport. Sam brought me. I paid you for a job?"

Smith paused, letting the memory fall into place.

"Stanhope," said Smith. "The job will be finished."

"That's what I'm here about," said Nardo. "You don't need to."

"The job will be finished," Smith said. His eyes drilled through Nardo and past him into the middle distance.

"I don't want the job finished, that's what I'm saying," said Nardo. "Just forget about it, forget Stanhope."

Smith snorted. "Forget Stanhope."

"That's it," said Nardo. "That's the idea. Just forget him. You've been paid, we don't want the money back, you can keep it." Nardo started to sit up. Smith lifted the gun from his knees, holding it with both hands, arms extended, like a marksman on the target range. Nardo sank back to the floor so fast his head hit the carpet. A scent of musk and dust rose from the carpet, and Nardo once again had the feeling of being in an animal's den, his head resting where the animal rutted and ate and slept.

"I don't want to forget Stanhope," Smith said. "I want to kill him."

"You don't understand," Nardo pleaded. For God's sake, the man was insane, no wonder Sam wouldn't come to see him. "We need him now. We need to make him talk. You can help us. You can make him talk. Afterward you can make him do whatever you want with him. . . ."

Smith was beside him, gun pressed against Nardo's temple, his tumescent penis rubbing Nardo's arm.

"How did you find me!"

"S . . S . . Sam told me. . . ."

"Were you followed?"

Nardo had begun to tremble. Nothing he said seemed to be the right thing. The man was going to kill him, he knew it.

"Followed? Why would anyone follow me?"

"You didn't check!"

"No," croaked Nardo.

Smith stood up. His demeanor suddenly changed, turning

224

from fury to guile in a moment. For the first time he lowered the gun, turned it away from Nardo.

"You must always check," he said mildly. "Come on, we'll see now." When he smiled, Nardo was the most frightened he had been since the man dragged him into the apartment.

# 18

When the man from Stanhope Security arrived at her door, Margo was ready. Her bags were packed and aligned neatly by the door. Mr. Stanhope had told her to pack only what was necessary, he wanted her safely in his house as soon as possible. A man would be sent to gather her other things later. She had done as told, although she realized three suitcases might seem excessive as bare necessities to a Stanhope, but then none of the Stanhopes were women.

She did not recognize the Stanhope employee, but he had the familiar crisply neat look of all the SSC men. He carried her bags easily, despite his slight build, and escorted her quickly to the waiting limousine. She reflected later that he managed to convey courtesy, deference, and even a sense of sympathy for her position, while barely saying a word.

He put her in the front seat, then began to stow the bags in the trunk. Margo got out of the car and went back to ask him to be particularly careful with the suitcase that contained her cosmetics. She thought she glimpsed a body in a business suit scrunched into one corner of the trunk, partially covered by the suitcases.

The idea was too preposterous to mention, and Margo could manage only a slight nervous laugh as the man closed the trunk. He smiled at her briefly, then once more escorted her to the door and put her in. By the time they pulled away from the curb, Margo had convinced herself that she was wrong, that she had allowed her imagination to transform a car rug into the body of a man.

They drove in silence to the Stanhope estate. When the high brick fence came into view, Margo felt relief. She had been anxious since the shooting at the wedding, of course, and Mr. Stanhope's insistence that she come live with him for her own protection had only heightened the anxiety. But there was something about the driver that made her more uneasy still. He had spoken little, had been cordial when he did speak, but there was something about his stillness, some tension in his repose, that reminded her of a snake watching a bird.

She had seen his lips move once, heard him say something unintelligible. When she asked him, he gave her a blank look for just a second, then smiled flatly and said it was nothing. She didn't know why but she didn't like the man, and she didn't like herself for forming an opinion on the strength of so little. Margo feared it was a trace of snobbery on her part. She had an inclination to look down on people who waited on her, a disposition drilled into her by her mother, who treated servants as if she were the dowager queen. Margo hated the tendency in herself and fought against it. When it occurred, she usually went out of her way to befriend the person.

They arrived at the gate.

"Would you do the honors, Miss?" the driver asked.

Margo was surprised, but glad for the chance to prove herself democratic.

"It's Margo," she announced to the intercom. The gate was electronically released, and they drove into the estate, past the closed-circuit television cameras, past the elaborate security systems.

The elder Stanhope was at the dining table. He rose as she entered, touching a napkin to his lips, then kissing her cheek. It always pleased her that such a strong man could be so courtly, too. He never failed to take her hand in his when they met, holding her fingers gently as if he would kiss them if they were in another time or place. When he kissed her cheek, he actually kissed it, not the air somewhere beside her ear. For the hundredth time she thought that she had chosen the wrong Stanhope. She loved Austin, but he was not the man his father was, and no amount of love would change that.

"Will you join me for dessert, my dear?" he asked. "No? Coffee then . . . yes?"

Stanhope turned to address the driver, who stood just inside the dining room. The driver put the bags on the floor and pulled a pistol from his pocket. Margo looked at Stanhope, bewildered, but Stanhope seemed to understand the situation immediately.

The man pointed the gun directly at Stanhope's heart. Despite the awkward-looking silencer on the muzzle, the barrel never wavered.

"Where is your son?" the man asked.

Stanhope glared at the man, contempt written all over his face. The man came closer, and Margo noticed for the first time that he had a slight limp.

"Where is he?" he demanded again.

"I don't know," Stanhope said.

The man turned to face Margo, but the gun never left Stanhope.

229

"Where is he?" he asked Margo.

Margo shook her head. Her throat seemed to have closed of its own accord, choking off the words.

"I don't know, he wouldn't tell me!" she finally blurted, but by then the man had returned his full attention to Stanhope. He never looked at Margo again, having dismissed her as knowing nothing and thus totally irrelevant to the business at hand.

"You know some numbers," the man said to Stanhope. "Tell them to me and this can be over very quickly."

Stanhope refused to speak at all, as if his stony silence could negate the threat of the gun. Without warning, the man lowered the pistol and shot Stanhope in the right knee. Margo heard the apologetic cough of the shot, but it seemed too soft, too harmless to connect with what happened next. Stanhope fell as if his legs had suddenly died, crashing onto his hip, then his shoulder. He landed heavily, his face colliding with the polished wooden floor.

Margo started forward to help, then stopped immediately as the man raised his free hand in her direction, as if he could harm her as surely with his bare finger as with the gun.

Stanhope slowly pulled himself upward, leaning on the chair. There was a large welt on his cheek where he had struck the floor. At first Margo didn't even notice the blood slowly welling into the fabric of his trousers around his knee.

Stanhope stood erect, his weight on his hand on the chair. Margo thought he was too proud to admit he was wounded.

"Where is your son?" the man asked again.

"I don't know," said Stanhope, his voice giving no trace of the pain he must have felt.

"Tell me the numbers," said the man. His tone was calm, reasonable.

Stanhope was silent. This time the man pointed the gun at the other knee, very slowly, giving Stanhope time to consider. Stanhope's eyes flickered toward Margo. For just a moment she thought she saw the pain and the fright show through. Was he looking to her for help? What could she do? She knew nothing.

"Tell him!" she urged. Even as she spoke she could see his eyes harden again. The frightened soul was gone, replaced by a man as hard as granite.

When the man shot Stanhope's other knee, there was nothing left to stop his fall at all. He fell straight forward, onto his face. For a long while he was still. The man with the pistol waited patiently. Margo began to cry.

"Please!" she said to the man. "Please, he doesn't know anything. He'd tell you if he could, he doesn't know. I don't know. Nobody knows. Let me get a doctor, you can get away . . ."

The man seemed to be paying no attention to her at all. Margo was certain the only way to get to him was to touch him, shake him—but she was afraid to go near him.

Stanhope slowly pushed himself into a sitting position, groaning with the pain. He did not try to stand again, but he did not cry out or plead. When at last he lifted his head again, blood dripped from his nose. His lips were drawn so tautly against his teeth, they had turned white. Stanhope raised his eyes to look at his tormentor and regarded him with contempt, as if he weren't human but some beast, dressed as a man but still trailing the stench and filth of the primitive world.

"Last chance," the man said.

Stanhope looked the man directly in the eye. He moaned with the pain, but the sound seemed to come of its own, as if Stanhope were not aware of it, had nothing to do with it, as if the noise sprang directly from his mutilated knees and did not issue from his mouth.

The man knelt beside Stanhope, his voice a fierce hiss. "Your son, old man. I want him."

Stanhope stared at the man's face as if trying to memorize it.

"Him or you," the man hissed. "Him or you."

Stanhope spat in the man's face, then grabbed for the gun. The man didn't react to the spit at all, almost as if he expected it, and when Stanhope reached for the gun, the man moved with great speed, catching Stanhope's arm with his own free hand, never moving the gun so much as an inch. He held the disabled Stanhope, his own strength the greater, and then laughed at him, mocked the older man.

Margo broke down completely, crying, begging, crawling to the man, pleading for mercy for Stanhope. The man acted as if she didn't exist, as if he neither saw nor heard her.

"Where is he? What are the numbers?"

Stanhope tried to spit again, the spittle dribbling down his own chin. The man pulled the edge of the tablecloth over Stanhope's head to prevent the gore from splattering on his clothes, then shot him in the head.

Margo buried her face in her hands and screamed. For what seemed an age she expected to feel a bullet smash into her. When she finally lifted her hands and looked for her tormentor, the man was gone. From under the tablecloth, where a stain of dark red was spreading through the white damask, she heard a moan.

Peter clutched his father's hand, amazed at its warmth. Stanhope was dying, but his hand seemed to be burning up. Peter had sat by the hospital bed for more than a hour, holding his father's dry, raspy hand, trying to communicate his love to the older man, trying to instill some of his own vitality into him. Peter's eyes were red from silent weeping, yet seemed to scratch his eyelids. He had not slept for two days as he kept his anxious vigil in the hospital, spending what time they would permit him with his father, the rest in pacing the corridors.

Stanhope had undergone two emergency operations in as many days. Smith's bullet had entered the cranium in the parietal eminence just above the upper temporal ridge and exited through the sphenoid bone, as the doctors first explained it to Peter. Or, as Peter pieced it together, the bullet went in the side of the head, careened around the inside of the skull, and came out at the base. There was a great deal of hemorrhaging, which was what threatened Stanhope's life, for miraculously very few of his motor functions were affected. That Stanhope hadn't died immediately was due to the relatively small caliber of Smith's Browning, the velocity of which was greatly diminished by the silencer.

After the second operation Stanhope had slipped into and out of consciousness, waking suddenly as if roused from slumber, his eyes fastened clearly on Peter. The moments would not last long before Stanhope's eyelids would flutter and he would slip back into unconsciousness. Occasionally the older man would speak in snatches of unrelated words that Peter could make no sense of.

It was in these brief moments that Peter tried to convey all his love, all his regret at their estrangement, all his forgiveness. He knew he couldn't do it with words, the time was too short, he wasn't even sure his father could hear, so he tried to do it with his eyes, and with the pressure of his hand. It was all he could do, but he knew it was not enough. He prayed that somehow his father would understand.

Suddenly Stanhope's eyes were open again, staring at Peter. "Dad," Peter said softly. "It's Peter. I'm here."

Tears fell from Stanhope's eyes and ran down his cheeks to the plastic tubes that were inserted in each nostril. He was crying as if he had awakened from a sad dream. Peter had never seen his father cry. The sight brought tears to his own eyes again.

He clutched his father's hand. "It's all right, Dad," he said thickly. "You're going to be all right."

"I tried," said Stanhope, his voice surprisingly clear and strong. "I tried."

Peter thought he sensed forgiveness in the old man's eyes. Tried what? Tried to love you, too? Tried to be a good father? Was it an apology for his human shortcomings? Peter chose to think it was. He squeezed his father's hand.

"I tried too," he said.

The old man seemed relieved, a faint smile pulled at his lips. It was late, but it was a moment of understanding, Peter thought.

Stanhope's eyelids fluttered, then closed. Peter clasped the hand harder, choking back a cry. Each time his father closed his eyes Peter feared they would not open again. But they did open, almost immediately.

Stanhope looked Peter directly in the face, his eyes no longer fixed but roving the features as if making sure whom he was talking to.

His eyes seemed more alert than ever, but his voice was suddenly weak, fading, the voice of a dying man.

"Peter," he said, using Peter's name for the first time. "Peter . . ."

"Yes? Dad?"

Stanhope squeezed Peter's hand, a pathetically weak tightening from the man Peter had once thought the strongest in the world.

"Good-bye," he said, the word slurring.

"I love you!" Peter cried, his voice catching.

"Good-bye," the old man repeated. "Good-bye." He seemed angry.

Peter lifted his father's hand to his face, pressed it to his cheek where his tears fell on it.

"I love you, Dad," Peter said again. He did not remember ever having said it before in his life with his father.

Stanhope's eyelids fluttered again, he strained, moved his head slightly to the side, at what cost in pain Peter could only guess.

"Goo—bayee," he said.

It was not until Peter left the hospital, not until his grief had collapsed into a pain that he would carry within his chest for months to come, not until he had reached his hotel, that Peter realized what his father had been saying. He had not been saying good-bye. He had been saying Ghoubadi.

# 19

"Oh, it's you," Anne said, feeling silly since there he was, standing in front of her. She had gotten along perfectly well while he was gone without feeling foolish with anyone. And now, the sight of him, a simple hello, and she was blushing and feeling foolish again. She was not entirely sure that the sensation of excitement he brought out in her entirely offset the rapid deterioration of her personality into that of a love-sick teen-ager.

"How did you find me?" She had acquired a new apartment and an unlisted phone number since she had seen him last. She had hesitated about the unlisted number, primarily because he might want to call her. But then she had realized that he would find her if he wanted her. And he had.

"Actor's agents can be very accommodating," he said. "Particularly if you lie to them."

"I think they prefer it," she added. "Nobody in this business goes very far on the truth."

*Or in my business either*, Peter thought. "Would you like to go to a little dinner party this evening?"

"I have a date," she said "But I can break it," she added,

thinking, *I should have at least waited for him to ask me to break it.*

"Where is it?"

"The Egyptian Consulate."

Anne looked down at her outfit. She was wearing leotards and a very old long-sleeved man's shirt tied at the waist. There was a rip in the knee of the leotard and another just above the navel. It was fine for dance class, but not quite right for the Egyptian Consulate.

"Informal, I hope," she said.

The Egyptian Consulate was just off Fifth Avenue, no more than a pistol shot from Central Park. The shot would have to be very well aimed, however, for the consulate, like the many other consulates that proliferated in the area, had been very discreetly but thoroughly fortified since the increase of international terrorism focusing on the Middle Eastern nations. All glass windows were two inches thick and of bulletproof glass. Steel shutters, never used, were in place and ready to be dropped across all glass surfaces at a moment's notice. All doors had been reinforced with steel, in many cases on both sides, but on the main entrance just on the interior, so the ornately carved wooden frame was still visible to the passerby. The number of security forces within the consulate had been tripled in the past four years, many of them serving as chauffeurs and other servants, but some prominently displayed in military uniform. It never hurt to have a show of strength if you feared attack. Detection systems to thwart penetration of either weapons or bombs were employed at all entrances. New York City had also quietly done its part, doubling the strength and frequency of patrols outside the consulate, although this information was not widely spread during a time of continual cutbacks in manpower elsewhere in the city.

The consulate was prepared to withstand attack by just about any force short of heavy artillery. Every member of the staff, from the Consul General down, had been trained in antiterrorist tactics. They were prepared, at least theoretically, to deal with any event ranging from an angry picket line to a kamikaze PLO attack.

Thus far their defenses had been tested only once. In 1979 a lone fanatic got as far as the inner foyer, six feet past the main entrance, with a plastique bomb molded to his torso like a brace for a slipped disc. Noticing a certain stiffness in the man's gait, the chief security officer on duty questioned him. The man became nervous, which alerted the officer even more. Under more direct questioning the man panicked and tried to detonate the bomb. His mistake was in waiting so long. If he had walked through the door and set himself off, he might at least have done some damage. As it was, his hand never reached the detonator in his coat pocket. The security officer shot him in the face, and the second security man, who had come up behind him, shot him twice in the upper back. Both of the bullets in the back missed the explosive, or the human bomb might have succeeded after all.

The man was dead by the time he hit the floor—or should have hit the floor. The chief security officer caught him as he fell, and together the two guards hustled him into a secure room, well away from the door—and the police in the street. The man had no identity papers, and his purpose, other than the obvious intent of destruction, was never divined. It was decided for security purposes to keep the matter a secret. It would not do for word to get around that it was that easy to blow up, or nearly blow up, a bomb in the Egyptian Consulate. Since that time new procedures had made it a good deal more difficult to get six feet into the front foyer.

When Anne and Peter arrived, the security precautions

were as discreet as possible while still being effective. Their names were checked off the invitation list at the front door by a smiling functionary. They were halted again within the foyer while another functionary checked their names again. As they stood in the foyer they were actually within the field of a metal detector recessed into the walls and ceiling of the building. A security guard ostensibly dealing with coats and hats in the cloakroom was actually studying the readout on the system. The second butler, a rather senior security officer, stood just inside the main hall. It was his job to identify at least one of every couple who entered by personal recognition. If he did not know a guest or recognize him from his file photo, he would delay the guest, politely, until someone could be summoned who did.

The second butler murmured deferentially to Peter and Anne, guiding them to the ballroom. He had been obliged to pull Peter's picture from the file this afternoon, since Peter was a last-minute addition to the guest list. He didn't know all the details, but apparently the man Stanhope was a friend of a friend of someone and had more or less asked to be invited. The social niceties were not his affair. He just wanted to know if Stanhope was safe, and his file said he was. As for the girl, she was so beautiful it was hard to imagine her as anything more dangerous than a threat to an aging security officer's sanity. He wished she would do something suspicious so he could have an excuse to search her.

"Christ, I'm dressed wrong!" Anne whispered as she saw the other guests. She had chosen a simple black sleeveless dress with a scoop neckline. A strand of cultured pearls partially disguised her décolletage—but not too much. It was not that she was following Chanel's famous advice about the little black dress being appropriate for just about anything; it

240

was that she didn't have any choice. The dress was not only simple, it was the only thing she had to wear.

All around her were ladies of the various delegations and a number from New York society, many of them in designer originals, all of them elegantly and elaborately made up and coiffed. Anne had worn her hair loose, the auburn mane flowing over her shoulders and down to her bare shoulder blades where it curled up and in as if it had decided it had strayed too far from home and wanted to start back. She seldom wore makeup except on the stage. Partly it was to play down her appearance, to be accepted for herself rather than her image. And partly it was vanity. She knew she didn't need it, that cosmetics could make her appear more elegant, perhaps, more sophisticated, but they would diminish the freshness, the dewy cleanliness of her skin that only youth and no bottle could duplicate. Women over thirty hated to look at her. Even when they got to know her and like her, they preferred never to have to stand next to her, unless it was very dark.

Peter looked at her and smiled. "I think you'll do," he said. "There's not a woman here who wouldn't trade appearances with you."

"You don't know what you're talking about," she said, surprising him with her brusqueness. She felt awkward and underdressed and totally out of place among the roomful of sophisticates, and she didn't want anyone to jolly her out of it by telling her how beautiful she was. Beautiful, maybe, but damn it, wouldn't it be nice to have a handful of those emeralds and diamonds and look spectacularly gaudy.

"Right now I'd rather look rich," she said. Peter laughed and took her to meet her hostess.

The wife of the Egyptian Consul General, Madame Fahin, was well educated, sophisticated, discreet, and a little embarrassed by her fellow countrymen. Schooled throughout Europe and reared during most of her formative years in Switzerland, she seldom spent more than two months at a time in her native land. Which was the way she liked it. She never apologized for what she thought of as her country's backwardness. She was far too proud for that. If anyone forced the topic on her, she could discourse intelligently on the glorious past of the land of the pharaohs, the evils of French, then British, colonialism, the vision of Nasser, the courage of Sadat, the great strides Egypt has made in modern times. She could do all that, and convincingly—if she had to. But she would rather not talk about it, rather not think about it at all.

Madame Fahin greeted Anne graciously, talking to her just long enough to fulfill her duties as a hostess, but as a woman, hurrying to get this radiant girl as far away from her as she could.

"What the hell are we doing here?" Anne asked when she and Peter were alone again. "I mean, what am *I* doing here? I feel like a third foot. I don't know what to say to these people, I don't know anything about Egypt, I don't know anything about anything, come to that. I'm glad you wanted to be with me, but I'm more the kind of date you take to the movies, don't you think?"

"I think you're the kind of woman I'd take anywhere," Peter said. "Besides, haven't we gotten a bit beyond the date stage?"

As he spoke his eyes roved the room, searching. The crowd was constantly moving, shifting from group to group, enclaves dissolving, forming again elsewhere. Other rooms were in use, and many of the guests moved in and out of them. There were close to 150 guests, Peter guessed. And none of them, yet, was the man he wanted.

242

"Christ, don't be nice to me," Anne said. "I'm too nervous for that."

"What are you nervous about?"

"I'm afraid someone will talk to me. . . . I'm afraid no one will talk to me. Never leave my side for an instant." She took a drink off a tray circulated by a liveried servant and drank half of it too fast, then struggled to keep from gagging.

Peter's body tensed beside her. For a second she had the same feeling of impending danger that she felt when they were in her bedroom and she felt his body freeze. But surely not here. She looked around; the room was filled with guests in elegant gowns and evening clothes. Surely nothing could happen here.

Ghoubadi drifted into the main room, a drink in one hand, a plate of appetizers in the other. Nominally a Muslim, like most upper-class followers of that strict religion he observed the dietary laws or not, according to his whim. If the Egyptian Consulate, also Muslim, after all, chose to serve alcohol and hors d'oeuvre canapés wrapped in bacon, then he would choose to eat and drink them. He was not a fanatic about it; in fact he was not a fanatic about anything, except, lately, staying alive. He had to admit he was rather devoted to that goal. When the Shah was still in power and Ghoubadi had acted as one of his primary agents abroad with the duty of locating and silencing critics and dissidents, staying alive had presented no problem. He had traveled with a phalanx of very tough, very devoted agents, none too bright, most of them, but obedient to a fault and peculiarly fond of their work. Ghoubadi had on occasion ordered a dissident to be hung by his ankles like slaughterhouse beef in order that a hose could be inserted in his rectum and water pumped in until the victim's intestines burst. It had fallen in the line of duty, but Ghoubadi had not relished the work as his loyal bodyguards had. They had their uses, those burly, low-browed men, but all in all they were a good deal too brutish for Ghoubadi's taste.

He wished he had them with him now, however. He saw Peter almost immediately, the length of the large room away, but closer to the exit than Ghoubadi was. He could never beat Peter to the door, and Peter was moving in his direction already. Smoothly Ghoubadi turned and headed back the way he had come, placing the cocktail glass on a servant's tray as he passed. He slipped several toothpicks from the bacon-wrapped cherry tomatoes on his plate and slipped them into his pocket.

Since the fall of the Shah, Ghoubadi, like all SAVAK agents, had become a marked man with a price on his head. Agents of the Ayatollah Khomeini, many of them low-level functionaries in the Shah's regime who now found themselves propelled upward as the revolutionary council swept away the upper tiers as one would ladle cream off milk, were hunting down expatriates like Ghoubadi, returning some to Iran for "trial" or simply killing them after the ritual torture in any convenient basement. The revolutionary council could not afford to dispose of all trained agents but the ones who were kept were naturally suspect of imperialist sympathies and thus were forced to become all the more fanatical to prove themselves trustworthy. Ghoubadi was a prime target on their hit list, and he knew it.

Suddenly finding himself an agent without portfolio—and returning home out of the question—he had been forced to sell his services where and when he could. Thus far he had done rather well. There was no lack of work for a man experienced in the seething pot of Middle Eastern politics. Much of the work had been a bit more on the strong-arm side than

Ghoubadi liked, but inasmuch as his bullyboys—being stupid —were now also largely dead, he didn't have a great deal of choice.

He was still welcome in many embassies and consulates, he had a large network of contacts from his years in the country. He had been careful and he had survived. Warned by associates that someone had been asking about him in the last two days, he had been more careful than usual. He definitely had not expected anything to happen at the consulate party, however. For one thing, it was unlikely that anyone could manage to get any weapons into the consulate, and for another, all the guests were carefully screened.

Making his way quickly toward the men's room, Ghoubadi tried to analyze his situation. He didn't know why Peter Stanhope had been asking about him, why he wanted him, but survival dictated the assumption that it was for no reason healthy for Ghoubadi. He might be acting for the revolutionary council as a mercenary, he might be acting for the U.S. government, a prospect that chilled him almost as much as the former. Ghoubadi was subject to deportation at any moment, and that meant return to Iran. Detention of any sort was very dangerous since it gave his assassins a chance to get at him. He couldn't afford to be hauled in for so much as a traffic violation; any check of his record put him in extreme jeopardy.

For the same reasons he could not afford any kind of incident in the consulate. His welcome depended on keeping a low profile. If he called attention to himself, he would be too much of an embarrassment to keep around. His problem was to get out of the consulate and disappear into the city without bringing attention to himself in the process.

A security guard acted as washroom attendant. Ghoubadi walked directly to one of the sinks in the marble counter.

With a display of combing his hair he located what he was looking for, a safety razor neatly arranged with its attendant shaving cream, shaving brush, and soap mug. The old-fashioned blade rather than an electric shaver was evidence of Madame Fahin's style. Her father had shaved with the brush and blade, and she felt it had an elegance that electricity sadly lacked. Her husband used canned shaving cream and a disposable blade, but then she had never looked to her husband for style, only security.

Ghoubadi loosened his belt and dropped his pants slightly, tucking in his shirt. As the security guard discreetly looked away Ghoubadi slipped the razor blade into his pocket. Outside the washroom he pushed two of the toothpicks through the central aperture of the blade. He placed the blade between the first and second fingers of his left hand, the toothpicks on top of the fingers, the blade held securely on the palm side of his hand.

As he returned to the main room Ghoubadi saw Peter waiting for him. Too bad, he thought. He had hoped it was all his imagination, that he could avoid all this. Survival did not hinge on wishful thinking, however. One had to be decisive. The object was very simple, get the man out of his way, away from the door so that Ghoubadi could leave and the man could not follow. And do it quietly.

"Mr. Ghoubadi," Peter said, approaching him, "I'd like to talk to you."

"My dear fellow," said Ghoubadi, smiling broadly. "What an excellent idea! Let's slip over this way, shall we? Not nearly so much noise. And how have you been? How good to see you again!"

Ghoubadi grasped Peter's right hand with his own, pumping it enthusiastically. His left hand slipped inside the jacket of Peter's tuxedo with a gesture that from a distance looked as if

246

Ghoubadi was giving an affectionate pat to an old friend. The razor blade sliced smoothly through the shirt and into Peter's skin, carving a thin furrow from just under his right armpit down to his waist. When Ghoubadi removed his hand, the jacket fell back to cover the wound entirely. *A very neat and tidy job*, Ghoubadi thought, releasing Peter's right hand. *He doesn't even know he's been cut yet.*

From across the room Anne watched Peter and the foreign-looking man. Why, if the man greeted him so affectionately, had Peter seemed so tense, she wondered. Still smiling broadly, showing a flash of white in his dark face, the foreigner was disengaging now, stepping away from Peter.

"Gustave Arpel," said a voice at her shoulder. She turned to see a man introducing himself, bowing slightly.

"What?" she asked, glancing back at Peter. The foreigner had put his left hand in his jacket pocket, then pulled it out again like a magician pocketing a hidden card. Peter had become strangely immobile for a second. She could not see his face, but from the rear he looked puzzled. Then he reached a hand under his jacket.

"My name is Gustave Arpel," the man at her shoulder repeated. "I am with the French Consulate."

"Hi," said Anne.

"Yes, hi. I have seen you standing here alone, and I have said to myself, this must not be." Gustave Arpel maneuvered until he was directly in front of her, partially cutting off her view of Peter. She saw him move after the foreigner, his right arm clamped rigidly to his side, then she lost him in the shifting crowd. Reluctantly she turned her attention to Arpel, annoyed with Peter for leaving her to fend off smiling Frenchmen.

Peter was fairly certain he wasn't badly hurt. He had seen nothing in Ghoubadi's hand, so it had to have been a small blade, a scalpel, a penknife, a razor. And he had sliced, not stabbed, which meant that it was unlikely any organ had been cut. If any muscles had been affected, he would have known it as soon as he moved, but there was no damage there. So he had only one immediate concern, to stop the bleeding. Already he could feel the warm ooze sticking his shirt to his body. He clamped his arm tightly against the wound. Once blood showed, someone would notice, a doctor would be called, people would cluster around him, creating exactly the kind of diversion Ghoubadi wanted. If he got out the door, the SAVAK agent would be impossible to find again now that he knew he was hunted. Peter could cause an uproar now, probably get Ghoubadi arrested, but once the police had him, he was no good to Peter. Peter needed the man alive, alone, and under Peter's control. And they both knew it. The main thing was to keep the blood from showing and not let the wound panic him.

Moving swiftly but without the appearance of haste, Ghoubadi made his way toward the exit. Peter was halted, at least for the moment, but to Ghoubadi's surprise he was not calling out for help, pulling a bloodstained hand from under his jacket, waving his distress to the crowd. To the casual observer he seemed perfectly all right, and now he was moving after Ghoubadi.

Almost to the door, the Persian was suddenly halted by Madame Fahin, who stepped in front of him, her aristocratic face pulled into a mock frown of distress.

"You are not leaving us, Mr. Ghoubadi," she said in a fair imitation of concern. She didn't care at all whether Ghoubadi stayed or not, but she did care for appearances.

"We all so looked forward to chatting with you," she said.

Ghoubadi glanced behind him. Peter was already within a few yards of him, appearing as calm and detached as anyone else in the crowd. There was no point in going now. Being alone on the streets with someone younger, stronger, and obviously very cool was the last thing Ghoubadi wanted. He was safer here in the crowd where he could wait for another opportunity and formulate another plan.

"Of course not, Madame Fahin. You shall have to drag me away with wild horses, as usual." He slipped his left hand into his jacket pocket, felt gingerly for the blade, and secured it between his fingers, although he knew it was unlikely that Peter would give him a chance to use it again.

Ghoubadi drifted off into the crowd, keeping an eye on Peter. He knew Peter would have to make a move soon and was working under the same rules and restrictions, that much was clear by his silence thus far. Peter could have gotten assistance with a word. The man was bleeding, he had to be, and was probably in pain as well. Ghoubadi had but to bide his time, it couldn't be long before that powder-blue shirt turned pink with blood. At the first sign of commotion, of people clustering around Peter, Ghoubadi would go. Give him a minute's head start and he would take his chances on the street against anyone.

The Frenchman had been joined by two other men when Peter came to Anne. He pulled her aside with a proprietary hand on her arm.

"Are you all right? You look pale."

"Listen carefully," he said, his voice in a whisper that drew her attention to it faster than any shout. "Go to the women's room and get some soap. Do it quickly and come right back to me." He didn't wait for her to respond, but moved off again, easing his way through the crowd, toward the table that held the appetizers.

As he listened to a member of the Liberian delegation deplore the state of American televison, Peter took a fork from the table. Working out of sight under the table, he bent the two outer tines of the fork down and back toward the handle, then forced the two central tines together, forming a crude knife. It was good only for stabbing, but it would penetrate the skin, it was a weapon.

Ghoubadi had joined a group, standing on the fringe, laughing at the right time, giving the impression of belonging, but actually keeping an eye on Peter all the time. Peter could feel the blood spreading. It was beginning to trickle slowly down his leg.

"This was all I could find," said Anne, hurrying up to him with a small bar of soap in her hand.

"It will do," he said. He broke the bar into small pieces and dropped them into a goblet, then poured mineral water on the pieces. Anne looked at his stomach where the first stain of pink was leeching itself across his shirt. Noticing her look, he buttoned the jacket closed.

"What's wrong?" she whispered.

Peter swished the soap back and forth in the effervescent mineral water until he had a fine lather of soap bubbles. Several people were watching him but he no longer cared, he was running out of time. The blood was soaking into his sock and he could feel it squish when he moved.

"Peter?" His attention was nowhere near her. She turned to see where he was staring so intently.

Ghoubadi was moving toward the door again. Peter grabbed a handful of suds and put it in his jacket pocket, then walked quickly after Ghoubadi, leaving Anne at the table.

Within a few feet of the door Ghoubadi realized that Peter was too close again. He stopped, moved back, smiling resignedly in Peter's direction, shrugging slightly as one player of the game to another. Stymied this time, perhaps not the next, his look seemed to say. But to his astonishment Peter kept coming, faster, then broke into a run when fifteen feet away.

"Help him!" Peter yelled, running toward Ghoubadi. "Help him!"

For a second, Ghoubadi was too stunned to move. He had thought he understood the rules. Discretion was the game. The last thing he expected was a screaming head-on attack. Then he saw Peter holding the makeshift knife in his left hand, swinging it wide to come at Ghoubadi's chest. The SAVAK agent threw up his hands defensively, parrying the attack, but at the last moment Peter's left hand dropped, the attack was only a feint, and he clubbed Ghoubadi with the heel of his right hand in the small of his back. The effect was the same as a blow in the solar plexus. Ghoubadi gasped, stunned, the wind momentarily knocked out of him. Without hesitation Peter's right hand flew up to the base of Ghoubadi's neck. His fingers closed expertly with all their strength on the nerve endings radiating from the vertebrae in the top of the spine. The SAVAK agent began to buck and spasm uncontrollably. Peter dropped the fork, scooped the suds from his pocket with his left hand, and smeared them across Ghoubadi's mouth and down his chin to his throat.

The entire attack had taken less than two seconds from Peter's first shout to Ghoubadi's lying helplessly on the floor, his extremities twitching, foam dribbling out of his mouth. It all happened too quickly for anyone to see what had really transpired, and for anyone who doubted the bucking body, Peter added the conclusion.

"He's having an epileptic seizure," Peter said as those nearest crowded in. Under Ghoubadi's neck, apparently cradling the head to keep it off the floor, Peter's fingers applied remorseless pressure on the nerves.

If anyone was inclined to doubt or interfere, the sight of the foam on Ghoubadi's face changed their minds. Peter was relying on the assumption that only a trained physician would overcome his wish not to become involved in something so messy and repellent. A twisted ankle on a tennis court will bring dozens of volunteers. Show them blood, vomit, or any real danger and they will gladly leave the matter in the hands of anyone competent.

Peter grabbed the fork from the floor and put it sideways across Ghoubadi's tongue.

"To keep him from swallowing his tongue," someone in the crowd offered. Peter's hand moved up higher on the neck, squeezing the carotid arteries. Ghoubadi tried to speak but only garbled unintelligibly with the fork on his tongue. His eyes flickered, the eyeballs rolling upward as the pressure on the carotids began to take effect. Two seconds later he was unconscious.

"He'll be all right, but I'll need help getting him to a bedroom," Peter said. Two guards hurried forward and lifted Ghoubadi, carrying him out of the ballroom and up the stairs. Peter followed, his hand cradling the agent's head, maintaining just enough pressure to keep Ghoubadi out.

"He needs to rest. Just leave me alone with him," Peter said, and the guards were only too happy to oblige. They withdrew, closing the door behind them.

When Ghoubadi awoke, he found Peter sitting on his chest, the tine of the fork in his ear.

Peter moved the fork just enough for Ghoubadi to know it was there. "This won't kill you if I push it in—maybe. But I dare say it will hurt a little."

"Yes," said Ghoubadi, careful not to move his head.

A fresh towel was pressed against Peter's wound and secured with a torn pillowcase. He knew now that he would not die

from loss of blood. Ghoubadi, however, was not sure that he
wouldn't die, despite Peter's assurance.

"I just want some information from you," Peter said. "If
you tell me what I want, you won't be hurt."

"I am hurt already."

"If you don't cooperate, you will be hurt. And when I am
finished hurting you, I will turn you over to the police. Do
you understand?"

"I very much want to give you information," Ghoubadi
said through dry lips. "What do you wish to know?"

"What do you know about Austin Stanhope?"

"Ah, yes," said the SAVAK agent. So it was not the revolutionary council, after all. "If only you had mentioned Austin
initially, we might have avoided all of this melodrama."

"You know who I am," said Peter.

"Of course, but not whom you work for. The Stanhopes
are mercenaries, are they not?"

"Not this Stanhope." Peter moved the fork within Ghoubadi's ear. The man shuddered involuntarily. "Tell me about
Austin."

"Austin came to me, you understand. It was not my idea,
it was his. He was working in the communications section of
your father's firm. A message came—someone must have
panicked, because it came in the clear. Well, there was a
revolution, the sky was falling, as you say. Many people panicked. It was understandable."

"What was the message?"

" 'Commence Operation Sanctuary. Merchandise installed.'
Very simple, you see, but not very enlightening unless one
knows what Operation Sanctuary is. Austin knew the message
came from Tehran. He knew it was sent to your former great
leader"—Ghoubadi said the phrase with no trace of humor—
"but he did not know what it meant. He did understand that

merchandise meant funds. Austin has an excellent nose for funds."

Now that Ghoubadi realized he was not going to be killed or turned over to the police, he began to relax as much as possible consistent with his position. He rather enjoyed the telling of the tale, it was so preferable to the confessions his own country's agents would have been extracting.

"How should it be that a young man like Austin, already wealthy, with his future assured, should covet more money? Well, that is human nature, is it not?"

"I'll draw my own morals," Peter said. "So Austin came to you to find out what Operation Sanctuary was."

"Just so. I have a certain expertise in matters Persian. Operation Sanctuary was a contingency escape plan for His Majesty, the Shah, to come to this country in time of need. It had been arranged earlier with the help of the CIA, a recognition of mutual friendship between your former great leader and mine. In exchange for certain merchandise, your leader 'convinced' a number of influential politicians and bureaucrats to welcome His Majesty to the United States. The Shah anticipated a certain hue and cry about inhumanities on his part if he were ever deposed—which was ever a possibility in my country. Uneasy lies the head that wears the crown, is it not—and he wished to be assured ahead of time that there would be friends at court in America who lent a kindly ear to his version of things."

"So he was buying a safe exile here."

"We all must plan for the future and our old age."

"And you explained all this to Austin, betraying your Emperor."

"Operation Sanctuary covered His Majesty and his family—but unfortunately it did not cover his loyal servants, either at home or abroad. It was axiomatic that as soon as Operation

Sanctuary was initiated, he was no longer my employer. I, too, must plan for my future and old age."

"What was the merchandise?"

"There was a certain down payment, of course—'retainers,' as you say, to certain officials—but the bulk of the merchandise was to be paid when the operation commenced."

"How much was the bulk?"

"Sixty-nine million dollars. The figure was established in 1969, I believe, so you see there was a bit of whimsy in selecting the numbers. Of course, it was in 1969 dollars, so with inflation the Shah purchased a bargain."

"Sixty-nine million dollars?" The sum was so large it had no meaning for Peter.

"There were many people to be convinced, you must understand. There was no guarantee that your leader would still be in office—in fact he left it sooner than expected, did he not? We all had trouble understanding that turmoil, you know. Such a minor corruption on his part, lying and what not—so many politicians had to be convinced of the Shah's welcome, congressmen, senators, not all of them, of course, only enough to quell any uprisings in the ranks. And the CIA felt they deserved a piece, a finder's fee, as it were. Certain authorities at the FBI were essential, as with the other security branches. Well, you can see how these things can spread. Security is expensive, and secrecy costs nearly as much. Of course, it is not a very large sum to a man who has over a billion, but one can understand that to Austin it seemed rather a lot. He felt there was enough for him to share."

"So you tried blackmail. On whom?"

"On your former leader, of course. He was the conduit for the funds, was he not? I was not a principal in this matter, you understand. I was merely an adviser, merely trying to complement my pension fund, as you say. The Shah in his hasty departure had failed to insure my retirement, you see, despite eighteen years of most effective service. So one does what one can, and what one must."

"You're a blameless pawn of history," Peter said.

"Just so."

"Was the payment made?"

"Well, that I cannot say. Austin threatened to tell your very scrupulous newspapers, you see, if he did not receive what he felt to be his fair share. That may have held up the payments, of course. Austin may have appeared something of an impediment. Someone may have taken a shot at Austin."

"And hit me, at the wedding."

"That may be. I did not remain behind to find out. Once the shot was fired I felt my role as adviser was no longer necessary."

"So you ran."

"Just so. Very fast. The wedding was a bit of bravado I had advised against in the first place, but Austin was feeling very celebratory, you see. Counting his chickens, as you say. . . . I have been cooperative, have I not? Perhaps you could release me."

"Have you seen Austin since the wedding?"

"No."

"Do you know where I can find him?"

"No."

Peter wiggled the fork.

"I assure you, I do not know!"

Peter was convinced that Ghoubadi was telling him the truth, at least as far as he knew it. But it wasn't enough. Something vital had been left out. Why would Austin be blackmailing anyone? He didn't need the money, Ghoubadi had pointed that out himself. He would not be risking his life for money, nor would his father have condoned it for a second.

Thanks to Ghoubadi, Peter knew who the enemy was, at least, but he still did not know why.

Peter slept that night with Anne in a motel in Queens. He drove her there over the Triborough Bridge, using the delay at the tollbooth as his opportunity to shake any tail. He had not been followed and hadn't really expected that the killer would have found him yet, but security is effective only if applied all the time.

They stopped first at a hospital and had his wound tended. It was clean and neat and would leave only a pencil-thin scar running the length of his right side like a zipper. Anne made love to him gingerly, more concerned with the stitches than he was. Despite her tenderness the fury of their passion was still there, all the more vibrant for being held in check. As before, Anne was astounded by the depth of her feelings. She had made love to this quiet man like a harlot and like a nurse. She had seen him take stitches the length of his upper torso without a wince. She had made a fool of herself for him and was ready to do it again, but she still didn't know him. Perhaps she never would know him, but she realized as she eased herself over him, moved his hips with her hands, that she would stay with him for as long as she could.

**HEADLINE,** *THE NEW YORK TIMES*:

# Shah Arrives in N.Y. For 'Compassionate' Visit

# 20

---

The bus was crowded and slow and hot, and the woman next to him smelled of warm bologna. Nardo wrinkled his nose, but the odor would not go away. He got off at the next stop, deciding to walk an extra two blocks. He hated buses almost as much as he hated subways. The only sensible way to get around in New York was by cab, but cabs could be difficult to follow. Someone determined enough could keep track of a bus on foot if it came to that.

As instructed, Nardo was making himself very easy to follow. The suggestion that someone would be following him made him feel horribly nervous; he kept wanting to scratch his back. But Smith had told him to do it, and he was so frightened of Smith that he wouldn't question anything he said. He was incapable of thinking of Smith without shivering at the memory of the naked maniac leaning over him, pressing the cold muzzle to his ear.

In order to be followed he first had to be found. Nardo still had a few friends among the press, recipients of the odd favor years ago when he was in a position to dole them out. The gossip-around-town columns in both the *Post* and the

*News* had printed little squibs about his presence in the city. The *Post* had him quoted as the source of a one-line joke he'd never heard of, and the *News* felt obliged to make a nasty remark about the Washington years. Both of them used his name, however, that was the main thing, and the *Post* had even mentioned that he was at the Plaza. The *Times*, of course, had treated his presence with the same disdainful lack of interest they had always shown him. Short of assassinating the mayor and hanging around for an interview, he doubted that he would ever interest the *Times*. But he had done what Smith had told him to do, he had made himself as conspicuous as possible.

As far as he could tell, it had all been for nothing. No one was following him. Stanhope was as invisible as he had been since the fiasco at Grand Central. Maybe they had frightened him right out of the game. Maybe he had fled to South America, taking the bank code with him. Nardo felt his stomach plunge at the thought.

At the corner newsstand Nardo bought a copy of the *Daily News*. The Shah was still front-page news. He had undergone another operation. Christ, he was right here in the same city. Nardo could hop a crosstown bus and go into the hospital and ask him the code. Except of course the combined federal, city, and personal security forces wouldn't let him get within shouting distance of the Shah. Nor would it do Nardo any good if he could get close enough to shake his hand; the Shah didn't know any more about this particular cache of money than Nardo did, and probably less. Details were not the province of the state ruler, they fell to the responsibility of lesser men. All of those lesser men, unfortunately for Nardo, were dead.

What could he expect the Shah to say to him, anyway? "You say you've lost that sixty-nine million dollars, Tom? Not to worry, I'll give you another." Not likely. Meanwhile, time was running out. The Shah was only in the country for "compassionate" reasons of health. Already there were rumblings of discontent, angry voices calling for him to be ousted. He no longer controlled the oil America coveted, a religious fanatic did, and the fanatic was calling for the Shah's regal head on a platter. If the Shah was to extend his stay, the Man had to start greasing a lot of palms, heavily and fast. And that couldn't happen until the Swiss gnome unlocked the treasure vault.

Nardo didn't doubt that the money would be released if everything was done as it should be. He also didn't doubt that the Swiss would hold onto it if they reasonably could. The Iranian revolutionary council was already clamoring for the return of the Shah's fortune that was reportedly secreted in the mountain country. The Swiss wouldn't want to give it up to anyone, of course, but given the hard choice—well, the Shah was deposed and the religious revolutionaries had the oil. Switzerland needed oil as much as any modern land. If Nardo didn't turn up with the proper information within the proper time, it wasn't hard to guess what choice the bank would make.

Austin was amazed at how easily it had gone so far. The incident in Grand Central had so shaken him at first that he had nearly quit. But the thought of returning home with nothing to show was too humiliating. He had begged his father for a chance to prove himself; if he gave up now, all he would nave proven was that he wasn't up to it.

For three days Austin had recovered from the shock and wondered what to do next. Then, providentially, he saw the newspaper mention of Nardo. The man's name had practically flown off the page. All the names in the gossip column were printed in darker ink to do precisely that.

He had picked Nardo up at the Plaza. Following him had been as easy as taking a stroll through the park. Austin knew he was in town for the money. He would follow him until he established a safe way to make contact. Nardo knew someone handy with explosives and a rifle, and Austin wanted to isolate that person before exposing his blind side. Once he had something concrete, then perhaps he would answer Peter's ad in the paper and they could work out a plan together. The main thing was to come back to the family with *something*.

Austin saw Nardo meet a man on a street corner. The man was dressed in a conservative business suit, but sported a Stetson, like a parody of a Texas oilman, Austin thought. The man with the hat had his hand on Nardo's arm, and Nardo appeared nervous.

The two men came toward Austin. He would allow himself ten more paces before turning into a shop. He wanted to see their faces clearly. The man with the hat was smiling, a particularly cold grimace, and talking slowly to Nardo, who nodded too much, too rapidly. Nardo seemed anxious to accommodate the man with the hat.

Austin stepped into a men's clothing store. From within the store he studied Nardo's companion's face, bland, nondescript, a face to forget or to be confused with hundreds of others. The cowboy hat would be much easier to remember than the face. The man's eyes flicked this way and that as he walked. His face was turned toward Nardo and his voice was directed toward him, but the eyes took in everything. As they glanced into the men's store they scanned the clerks and customers, jabbed a second at Austin, catching and releasing Austin's eye contact so swiftly that Austin was sure it hadn't really happened at all. To be safe Austin turned away and picked up a shirt, pretending to look at the price.

After a few moments Austin brushed aside a clerk who had

come to help and stepped out of the men's store into the street. He could see the Stetson bobbing among the pedestrians half a block away. Austin followed.

As they turned a corner Smith stopped and spoke ardently to Nardo, clapping him on the shoulder as he did. This motion allowed him to look back the way he had come without seeming to turn around. Smith saw a man enter the street from the men's store. Passing it only moments before, Smith had taken in the familiar face watching him, and now here was the man himself, dawdling along in Smith's wake, studying the retouched wedding photos in a photographer's studio window with too much absorption. Nardo had been effective bait.

There was an anomaly about this situation that Smith puzzled over for a moment as he turned Nardo once more and continued walking. The man tailing him was clearly a Stanhope, he had the look of the Stanhopes, which Smith had studied on the face of the difficult, haughty old man he had assassinated and again on the face of his son whom Smith had followed and lain in wait for in the girl's darkened apartment. But this man was obviously not cut from the same cloth as the other two. The old man in his stony, suicidal silence had earned a measure of Smith's respect. He had probably known he was going to be killed whether he spoke or not, but few would have had the courage to defy Smith to the end. And his son, the one who had faced Smith in a test of wills in the darkness—and won; he was tough and smart and altogether dangerous. A lesser man than Smith might even have feared him. But this man trailing him now was not like the others. He was sloppy, incompetent. He seemed to credit Smith with no intelligence. He was either arrogant or a fool, or both, and really in this business the one amounted to the other. He who did not approach his opponent with caution and respect frequently paid with the price of his life. However, even a fool had his uses.

Such as the fool beside him now. Nardo was so frightened, as paralyzed as a bird by a snake, that it was all Smith could do to keep the fool from bursting into tears. Nardo could still walk, however, and that was all Smith required of him right now.

"I'm going to leave you for a few minutes," Smith said, his voice low and soothing. "I'm going to drop back and walk a few paces behind you. I'm not going far," he said, anticipating Nardo's hopes and dashing them immediately. It would not do for Nardo to get hopeful. "I'll be right behind you but you won't see me. Don't look back, just keep on walking. You know where you're going, keep going there and that's where I'll meet you. Do you understand?"

Nardo nodded mutely.

"Tell me."

"Just keep walking," Nardo said. "Don't look back."

"Very good," Smith said. He squeezed Nardo's arm, but whether in approbation or warning, Nardo could not have said. He was so terrified of Smith that he yearned for his approval.

"I will be behind you, watching you all the way," Smith warned. "Don't disappoint me."

"No. I won't!"

They turned a corner and for a moment were out of sight of Austin. Smith put his Stetson on Nardo's head.

"Keep going," he said, then stepped into a florist's shop. Smith walked to the rear of the shop where an assistant was making bouquets of daisies, mass-producing them to sell for $1.50 a bunch, tying the stems quickly with wire and thrusting them into a bucket.

Smith picked up a bouquet from the bucket. Only when he started to pay for the flowers did he allow himself to turn and look through the plate glass windows at the store front. He held the flowers up near his face to screen his features on the off chance that Austin might glance into the shop. He needn't have bothered. As Smith had expected, Austin was still following the bobbing Stetson, a little breathless from having sprinted the last few yards to get around the corner. He would catch on eventually, of course, perhaps even soon. But it would be too late. Smith paid for the flowers and walked briskly out of the florist's shop without waiting for his change.

Halfway down the block Austin began to realize something was wrong. The man with the hat wasn't Smith, his walk was different, too stiff, like a man who knows he is being watched and thus has lost his unconscious stride and must will himself to take a step. Smith had peeled off, doubled back, must be behind him. The important thing was not to panic, not to do anything too abruptly. He had to think of a way to loop around again, find Smith, and stay behind him. There was no reason to think Smith had spotted him. Maybe the two of them had simply gone separate ways. That didn't explain the hat, but then . . .

He felt the muzzle of the gun pressing directly into the base of his spine. A shot there would paralyze him for life if it didn't kill him. Smith's face was pressing in on him, smiling, holding out flowers, of all things.

"Take them, won't you?" Smith said. "They're very lovely. Consider them a gift. . . . *Take* them."

Smith emphasized the command with a nudge at his spine. Austin took the flowers in his left hand.

"Use both hands," said Smith. "They're fragile."

Austin wrapped his right hand over his left, which held the flowers. Smith nodded approval as he saw Austin's hands im-

267

mobilized and in plain sight, clasped around the flowers like a desperate suitor, or an altar boy.

"We're all of us very fragile, in our way," said Smith. Austin felt the muzzle being withdrawn from his back, but he could still feel the impression in his mind.

# 21

---

The two-line ad had run at the bottom of the front page of *The New York Times* for a week. On the eighth day there was a response waiting when Peter called the newspaper.

Inside the envelope was an advertisement for a newly released movie, also clipped from *The New York Times*. The times for feature showings were listed in the ad and one of them, 4:40, was circled. The single word "sat" had been clipped from elsewhere in the paper and lay loose in the bottom of the envelope. There was nothing else.

The movie house was on Fifty-sixth and Lexington, and there was a large weekend line waiting to get in when Peter arrived for the 4:40 P.M. showing Saturday. He took his place in line and waited.

A hooker, young and brash in skintight purple toreador pants and a leopard-spotted shirt open nearly to the navel, made her way slowly down the ticket line. Sashaying somewhat unsteadily on spiked heels, she studied each face she passed with a defiant scorn. She looked to be not much more than sixteen, and was much too obvious for East Side tastes. The girl paused in front of Peter.

269

"Wanna come with me?" she asked. It was not a question. Peter stepped out of line and fell into stride beside her, feeling the amused eyes of the others in line watching him.

Without a word she led him to Bloomingdale's. They crossed the ground floor of the department store to the accompaniment of raised eyebrows, and stopped in front of the elevators. Here she turned and looked at Peter, her eyes ranging over him, sizing him up, all the while smiling a derisive grin. Peter wondered if she still sneered at the world when she went to sleep at night. Having satisfied her curiosity, she returned her eyes to the elevators. One came, and opened, and filled with people, but the hooker did not move. When the second one came, she led Peter in.

They rode the elevator all the way to the top. At the last floor she touched Peter's arm lightly, a restraining gesture, but it was unnecessary, Peter had made no move to get out. The elevator emptied of people, took on more passengers, and started back down. On the fifth floor a man stepped on whom Peter recognized. It took him a few seconds to place the clean-cut, collegiate face, then Peter remembered him as a security man who had barred him from entering the SSC plant on the day of the wedding.

They rode up and down on the elevator twice more. The man would have been following him and the hooker from the movie line, Peter knew, checking to make sure they weren't followed. The yo-yo ride was sound procedure to double-check, and it may just have been caution, but Peter had the feeling that the young man was doing it to impress Peter with his trade craft.

The young man finally stepped off the elevator on the seventh floor. Peter let several others go in front of him, then followed. The young man walked straight down the aisle, as if he had proved what needed proving and now was too impatient to bother with caution, but Peter followed slowly, ambling circuitously among the counters, scanning the merchandise speculatively like a shopper with money to spend, time to kill, and no definite purchase in mind.

The young man was waiting among the beds. "My name is Richter, sir." Peter nodded. "I work for SSC, we met briefly . . ."

"I remember," said Peter. "How did you know how to get in touch with me?"

"Your father had instructed us all about planting messages in the *Times*, sir," he said. "I didn't know your particular code, of course, so I answered all of the ads. Yours was the fourth I tried." Richter smiled. Peter could see he was proud of his thoroughness.

"I thought it best to do this on a full security footing, sir."

"Quite right," said Peter.

"I checked you out carefully, there was no one following you."

The young man seemed to be looking for a compliment.

"Very pleased with your performance," Peter said, realizing after he said it that it was exactly the way his father spoke.

Richter beamed. "Thank you. Thank you . . . uh, Mr. Stanhope, I want to say how very sorry I am about your father."

Peter nodded, making a vague gesture with his hand.

"Thank you," he murmured. He did not feel ready to accept condolences. He was not ready to admit the fact of his father's death yet.

A salesman hurried toward them, thinking Peter's gesture was directed at him.

"Just looking, thanks," Peter said. "We'll call you when we need help."

"Was there anything in particular you're looking for?" the salesman asked.

"We'll call you," said Peter dismissively. Peter and Richter moved slowly through the beds, keeping up the appearance of shopping.

"We received a message for you, sir," Richter said. "It came in over the telephone from someone asking to speak to anyone in charge. I was on duty, so I took it."

"A man's voice?" Peter asked.

"Yes, sir. It was very brief. He said he was ready to swap Stanhopes."

Peter looked at him. "I know it sounds odd, sir," Richter said uneasily. "But I wrote it down as soon as he hung up." Richter pulled a note from his pocket, glanced at it to verify what he had said, then passed it to Peter.

Peter sat on one of the mattresses as if testing it while he looked at the paper. "Tell Peter Stanhope I'm ready to swap Stanhopes," the note read. "The Palm Court of the Plaza Hotel, Saturday, 2:00 P.M."

"He hung up before I could use a trace," Richter said. He yearned to ask Peter what it was all about, but he knew he would not get an answer.

"You did well," Peter said dully, too concerned to pay much attention to Richter's ego needs.

"Under the circumstances, with your father and everything . . ." Richter paused. "I think everyone at SSC would like to help, sir."

Peter looked up and managed a smile. "I'll let you know if I need anything, Richter. Thank you."

But Peter knew there was very little anyone else could do at this point. Someone had Austin, that much was clear. He was a very good professional, very good. Whatever he had planned, it was doubtful that a few dozen SSC operatives staked out at the Plaza would be able to do much about it. Whoever he was, he was too smart for that.

He had Austin, he wanted Peter. First his father, then Austin. It was a bloodbath, carnage. And Peter still did not know why.

The clerk at the message center of the National Security Agency was miffed. He might be only a clerk to some, a sort of human answering service, but he had his own highly calibrated sense of dignity. He knew when someone wasn't showing him the proper respect, and the man who had relayed this last message was—well, downright snippy.

He knew the agents only by voice, but that was enough to tell who was a gentleman and who wasn't. No matter how urgent your business, it never hurt to be polite. The clerk, whose name was Chris, punched the numbers for agent Rimbaud in New York. Rimbaud fell into his less-than-a-gentleman category, somewhere above sullen-clod, but definitely no gentleman, not someone Chris would go out of his way for.

"Message center for agent Rimbaud, please," he said when someone answered. After a pause Rimbaud came on the wire. "Rimbaud," he said.

"Procedure, sir," Chris reminded him. When Rimbaud answered, he sounded annoyed, as they usually did when he reminded them of procedure. For heaven's sake, it was *their* procedure, not his.

"Nighthawk, for Chris' sake," said Rimbaud testily.

"Night owl," said Chris.

"Yeah, yeah, okay, what's the message?"

"A 'person' has been trying to get in touch with you, Mr. Rimbaud," Chris said with a disapproving emphasis on the "person." "A Mr. Stanhope wants you to call him in New York City."

"Give me the number!"

"I was about to . . . sir," Chris said. He repeated the num-ber Peter had left.

"Is that it?" Rimbaud asked.

"Yes, sir, that's the message . . ." The line went dead in midsentence. Rimbaud had hung up. "You're very welcome, sir," Chris said to the dead line. He slipped Rimbaud into the ungrateful-bastard category.

"You said you wanted to help," Peter said on the phone.

"What do you need?" Rimbaud asked

"Is this line secure?"

"Yes, go ahead."

"I want to know the identity of an agent, maybe yours, maybe CIA, who goes by the code name of Max. He used a false-flag recruitment on a friend of mine to rent that apart-ment where the cop was murdered."

Rimbaud paused, then spoke very carefully. "Naturally I cannot give you such information," he said, speaking in a forced, formal tone. "Such information is classified and I can be of no assistance to you. . . . Will you be at this number for another five minutes?"

"I can be," Peter said.

"I will call you back," Rimbaud said. "I would like to im-press upon you the gravity of your situation."

Without waiting for a reply Rimbaud hung up and left his office. He was sure the line was secure from outside taps, but he wasn't all that certain that Levy didn't have someone listening in. His categorical denial of Peter's request would look good on the transcript, but he hoped that Peter could read between the lines.

As he hurried to a pay phone Rimbaud thought of Levy and his constipated air of superiority. Rimbaud had done

David Wiltse

what he had been told, he had pulled his horns in on the Stanhope case, practicing the director's version of benign neglect. Which meant giving Stanhope the shaft, he realized. Well, it wasn't often that he had a chance to do something to the tall, cadaverous Levy, but when one came along, he wasn't going to pass it up. Levy was pretty clearly lining his pockets in this deal, if not financially, then politically; otherwise there was no explanation for his attitude. Rimbaud couldn't prove it, of course, but then Levy couldn't prove that Rimbaud was about to slip it to him, either.

"I was very sorry to hear about your father," Rimbaud said on the pay phone. "He was always very straight with me."

"He was straight with everyone," Peter said.

"Yes," Rimbaud said, then paused. Christ, he could get hanged for what he was about to do. "You didn't hear this from me," he said.

"I didn't hear it at all," Peter said. Rimbaud had seen Peter in action. He believed him.

"Max is the code name for a CIA agent who acted as a roving troubleshooter throughout Europe and the Middle East. Had a mission or two in Africa, I understand. Specialized in heavy-duty stuff. Do you know the expression 'wet affairs'?"

"Yes."

"That was his territory. Just a supervisor, though, not an active."

"Where do I find him?" Peter asked.

"Just look in the Washington phone book," Rimbaud said. "He's retired now. He's not Max anymore. He's just plain Sam Bobrick."

Austin awoke to fear. He climbed to consciousness unwillingly, his mind struggling to stay insensate. As he came slowly to himself he felt the fear first, and only later came the

275

pain. The fear was only partly because of the pain. The other element of his terror was in knowing he was at the mercy of an animal. This animal looked like a man, moved like a man, but he did not have the feelings of a man. He was not torturing Austin as one man tortures another, to extract information, or even as a sadist might, to inflict pain. Smith seemed oblivious to any of that. He was gnawing at Austin with his instruments with the indifference of a spider gnawing on its prey, not caring at all if it were living or dead.

As his head cleared Austin realized he was still in the closet, hanging from a coat hook like a piece of meat, slung with his feet off the floor by a rope that passed under both elbows and forced him to jut forward at the waist. At first the strain on his back and shoulders and arms had been very painful, but by now they had all become numb. And of course there had been many new pains to replace them.

Smith was sitting in a straight-backed chair at the entrance of the walk-in closet. Sheets had been draped over all the walls and the floor, and they were now spattered red. Austin was amazed at the distance and angles to which his blood had spurted. Smith himself was naked. Speckles of blood dotted his skin. His right hip was a smear of red where he had wiped his slippery hand.

Smith was watching Austin, and when he saw his eyes open, he picked up his tools. He had bought them all at a hardware store, a pair of pliers, poultry shears, a paring knife. They were not designed for subtlety.

"If you're ready to tell me, blink your eyes three times," Smith said.

Austin muttered something unintelligible through the gag in his mouth. Smith made no attempt to understand, but returned right to his work. He reached for Austin's hand, which was hanging down and back against the wall, out of Austin's sight.

*Oh, my God, it hurt, it hurt!* Austin's mind was filled with agony. For several seconds there was nothing at all in his mind but the pain. He struggled to remember the techniques for enduring torture, the tricks of breathing, the methods of concentrating the mind elsewhere. But it hurt too much!

He could not see what Smith was doing, only Smith's face, brow furrowed with annoyed concentration, like a mechanic who can't quite get a bolt loose. Smith tugged and Austin felt it in his arm, a dull feeling, with no pain attached. Austin thought, *I've made it, I'm numb, I've suffered all the pain there is, and now it's over.*

Smith tugged again and Austin felt something pull free. For a moment Smith studied something out of Austin's sight, his head tilted to one side, a bird remarking something curious. Then he held it briefly in front of Austin's face, as if Austin, too, might be interested, before he tossed it negligently over his shoulder.

The thing rolled across the sheet on the floor and stopped against the leg of Smith's chair. It was small, no wider than a man's finger, but much shorter, only the length from one knuckle to the next.

What could it be, Austin wondered dully. Where had it come from? Smith took a step back and surveyed Austin critically, turning his head from side to side. Austin still could not see what Smith was looking at, but suddenly his arm came to life again and he felt the waves of pain pulsing upward from his hand, wave after wave.

Smith left the closet and Austin thought again, *This is it, it's over, I've held out long enough and he's given up. All I have to do now is get through this last spasm of agony. He's done his worst and I've taken it. He can do nothing more to me now.*

His tormentor came back into the closet, holding a large mirror. He positioned the mirror in front of Austin, holding it impassively, like a barber showing his customer the back of his neck. Smith maneuvered the mirror so Austin could see his own hands.

Austin looked at the mirror. For a moment he did not recognize the bloody, misshapen lump as his own. When he realized what he was seeing, he began to scream.

When the muffled screams subsided, Smith spoke.

"If you're ready to tell me, blink three times."

Austin slowly opened his eyes, which he had squeezed shut to close out the sight of what had been his hand. He blinked.

# 22

Sam Bobrick heard a noise from the kitchen, a faint clunk, as of something falling. His refrigerator had an ice maker, the legacy of a former owner, and Sam attributed the noise to freshly made ice cubes dropping into the bin. It reminded him that he wanted to freshen his drink. Alcohol, in moderation, was good for you, his doctor had said, and Sam was not going to argue with that advice. He allowed himself two Scotch and sodas per evening, one at the beginning of the local news program at six o'clock, the second at the end of the national news, an hour and a half later, just about now.

Sam had been glued to the news, getting what scattered and frantic reports there were about the seizure of the embassy in Tehran. He could imagine the paroxysms of anxiety Nardo was going through now, wondering how this would affect his Operation Sanctuary. If the Shah were to be secure, the work would have to be done awfully fast.

At the commercial break he went to the kitchen. When he opened the refrigerator, a black bag fell over his head and something metallic pressed against his back. Already blinded by the bag, Sam did not struggle as he felt cords being tightened around the opening, securing the sack on his head. A hand touched his shoulder, moving him toward a chair, but the gun barrel never left his back until Sam was seated.

Resistance was idiotic as long as he was sightless, and Sam knew immediately that he was in the hands of someone very skillful. If the person had wanted him dead, Sam would have been dead by now.

The list of people who might in theory want Sam dead was a long one, but in practice old grudges weren't carried very long in his business. Retirement was more or less universally respected, except perhaps by the more fanatical terrorist groups or some of the South American countries. He had never had any dealings with either group. Even spies got old, after all, and wanted to live out their last days in peace as much as anyone else. That didn't keep one from dabbling in the business, keeping one's hand in, but the respect for a man's years was stronger in his trade than in most. The evil you had done was interred with your discharge papers.

Which meant that whoever had captured Sam as embarrassingly easily as one might catch a lobster in a restaurant tank was interested in something current. And Sam had only one current case, but he waited for the man to mention it first.

He had a long wait. Sam could hear the intruder moving around, faintly, for a few seconds, then silence. The bag over his head muffled his hearing as well as blinded him, and seemed to exaggerate the noise of his own breathing. It sounded stertorous in his ears. The silence on the other side of the bag lasted so long it became ominous. Was the other man still there? What was he waiting for? What was he doing? Sam was well aware of the dangers of letting your imagination run free under stress situations. It was a tactic any good interrogator would use, hinting at perils that lay in wait for the uncooperative that were all the more frightening for being vague. Sam had used variations of the tactic himself from time to time, but that didn't make it any easier to be on the receiving end. His breath continued to grow louder, despite his efforts to control it, and he began to wonder if he was getting enough oxygen through the fabric. It seemed as if he could hear his heart beat, and the pulse in his forehead was definitely throbbing much too hard.

"What's this all about?" he asked. He wasn't sure he could be understood through the bag.

"If you're after money, there's some in my wallet, I don't keep any around the house," but he knew the intruder wasn't after money.

"I'm going to take this bag off now," Sam said into the silence. He could very faintly hear the sound of voices on the television set from the other room, but not a sound in this room. When he spoke his voice seemed to echo back to him, but he wasn't sure if that was the effect of the bag.

Sam began to lift his hands toward the bag, but something, some motion which was in itself a complete cessation of motion, like a herd of grazing deer freezing simultaneously in place at the first distant whiff of the hunter, made him stop. He did not know how the other man had moved, or how he himself knew that the motion was threatening, but he knew. He eased his hands into his lap and waited again.

Sam tried to fight the rising sense of panic as the silence stretched. He tried to count, to keep some sense of time that way, but all his senses kept jumping back to his situation. His brain craved information, but it received none. He tried to concentrate on something interesting to him, something to keep his nerves from jumping. Working very slowly and carefully, he began to dismantle his car, his beloved Porsche, part by part, placing each part just so on the tarpaulin spread across his mind so he would have them at hand when he started to reassemble the automobile in his head. But it was no use. He knew the man was moving, but he could not hear it, he could only feel it. The man was behind him now. It was like lying with your head on the guillotine, waiting for the blade to descend.

Finally the man spoke. The voice was close to his ear, a whisper, without characteristics, indistinguishable.

"Who killed Stanhope?"

"I don't know what you mean," Sam said. "I don't know anyone named Stanhope. What do you mean?"

The man had withdrawn from him again. Sam wanted to cling to the voice, to have it fill the void. Anything, threats, even physical abuse, was preferable to the silence that consumed itself.

"Was the name Stanhope?" Sam asked. "I'm not sure I heard you right."

But it was no use, the man had shut him off again. For a moment Sam thought that it might be Smith himself, trying to see if Sam would betray him. But no, Smith was not smart enough to bring a man's nerves to the point of screaming for release without even touching him. Smith was cunning, and deadly as a cobra, but he was not that subtle.

Sam resisted because of his pride. He had been trained for a lifetime to avoid telling anyone more than he had a right to know. His career had been built in part on his ability to keep his mouth closed, and he wasn't going to allow that to be negated now, not without a struggle. It wasn't a matter of betrayal. He owed nothing to Smith, the man had gone insane, out of control. Killing old Stanhope was completely uncalled for. No, he owed nothing to Smith—but he owed something to himself. He would not speak.

It was impossible to get any sense of time. He tried to listen to the voices from the television, but they were too muffled, he could make no sense of them, could not distinguish between narrative and commercial. He tried to get to know his prison, concentrating on the black bag that had so effectively sealed him off from his world. He smelled the cloth, noting a faint odor of laundry detergent. Turning his head back and forth slightly, he felt the cloth move across the end of his nose, soft, but with a raised quality to it. He touched it gently with his tongue. Velvet, perhaps, or velour. It might be a very large jeweler's bag.

The sound was so unexpected it startled him, and at first he couldn't place it at all. There had been a slight grinding sound, very high-pitched, almost a squeal, as of glass rubbing against glass. Then a pop, soft but distinct. A glass cork in a glass bottle. As he was trying to figure that out, he caught the first scent of it. The bottle must have been held close to the bag opening, and low, at his chest level, for the fumes to have penetrated. A sharp, penetrating odor, astringent and repellent. Sam jerked his head away involuntarily as the fumes burned at his nasal membranes. Even as he pulled his head away he heard the sizzle, a series of popping smacks, like bacon frying, but more subdued and faster. Acid!

"For God's sake!" Sam cried. He had been told of the pain of acid, the unbearable agony as the chemical ate its way through the skin, through the muscle, down to the bone, and into the bone itself. He had seen a face disfigured by acid, head seared as if thrust into fire. Sam fought to hold back a scream.

Suddenly hands smoothed back the bag over his head, pulling it more tightly against his eyes. He felt two drops strike the bag. Like rain drops on an awning they bounced, then settled into the fabric directly over his eyes. Sam could hear the sizzle clearly, could smell the sharp odor, could almost see the corrosive liquid eating its way through the cloth, through his eyeballs, into his brain.

"The man's name is Smith!" he called, his voice trembling. "For God's sake, take it off!"

"You have a little time," the voice said calmly. "It takes a while. Tell me about Smith."

Sam told him all he knew. About Nardo, the Man, the money, Austin, and the numbers.

"But no one told him to kill Stanhope! No one knew he would do that! I knew old man Stanhope, I liked him, I'm sorry he's dead, Smith was not ordered to do that! He's gone berserk. He hates Peter Stanhope, he's obsessed with revenge, he'll do anything to get him. Please take the hood off!"

As he said it Sam realized the sizzling had stopped. He was flooded with gratitude. His captor was a humane man, a reasonable man, a man to be trusted. Sam knew that he had been manipulated to feel that way, but still he could not resist the great sense of relief. He needed no further coaxing to talk; the vessel had been uncorked and information spilled forth.

"Why does he hate Peter Stanhope?" asked the voice, and Sam told him everything.

"Stanhope nearly killed him once."

"When? Where?"

"Iran, five or six years ago. Smith was working under me then, he was still a member of the agency. The Shah's regime was very shaky at that point, there was a lot of internal turmoil. There were dissident factions all over the place, Communists, socialists, Muslim extremists, you name it. The Shah was clapping them into jail as fast as he could find them, but he couldn't hope to stop them that way. The *people* were discontented, and all of the dissident factions were just reflecting that. The Shah had never been secure on the throne anyway, he'd been forced out once in the 1950s, and he could see it coming again. He needed something to pull the people together behind him, he needed an incident that would justify his shaking the country like a rattle till all the loose pieces fell out. It couldn't be an internal threat, because the people were in sympathy with most of those, so it had to be an external threat. He didn't have one at the moment, so he decided to invent one.

"What he needed was an invasion, a small one, manageable, since he was going to fabricate it. He asked us to stage a small invasion that he could squelch. Not possible. If we sent in our own men and it came out who they were, well, that would be a hell of a mess. We decided to scale things down. He didn't need an actual war, all he needed was a couple of bodies to parade in a show trial. Someone he could get to confess—and give his bullyboys time enough and anyone would confess."

"Who did you get?"

"*I* didn't get anyone. This was all done at the top; I mean at the very top. We'd had our Bay of Pigs and weren't about to go for another one. The agency recommended against it, but the Shah went over the agency's head."

"The President?"

"Must have been. The next thing we knew was a private agency was hired to slip into the country at night. I don't know what story they'd been told, but when they were caught, I know what they'd confess to. They'd been briefed in Paris— the Ayatollah Khomeini was in France at that time. They'd passed through Saudi Arabia and taken passage there. They were supposed to come ashore with Czech weapons. They had been told they were studying the feasibility of an invasion of the oil fields. They were known free-lance mercenaries. Well, you could put all of that together to spell any kind of Com-

munist-Khomeini-Saudi threat you like. What you had were
two spies sent to prepare for an invasion. It was just what the
Shah needed. We knew when they were coming and where,
and we were waiting.

"Two provocateurs weren't enough, of course, so we added
a couple dozen 'soldiers' for window dressing. They dredged
political prisoners out of the jails, men who'd been beaten and
tortured and never would have been released anyway, and
dressed them in uniforms and sent them in as an 'invasion
force.' When reporters were brought in the next day they'd
be shown the dead invaders with weapons in hand, and be told
that the rest of the enemy had escaped out to sea. That part
of it went well enough, but something went wrong with the
rest of it.

"The idea of course was to capture the 'spies' if we could
and put them on trial, but their corpses would have been almost as good since they could be traced to a mercenary agency.
But something went wrong. They slipped past us. Smith located them somehow and was half-castrated by Stanhope in
the process. He was hospitalized for a long time, and when he
came out, he was a psycho. Whether it was what happened to
him, the nature of the wound, the hospital drugs, or just being
that close to death, I don't know, but he was too dangerous
to keep around. We let him go. We use him now and again,
but I can see that has been a mistake."

"Yes," said the voice. "That has been a mistake. So Smith
killed Thomas Stanhope?"

"Yes," said Sam. The voice fell silent again. Sam was worried, felt he hadn't pleased him, hadn't told him enough.

"And how much of this did Austin Stanhope find out?" the
voice asked.

"He knew about Sanctuary, he was trying to scuttle it. He

knew Ghoubadi, who could have told him something about the 'invasion.' I think he had probably pieced it all together."

The man was still in the room, then at some point he was no longer there. Sam did not know how he knew, but when he heard a car drive past outside, he slowly reached up and removed the bag from his head. As he squinted his eyes against the light he realized for the first time that every muscle in his body had been tense during the whole ordeal, and he now ached all over as if he'd just run an obstacle course. Sam looked at the spots on the hood where the acid had been poured on his eyes. He smelled the spots, touched them. Water. Despite himself, he smiled. The man had been so very good at it. He looked at his watch. It had seemed like an eternity. It had been twenty-five minutes in real time.

# 23

Peter sat in the Palm Court of the Plaza Hotel, sipping a glass of mineral water. A bellman walked slowly through the lobby, paging someone. He made his way through the scattered tables and overstuffed armchairs of the lounge, calling out a name. When Peter was certain he was not being called, he relaxed and sank back in his chair.

The bellman wandered farther into the hotel, still mournfully calling for a Mr. Campbell, Mr. Shep Campbell, his voice finally falling off in annoyance and disappointment. It was the third call for Mr. Campbell since Peter had been there. The mystery man answered none of them, but still each time the bellman went dutifully forth.

Peter thought of Austin, the only other remaining member of his family. When he thought of him in the abstract, he thought of him still as a ten-year-old boy, a little spoiled by the loving attention of father and older brothers, but utterly trusting, serene in the certainty that the men in his family, so much older, so strong, would take care of him. His father was dead, one of his invulnerable brothers was dead; only Peter remained to protect him. For a moment a vision of that ten-year-old boy flashed through his mind, tied down, being tortured by Smith, a faceless embodiment of evil. Peter squeezed his eyes closed to blot out the picture.

If Smith was willing to swap Austin for Peter, then Austin must already have talked. Nardo probably had the numbers, maybe even the money by now. The Man had won after all. It sickened Peter to think of it, but it wasn't important, it wasn't the first time he had realized there was no real justice in this world. The only thing he had to think about now was freeing Austin and then, somehow, surviving himself. He felt the muzzle of the Walther TPH pressing against his abdomen under his belt. He didn't expect to get a chance to use it, but he knew Smith would expect him to be armed. If he disarmed him, perhaps Smith's caution would lessen a degree or two. And then Peter had but to await his chance.

The bellman passed again, this time calling Peter's name.

The voice on the telephone was calm and flat.

"Stanhope," said Smith. "I have your brother."

"I don't know that," Peter said.

There was a pause, then Austin's voice came on the wire, very weak, frightened and pleading. "Peter! For God's sake . . ."

He was cut short, then Smith came back on the line.

"I'll release him . . . but I want you."

"Where and when?"

"Now. Walk into the park, past the little lake, and keep going. I'll find you. If you have any friends with you, I'll kill your brother."

"I'll be alone," Peter said.

"I'm very good at spotting friends," Smith said. "Leave the hotel now." The line went dead.

\*　　\*　　\*

Crossing through the lunchtime crowd of loiterers, shoppers, vendors, and picnickers who crowded around the Plaza fountain and the walls of the park, Peter entered Central Park. The day was a bright, sunny one, and the park was filled with people. Peter scanned every face. "He looks like anybody," Sam had said of Smith. "He looks like your neighbor, your best friend, and he always looks different." Peter could not imagine a more frightening description of a killer. Smith could be virtually any of the men all around him. He could die with a knife in the back at any second and never know who did it. He kept walking.

Peter continued along a curving sidewalk. On one side was the pond that served as a moat to protect the bird sanctuary island in the middle of it. Tame, spoiled ducks clucked and competed for scraps of bread while, farther off in the water, a pair of swans watched disdainfully. On the other side of the sidewalk picnickers sat elbow to elbow on a phalanx of wooden benches. Secretaries eating their yogurt and junior executives bolting junk food and deli sandwiches sat hip to hip with old men and women, sweatered and buttoned in the heat, seeking the warming rays of the sun. They, too, sought safety in numbers.

As Peter passed the people on the bench an old man moved, shifting slightly from one haunch to the other, and throwing his features into such a perspective that for an instant Peter thought it was his father. A wave of loss and grief swept over him, so sudden and severe that he had to sit down, struggling against the tears that burned his eyes. It was not the first time he had fantasized seeing his father since his death. Like an amputee suffering the sensation of a phantom limb, some part of Peter's mind refused to accept the loss of his parent. He dreamed that he was still alive, woke expecting to find him there. He saw him at odd moments in the features of others, the back of a head, the familiar gait, the turn of a neck. Peter had suffered at the loss of his brother years ago, mourned as if a part of himself had died, but his grief for his father was different, colored as it was by Peter's deep sense of failure to let the old man know he was loved. Guilt compounded the grief, guilt that the old man had died with bitterness in his heart for Peter, guilt that he had died the way he had, staunchly defending a son who was nothing but a disappointment to him, a final testament of love that belied all the years of acrimony.

Just as suddenly as the wave of sorrow had come, it was replaced by anger, a deep, bitter fury at the man who had killed his father, killing him as a small boy kills an insect, pulling off a wing at a time before squashing him. Peter felt a hatred for Smith so strong that he began to tremble. He wanted to destroy the man, blot him out, crush him with the same sense of justification as he would a poisonous snake threatening his family.

The old man shifted his weight again. Just an old man, sunning himself like a lizard, not Peter's father after all, not anything like him, really.

The Sheep Meadow was filled with people, owners frolicking with their dogs, fathers playing catch with their sons, a young couple flying a Japanese kite, outlandish in its configuration yet wheeling through the sky like a hawk. Frisbees seemed to be everywhere, filling the air like a miniature invasion from outer space.

A bright red Frisbee hit the ground and bounced to a halt against Peter's foot. Peter stooped to retrieve it. As he stood up again he saw Austin, coming from the side, less than thirty yards away. A man walked to the side and half a pace behind Austin, one hand out of sight behind Austin's back. Peter realized immediately that it was Smith, that he had a gun in Austin's back, that he would kill Austin the instant either Peter or Austin tried to flee. Peter looked at the man's face and saw again the face that had been illuminated by the spotlight for a fraction of a second just before he shot Thomas years ago. Then Peter noticed the huge bandage that swathed Austin's right hand and realized Austin would not be able to help. Peter would have to kill the man again, by himself.

As they reached the border of Sheep Meadow, Austin heard Smith suck in his breath.

"It's him!" the killer murmured excitedly. "It's him!"

Austin saw Peter standing by the lake, watching him. At first Austin had not understood why he was still alive. He had given the code to Smith, Smith had passed it on to Nardo. Without the numbers Austin was useless to them, an annoying detail who would have to be expunged. But when he had heard Smith on the telephone, he realized why Smith hadn't simply snuffed him out. Austin had failed at everything, he had done it all wrong, and now he was being used to help kill his brother, his final failure before Smith killed him, too.

Smith stopped ten yards away from Peter, pulling Austin to a halt and standing behind him, keeping Austin as a shield between himself and Peter. Smith tossed a battered attaché case onto the ground in front of Peter.

"Put your weapon in there," Smith said. "Keep it out of sight." Peter removed the little Walther with his left hand and slipped it into the attaché case. He still held the Frisbee with his right hand.

"Take off the jacket, casually, as if you're too hot," Smith said.

"Are you all right, Austin?" Peter asked.

Austin could only nod. He was the reason his brother was going to die. He hated himself, he hated himself almost as much as he hated Smith.

"Hey!" One of the men from the Frisbee game, his long blond hair tied back in a ponytail, was walking toward them. "Throw it back!"

Peter looked at the Frisbee in his hand as if he had just noticed it for the first time. Smith glanced quickly at the Frisbee player, then back at Peter. He knew there was nothing anyone could see to tell them what was going on. The Browning was well concealed in his jacket pocket. "Give him the toy," Smith said.

Peter threw the Frisbee straight at Smith and charged. The Frisbee curved off, missing Smith and sailing harmlessly into the distance. Peter ran for Smith, ready to dive under the gun, but before he was halfway there he knew it was no good. He was too slow, too far away, Smith hadn't taken the feint. Austin was in Smith's line of fire. Smith shoved Austin to one side and pulled the Browning up. Austin swung his mutilated hand across his body and struck Smith in the face. The pain was too much, and Austin reacted immediately, falling to his knees. It saved his life as Smith turned instinctively and snapped off a shot through the cloth of his jacket that whizzed over Austin's head. Smith jerked the gun up to fire at Peter, who slammed into him, knocking him down and rolling clear immediately. Peter scrambled to his feet and kept running, then dived to the ground and rolled again. The silencer coughed discreetly again, and another hole was ripped in the cloth of Smith's coat. The bullet coursed three feet over Peter's head. Peter was up and running, changing direction with every step, zigzagging like a frightened hare. From the corner of his eye Smith saw Austin running in the opposite direction. Let him go. The one he wanted was streaking toward the lake, much too difficult a moving target from this range with the Browning still in his pocket.

Peter raced through the meadow like a halfback, scattering dog lovers and kite fliers and gathering curses in their wake. Peter glanced back and saw Austin break free, that was all he could do, all he had hoped to do. Now he had to run for his life, but even as he ran he felt that he had regained the initiative to a degree. He and Smith both knew there was no real chance for Smith to shoot him as long as he was running. Once Smith gave chase he made the possibility ten times as remote. Smith could not possibly hit anything while running himself, and if he stopped and tried to get off a shot, he would be breathing too hard, shaking too much from the effort of chasing Peter to hope to hit anything with a handgun. But both of them had to stop running sometime, and when Peter stopped, he knew that he had to have the upper hand.

The sidewalk skirting the lake was in front of him; beyond that lay the street and a thousand ways to lose a pursuer. But as Peter reached the sidewalk a small boy who had been sailing a toy boat in the pond stood in his way, momentarily panicked by the sight of a man running toward him. Peter jigged to the left to avoid the boy, but the boy moved that way too, dropping the boat. Peter leaped back to his right at the last second to keep from crashing the boy to the ground. His foot caught the edge of the boat and he fell forward, sprawling awkwardly on the fringe of grass between the sidewalk and the water. Even as he scrambled back to his feet, without looking back he could hear Smith slowing, preparing to steady himself for the shot. He was too close to miss now, too close for Peter to hope for the street. Peter plunged headlong into the pond, skimming flatly across the water in a racer's dive, then pulled his arms up through the water, propelling himself down. On the second rapid scissors-kick of his legs he vanished beneath the water.

Peter swam straight for the island, pulling with all his might. Every inch of water he could put between himself and Smith would deflect a bullet just that much more, slowing its lethal flight, blunting its accuracy. His head broke surface once, midway to the island, then plunged back under immediately after he had sucked a lungful of air through his open mouth.

Smith paused at the water's edge. He was not a good swimmer, but the island didn't look that far, and it was a dead end for Peter. Even from here Smith could see the cyclone fence that encircled the islet just inside the first rank of trees, keeping dogs and raccoons from plundering the sanctuary of its treasure of birds' nests and eggs. Smith could kill Peter as he tried to get over the fence, or better still, let him get into the trap where Smith could stalk him at his leisure, within the cover of trees, out of sight of the witnesses on shore. Even now the younger picnickers were treating the chase like a happening staged for their lunchtime entertainment, cheering happily as Smith waded into the water. There was still no gun in sight, no blood, nothing to cause them panic. An ordinary man in a business suit, wading waist-deep in the water, was a strange sight to be sure, an executive in crazy rebellion against conformity, perhaps, or having a breakdown, but nothing to get alarmed about, nothing to summon the police for. Like so many other things in the city, it was a sight to note but not get involved with.

The lake was not as deep as Smith had feared. He was already halfway there and the water was only chest high, he would be able to walk the whole way and not swim after all. He had not seen Peter surface, but he did catch a glimpse of motion where the shore curved out of sight, just a blur, then a loud report. Peter had probably tried to pull himself over the fence and the branch had broken with a crack. *Good,* thought Smith, *let him clamber into the trap.* The island was not large, no more than fifty yards long and probably not as wide. There couldn't be many places to hide. Smith would find him.

As the water receded from his chest to his abdomen to his waist, Smith went faster, forcing his body through the water. It was hard work, but he wanted to keep the pressure on Peter, keep him panicked, not give him time enough to think. The sun was bright and hitting the water at only a slight angle from the perpendicular, and the rays reflected from the surface as from a shining mirror, forcing Smith to squint against the glare.

The water fell below his belt, when suddenly Smith felt a searing pain in his knee. Something had struck him from beneath the water level, jabbing into the soft skin on the back of the knee, ripping through the flesh until it seemed to be scraping the kneecap from the inside. Smith lost his balance and fell heavily on his butt. Water splashed up and for a moment washed into his nose and eyes. He jumped up again, spluttering and coughing, panicked, one hand pulling the gun free while the other felt into the water, gingerly seeking whatever it was that had crippled him.

His fingers closed on something long and rough. He pulled it out with one forceful jerk, then lifted it above the water. It was a branch of a tree, nearly as long as a spear, the jagged broken end that had penetrated his leg still covered with gore and shreds of his pants. Peter must have shoved the thing from beneath the water with all his weight behind it. As the pain spread from his knee and up through the leg, making him dizzy, Smith scanned the surface of the water. It was like looking into a headlight, impossible to penetrate the glare. Smith knew that Peter had to surface again, but he felt terribly vulnerable, as if he had stumbled into shark-infested waters. Using the makeshift spear as a crutch, he hurried into shallower water.

Limping heavily, Smith struggled along the fence line, looking for a way into the island. He could hear movement in there, knew Peter was waiting. As he searched the fence Smith peered into the heavy woods of the sanctuary. Huge oaks and elms and maples were interspersed with slender ashes, ghostly birches, a sprinkling of hardy conifers. The soil, enriched by the guano of countless birds, supported scrub and brush, flowering azalea, and spreading laurel that covered the ground to the height of a man, broad leaves leaching out the sun that penetrated through the high canopy—and providing cover for an ambush. Unpruned, untended, un-"beautified," the thousand-odd square yards of the bird sanctuary resembled the forest primeval of a German fairy tale, threatening to those who did not belong, protective to those who did. Smith thought it was a jungle.

A seam in the fence had been pulled apart, ripped by desperate hands that left a random pattern of blood on the wire. The opening was low and narrow, and Smith would have to enter it bent double, vulnerable. He peered again into the miniature forest. Every leaf and branch seemed to sway slightly in the breeze, an effect heightened by the shift of shadows. The woods seemed alive, crawling with threat. Scanning the area closest to the fence, Smith decided it was safe enough. He glanced over his shoulder. He had come far enough around the island to be out of sight of the picnickers. To his back now was a stretch of water that ended abruptly in a massive outcropping of rock that made the sanctuary virtually impenetrable from its hidden side. He and Peter were definitely alone now, which meant he could use his silenced gun without fear of being seen.

Extending the spear through the opening in the wire first,

to support the weight of his bad leg, Smith bent and eased through, keeping the gun well out in front of him. For a second, ducking under the wire, he had to turn his face down and was effectively blind. It was the perfect time for an attack but couldn't be avoided. Smith went under quickly, jerking his head up too fast so the jagged edge of the wire caught him in the back, forcing him to bend again in pain. He hobbled one step farther in, safely free of the fence, and paused. He had made it, Peter had not seized the opportunity, he was not as smart as Smith had feared. He stood under the spreading lower limbs of a red pine.

Smith heard a whoosh from above and jerked his head and gun hand upward just as a branch of the pine, pulled back and taut as a spring, was released and snapped full force into his face. Hundreds of pine needles bit at his skin like so many tiny whips. Some of them raked the cornea of his right eye, and a broken twig gouged into his left eyebrow. As the limb recoiled upward Smith fell, clutching his eye. He saw Peter leap from the tree into the cover of the brush and fired a shot, hopelessly wild. A flock of grackles rose in a black cloud of alarm at the commotion, squawking indignantly, adding to the confusion.

The main blow to his forehead and nose had stunned Smith, sending bright lights flashing through his head, but the real pain was in his eye. It felt as if a pin were sticking into his eyeball. Tears were already filling his eyes because of the blow to the nose, and he tried to wipe them away, to clear his vision in the good eye while he kept the injured eye closed tightly.

Rising first to his knees, playing the gun back and forth in front of him, Smith unsteadily made it to his feet. The eyeball had been scratched, he realized, and he was going to have to live with the pain until he could get to a doctor. He tried to open the bad eye, but that made the pain worse, and even during the tiny glimpse he could tell he had lost the sight from that eye.

Pausing after every step to look and listen, Smith moved in the direction where Peter had fled, deeper into the woods. Something hot and wet was on his face. He touched it, saw the blood on his fingers, found the wound scooped out of his eyebrow. He wiped the blood away with his sleeve, but it continued to come. Even as he blinked he could feel the sticky fluid beginning to gum his eyelid shut. He had to stop the wound from bleeding or he would be completely blinded.

A bush fifteen yards ahead and to his right moved unnaturally. Smith fired a shot, knowing as he did so that he had been tricked, fooled into wasting a shot. That was three gone, one on the Sheep Meadow, one wasted wildly as Peter jumped from the tree, and now this one, fired at a bush that was probably being nudged by a branch while Peter hid safely several yards away.

His nerves were going, he was badly injured, perhaps blind in one eye, totally out of his element with an adversary who seemed as at home among the trees as any squirrel or fox. *That's why he didn't attack me when he had the chance,* Smith realized. *He thinks he'll have even better chances, he's confident he can work on me at his will. He's hunting me.*

As he stood in the middle of the darkling woods, in pain, crippled, nerves straining at every shift of the shadows, Smith realized that for the first time since he could remember, he was really afraid. He had caused fear many times, oh, many times, and had enjoyed watching it. He had been in danger many times, but his reaction then had never been more than a heightened sense of caution, a full awareness of the danger, but not real fear. He had always been sure he could handle it. Now he was not sure.

Smith gingerly touched his eyebrow. The bleeding seemed to have stopped. Just as his concentration wavered he saw Peter, standing alarmingly close, only a few yards away, his right arm raised as he stood, a club flying out at Smith. He fired as the club hit him, pulling him off the target, which was already moving anyway. Peter disappeared into the brush as the club slammed off Smith's protective forearm, one end of it continuing to twirl and catching Smith with full torque in the throat. As he turned, choking, his full weight fell on his injured leg. The leg crumpled beneath him, and Smith fell to his knees, gasping for breath.

Still Peter did not come. He wasn't just hunting Smith, he was toying with him, tormenting him. Again Smith felt the churning of fear in his bowels. What had made him think the man was unarmed? He had a forest full of fallen limbs, spears, clubs, as dangerous as bullets in this environment; and, unlike Smith, he had an unlimited supply.

A noise behind him sent him twirling around on his knees, leveling the pistol. A shape moved, a shadow? Stanhope? Smith no longer trusted himself, he had been wrong too much, missed too often. The next time he shot he would be close, he would be certain, and he would not miss.

When he heard the splashing of water, Smith began to move. This time he did not go directly toward the noise, but circuitously, avoiding any ambush that might be waiting. It was easy enough for Peter to throw things into the water to lure him on. He tried to move quietly, but with the bad leg it was nearly impossible, he was awkward and ill at ease on the uneven footing of the forest floor, his sodden clothes squished and slapped against the underbrush with every step. The attempts at stealth made him feel ridiculous; he was sure he was being watched the whole time.

Peter lay on his back in the muck of the pond bottom.

Only his nose and eyes were above the surface, his head tilted skyward, parallel to the water, presenting very little that could be seen above the surface. There was shade on this side of the island, a deep darkness cast by the towering trees and the rocky cliff. He had run through the water at shin depth, stirring up the mud from the bottom, which spread and cast a murky shadow just beneath the already dark surface. It was inpossible to see more than an inch or two through the haze that extended for twenty yards along the shore and four feet outward. Peter was squarely in the middle of the smokescreen he had created, resting like a crocodile, only his eyes to give him away, waiting for his prey.

Smith appeared at the opening in the fence, and Peter eased his head under water until two inches of water covered his eyes. Lying very still, he could breathe when he needed to by simply craning his neck enough to nudge a nostril above the surface. From beneath the surface he could see little more than a sensation of sunlight filtered through a thousand floating specks of mud—but he didn't need to see much. His ears would tell him all that he needed to know.

The stirred-up muck spread over the surface like a ink stain. *He wants me in the water again*, Smith thought. *He's trying to lure me in, to finish me there where I'll have no mobility at all. But I won't do it, I'll outwait him.* He leaned his back against the fence, taking weight off his throbbing leg. *If he's underwater, he'll have to come up. If he's still in the woods behind me, the fence will serve as a protection against his weapons. I still have the gun*, he thought. *He's only human, he'll make a mistake.*

Standing still only made the pain worse. The knee was bad enough, he would need an operation to fix that, but the eye was intolerable, he wanted to claw his eyeball out to make the agony go away. He was breathing heavily now through his open mouth, the blow from the club had done something to his windpipe. In the distance, over the sound of his troubled breathing, he could hear the voices of people in the park, doubtless having long since forgotten the bizarre sight of fully clothed men heading for the sanctuary.

But it was no sanctuary for Smith. He thought of going back, walking through the water to the safety of the crowd, but he was afraid that Peter was in there, somehow breathing, waiting for him.

Violent movement, the surface broke not ten feet away. Smith aimed, allowing for the deflection of the water, then cursed himself. A fish had jumped! He nearly shot at a fish!

Smith never carried extra cartridges with him. They were just one more scrap of evidence to get rid of in an emergency. If he couldn't kill with the six shots the Browning held, he couldn't kill with more. Now he regretted that decision. He had one shot left . . . but slowly he began to see his target. And this time he wouldn't miss.

As the sediment gradually precipitated back to the bottom of the pond, a form began to take shape in Smith's good eye. A man's back loomed just under the water, the dark coat darker than the water. It *was* a man, there were the arms! Smith fired from six feet, wading into the water to his calves, shooting point blank into the middle of the man's back. His last shot gone, Smith fell upon the man, clubbing him with the pistol butt.

It was just a jacket, held down and arms spread wide by a forked branch. A shadow of a man, a wraith. As Smith looked around desperately he saw a face come slowly up out of the water. Stanhope rose, covered with the black ooze of the bottom, not ten feet away. How could he have been so close! Between his hands, like a garrote, he held a red bandanna.

Smith screamed and ran. Peter had quickly stepped to the shore side, forcing Smith to go the only way he could, into the water, toward the cliff face.

The water was slightly deeper on this side of the island. It crested just under Smith's chin, but he kept hobbling forward, driving off his good leg, struggling against the weight of the water. He felt hands close on his right ankle, pulling the leg taut, sending a knife blade of pain the length of the leg, and dragging Smith under the water. He flailed out with his good foot and felt it make solid contact. The hands released his foot. Gasping for air, Smith broke surface again, looking vainly all around. He started for the cliff face again, mucous running from his nose, lungs bursting with effort, expecting to be dragged under again at any moment. He was screaming but didn't know it, didn't recognize the voice as his own as it reverberated off the stone wall in front of him. The noise seemed to Smith just like another part of the nightmare he was having.

For the first time he felt a glimmer of hope as he reached the sheer rock of the cliff. His fingers found a hold, he pulled himself upward, planted his good foot in a seam of rock, hauled himself entirely out of the water. He was going to make it! As he looked up the sheer rock face to find his next point of purchase, the hand struck again, reaching up from below the surface, encasing the ankle on his bad leg. Inexorably the hand pulled downward on his ankle, tugging him back toward the water. Smith kicked out with his other foot, his weight was too much for his fingers to hold, and he fell into the water, screaming.

Water filled his mouth, his nose, his lungs. Hands held his arms behind him in a grip as strong as a vise, a leg hooked his good leg and pulled it out from under him, a knee struck him in the back, forcing him down, down.

Just as he felt he was dead, that his lungs would tear apart, the hands released him. Smith broke the surface just long enough to get half a breath before he was pulled down again. This time he was forced to the very bottom, his face pushed deeply into the ooze. He felt the last of his strength leave him, he went limp, but then inexplicably he was pulled up, his face felt air, he gulped automatically. Again he was plunged under; this time it seemed he had gotten no breath at all. The beasts of Smith's imagination flooded in on him, serpents and dragons stormed through his head, tearing at him, devouring him. He gave up all hope and yearned to die.

Peter plunged Smith under the water once more, his form already limp and unresisting. Pity flickered in the back of his mind. He didn't need to kill the man, he was another human being. But then Peter thought again of his father, of Smith shooting the old man to death piece by piece. A black, angry hatred welled up in him, and he thrust Smith deeper into the water. Let him taste death, let him know what it is to die. Peter had shown him fear and pain, let him show him death.

# 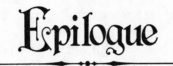Epilogue

The two cops splashed ashore from the rowboat. Slattery, the senior of the two, enlarged the hole ripped in the cyclone fence with his wire cutters, then peeled a section aside as his partner walked through.

The partner was nervous, and he kept his hand close to his holster. The details of the anonymous phone call had been unsettling—a man wanted for two murders. The dark woods had an eerie feel to them for a man used to the known evils of the city.

"Relax," Slattery advised. "Nine times out of ten these anonymous tips don't amount to nothing. Chances are there's no one here. . . ." But even as he spoke he heard the cries.

The cops split up and proceeded in a pincers movement to the middle of the bird sanctuary. They found a grown man huddled against the base of a tree, crying like a child in the midst of a nightmare. His forearms were crossed over his face, blocking out the light, his knees were pressed to his chest.

Slattery scooped up the pistol that lay on the ground at his feet. "It's all right, mister," he said soothingly, but the man didn't respond to them. They had to carry him toward the boat, he never came out of the fetal position, never removed his arms from his face.

God knew what terrors were in his mind, Slattery thought, but they must have been terrible. If the call was right, the man would have been here for half a day like this, too frightened by something to walk through the pond to civilization.

As they approached the water the man went berserk, screaming and kicking to get away. "He's in there!"

In the end they had to handcuff him at hands and feet and carry him bodily into the boat. Even then he nearly sank them twice on the row to shore, so great was his terror.

If the anonymous caller had been right, the man was guilty of two murders. The ballistics check on the gun might tell them the truth, but it didn't really matter. This guy would never stand trial. He was going to spend the rest of his life in a hospital for the criminally insane.

Smiling politely, her eyes slightly glazed with tedium, the stewardess pretended not to see Nardo's broad wink. There were two or three customers like this on every flight, frisky, hopeful, full of beans about being away from home. If she wanted to cheat on her husband, she could have her pick, she didn't need to take someone like Nardo. She had assessed him early on as someone flying first class on someone else's expense account. The stewardess feigned interest in maneuvering her dessert cart down the aisle until she was safely past Nardo's winks and innuendos.

*To hell with her,* thought Nardo. *If she knew how much I'm worth she'd be all over me like a dirty shirt. I can do much better than that. I can afford a small harem of airline hostesses now.* As he thought about his wealth he soon forgot about the woman. Money had a far more erotic effect on Nardo than sex, and he was in much too good a mood to let it be spoiled by a stupid airborne waitress.

By the time the aircraft touched down in Zurich, Nardo had actually forgiven her in his heart for her lack of taste and judgment. To prove it, he smiled broadly at her as he passed out of the plane. She said good-bye to a space just above his ear.

The trip from New York, a supersonic hop to Paris, then a conventional jet to Zurich, had been even shorter than Nardo had anticipated. There had been no delays, they were ahead of schedule with favoring tail winds. He had no luggage beyond his carry-on overnight case. Nardo breezed out of the airport and toward the bank with two full days to spare.

Herr Frischel seemed surprised to see him.

"I called you I was coming," said Nardo.

"Yes, of course," said Frischel. "But that was twelve hours ago."

"So what? My time isn't up. I've got two days left!"

"Yes, of course, but . . ."

Nardo pulled a memo pad from the Plaza Hotel from his inside pocket. On the pad was written a four-number sequence: 1, 2, 3, 4.

"Here are the numbers," Nardo said.

Frischel didn't look at him.

"Well?"

"Haven't you heard?" asked Frischel.

"These are the right numbers!" Nardo insisted.

Again Frischel didn't look at them. "I'm quite certain they are," he said. "But it hardly matters."

"Heard what?" Nardo asked belatedly. "I've been traveling."

Frischel handed Nardo the newspaper from his desk.

After a moment Nardo sat down.

"Naturally the account was closed immediately."

Nardo continued to stare vacantly in front of him.

"Do you understand me, Mr. Nardo? You are too late."

After another moment's silence Frischel realized that Nardo was silently weeping. It was most embarrassing. After all, it was only money.

**HEADLINE,** *THE NEW YORK TIMES***:**

# Shah Leaves U.S.
# Seeks Panama Refuge